big
NATE
GOES BANANAS!

Complete Your *Big Nate* Collection

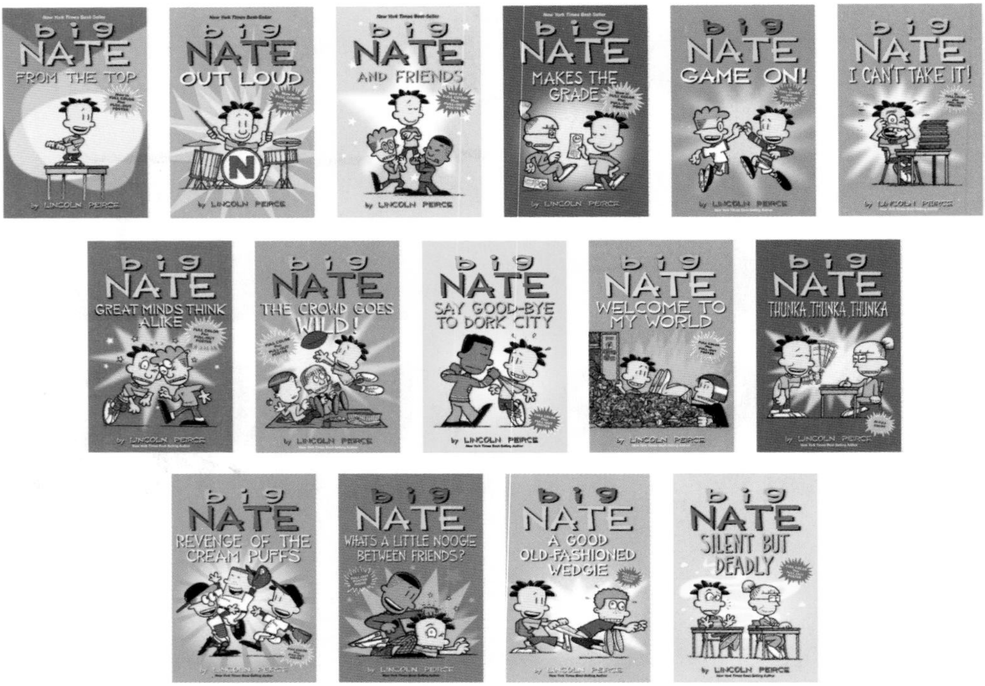
big NATE FROM THE TOP
big NATE OUT LOUD
big NATE AND FRIENDS
big NATE MAKES THE GRADE
big NATE GAME ON!
big NATE I CAN'T TAKE IT!
big NATE GREAT MINDS THINK ALIKE
big NATE THE CROWD GOES WILD!
big NATE SAY GOOD-BYE TO DORK CITY
big NATE WELCOME TO MY WORLD
big NATE THUNKA, THUNKA, THUNKA
big NATE REVENGE OF THE CREAM PUFFS
big NATE WHAT'S A LITTLE NOOGIE BETWEEN FRIENDS?
big NATE A GOOD OLD-FASHIONED WEDGIE
big NATE SILENT BUT DEADLY
by LINCOLN PEIRCE

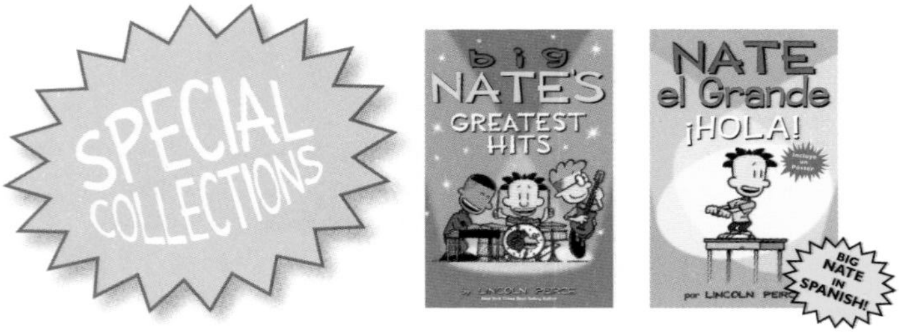
SPECIAL COLLECTIONS
big NATE'S GREATEST HITS
NATE el Grande ¡HOLA!
por LINCOLN PEIRCE
BIG NATE IN SPANISH!

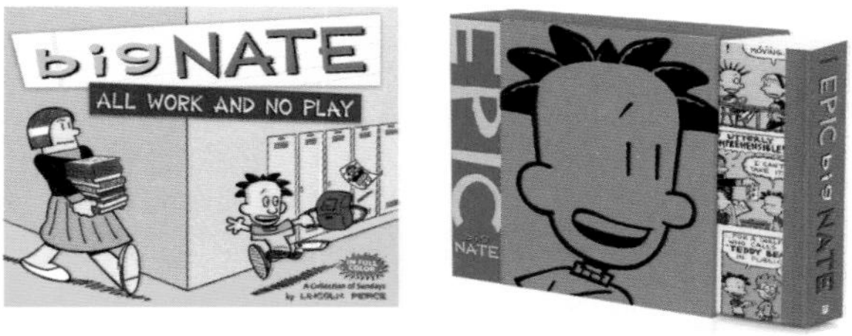
big NATE ALL WORK AND NO PLAY
A Collection of Sundays
by LINCOLN PEIRCE
EPIC big NATE

big NATE

GOES BANANAS!

by LINCOLN PEIRCE

Andrews McMeel
PUBLISHING®

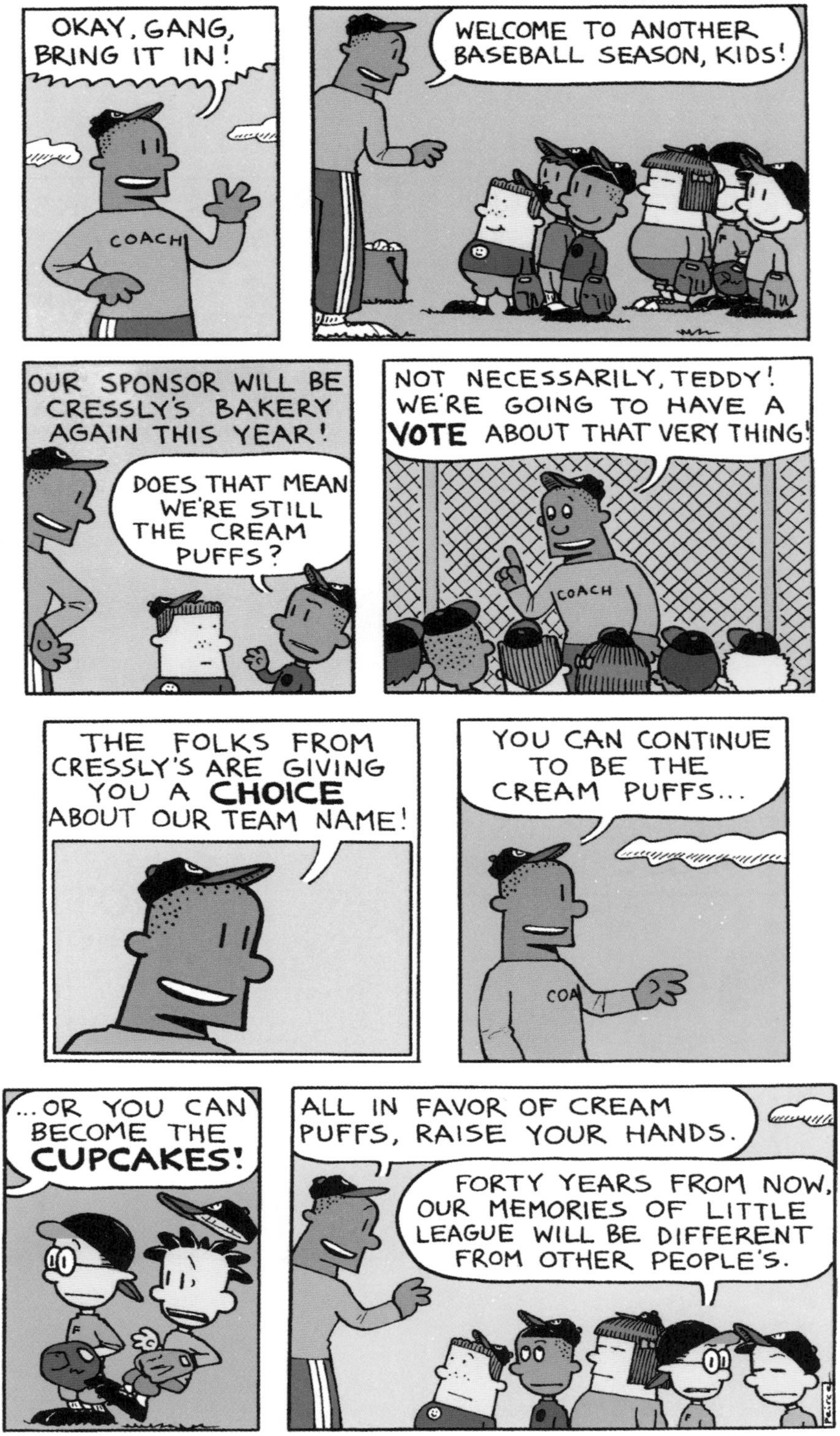
OKAY, GANG, BRING IT IN!
COACH
WELCOME TO ANOTHER BASEBALL SEASON, KIDS!
OUR SPONSOR WILL BE CRESSLY'S BAKERY AGAIN THIS YEAR!
DOES THAT MEAN WE'RE STILL THE CREAM PUFFS?
NOT NECESSARILY, TEDDY! WE'RE GOING TO HAVE A **VOTE** ABOUT THAT VERY THING!
COACH
THE FOLKS FROM CRESSLY'S ARE GIVING YOU A **CHOICE** ABOUT OUR TEAM NAME!
YOU CAN CONTINUE TO BE THE CREAM PUFFS...
...OR YOU CAN BECOME THE **CUPCAKES!**
ALL IN FAVOR OF CREAM PUFFS, RAISE YOUR HANDS.
FORTY YEARS FROM NOW, OUR MEMORIES OF LITTLE LEAGUE WILL BE DIFFERENT FROM OTHER PEOPLE'S.

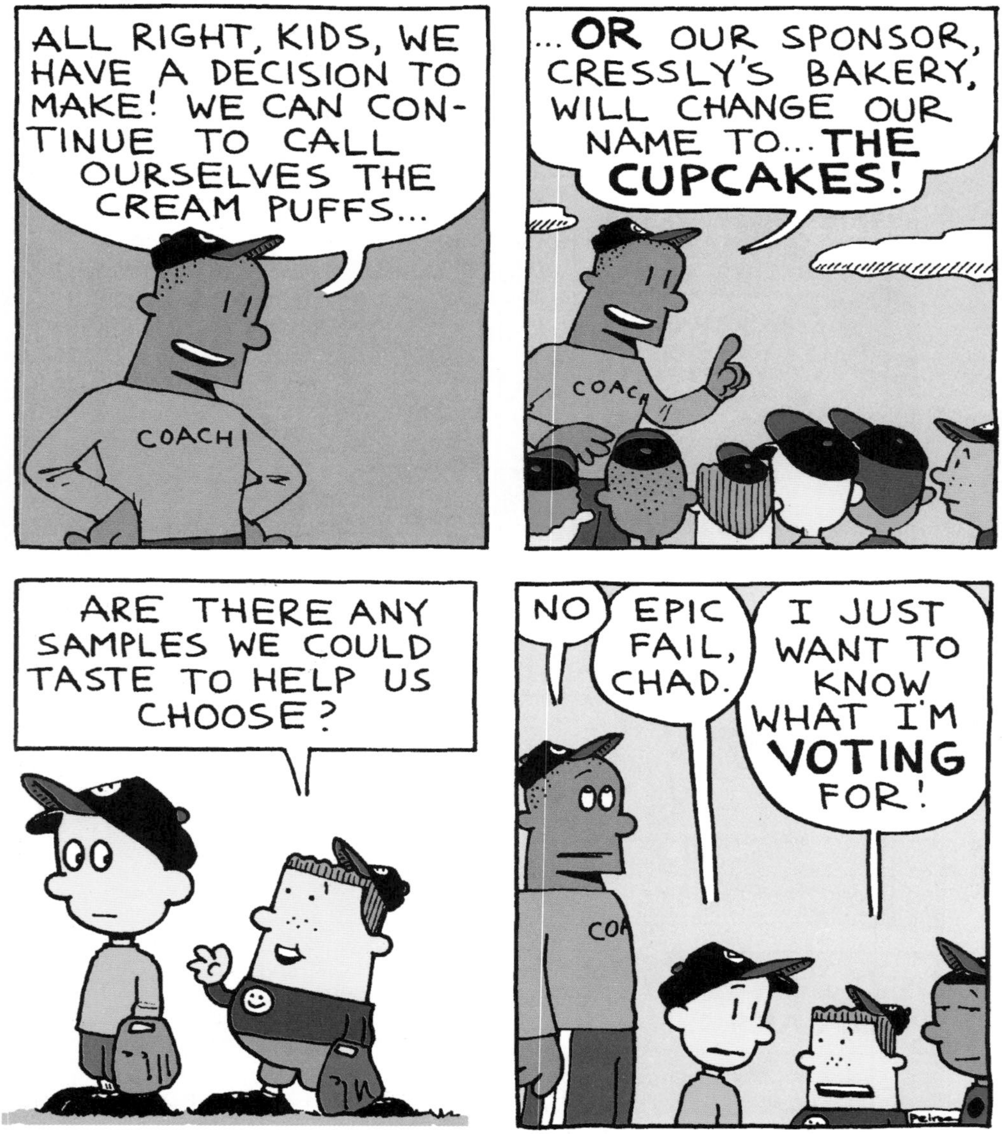
ALL RIGHT, KIDS, WE HAVE A DECISION TO MAKE! WE CAN CONTINUE TO CALL OURSELVES THE CREAM PUFFS...
COACH
...**OR** OUR SPONSOR, CRESSLY'S BAKERY, WILL CHANGE OUR NAME TO... **THE CUPCAKES!**
ARE THERE ANY SAMPLES WE COULD TASTE TO HELP US CHOOSE?
NO
EPIC FAIL, CHAD.
I JUST WANT TO KNOW WHAT I'M **VOTING** FOR!

...7...8...9... THAT'S IT! WE'RE OFFICIALLY NO LONGER THE CREAM PUFFS!
WE'RE NOW THE **CUPCAKES!** LET'S HEAR IT, EVERYBODY! HIP!...HIP!...
COACH
TEAM MORALE APPEARS LOW.
IS IT TOO LATE TO SWITCH TO LACROSSE?

KIM! CAN'T YOU DO SOMETHING ABOUT THIS?
ABOUT WHAT?
YOUR FAMILY'S BAKERY IS OUR SPONSOR! CAN'T YOU ASK THEM TO PICK ANOTHER NAME FOR US BESIDES CUPCAKES?
NO
IT'S GOOD FOR BUSINESS IF THE TEAM NAME IS SOME KIND OF BAKERY ITEM.
WE COULD BE THE WHOOPIE PIES!
MAYBE WE SHOULD QUIT WHILE WE'RE AHEAD.

WHAT A FIASCO!
WE FINALLY GET
RID OF THE NAME
CREAM PUFFS,
AND WHAT HAPPENS?
WE BECOME THE
CUPCAKES!

WHAT'S THE **DIFF**?
THEY'RE THE **SAME**
THING!

NO,
THEY'RE
NOT.

A CREAM PUFF — ALSO
CALLED A PROFITEROLE
OR CHOUX À LA CRÈME —
IS A FLAKY PASTRY
BALL FILLED WITH
CREAM, CUSTARD, OR
ICE CREAM.

A **CUPCAKE**, ON
THE OTHER HAND...

CHAD WATCHES
A LOT OF
FOOD NETWORK.

YOU WANT TO KNOW WHY I DON'T LIKE BEING ON A TEAM CALLED THE CUP-CAKES? LOOK!
ACCORDING TO THE SLANG DICTIONARY, A CUPCAKE IS "A PATSY, A WEAKLING, OR AN EASILY DIS-PATCHED OPPONENT."
THAT'S NOT ME! THAT'S NOT ME AT ALL!
HOLD IT, THERE'S ANOTHER DEFINITION.
"AGGRESSIVE OR THEATRICAL FLATULENCE"
THAT'S YOU!
Peirce

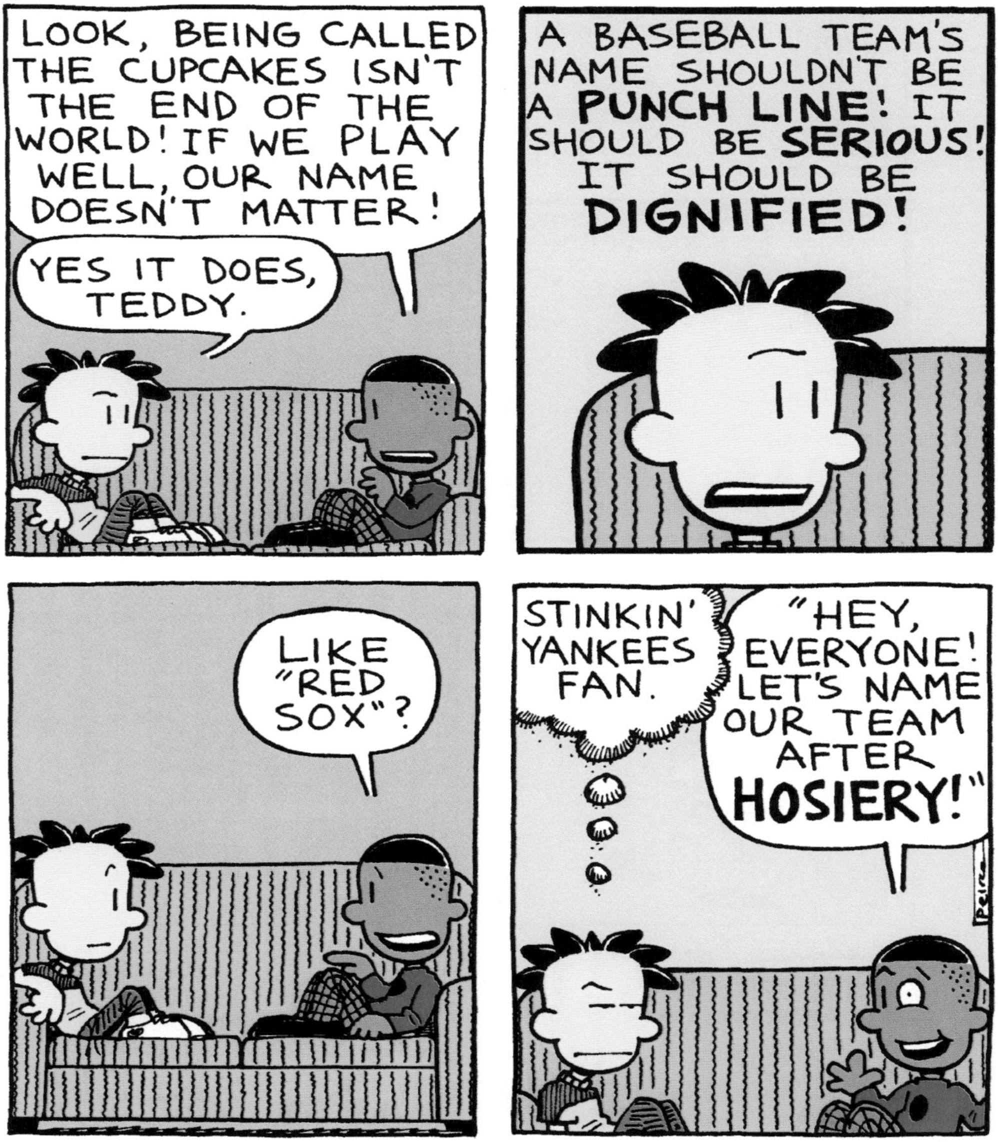
LOOK, BEING CALLED THE CUPCAKES ISN'T THE END OF THE WORLD! IF WE PLAY WELL, OUR NAME DOESN'T MATTER!
YES IT DOES, TEDDY.
A BASEBALL TEAM'S NAME SHOULDN'T BE A **PUNCH LINE**! IT SHOULD BE **SERIOUS**! IT SHOULD BE **DIGNIFIED**!
LIKE "RED SOX"?
STINKIN' YANKEES FAN.
"HEY, EVERYONE! LET'S NAME OUR TEAM AFTER **HOSIERY**!"
Peirce

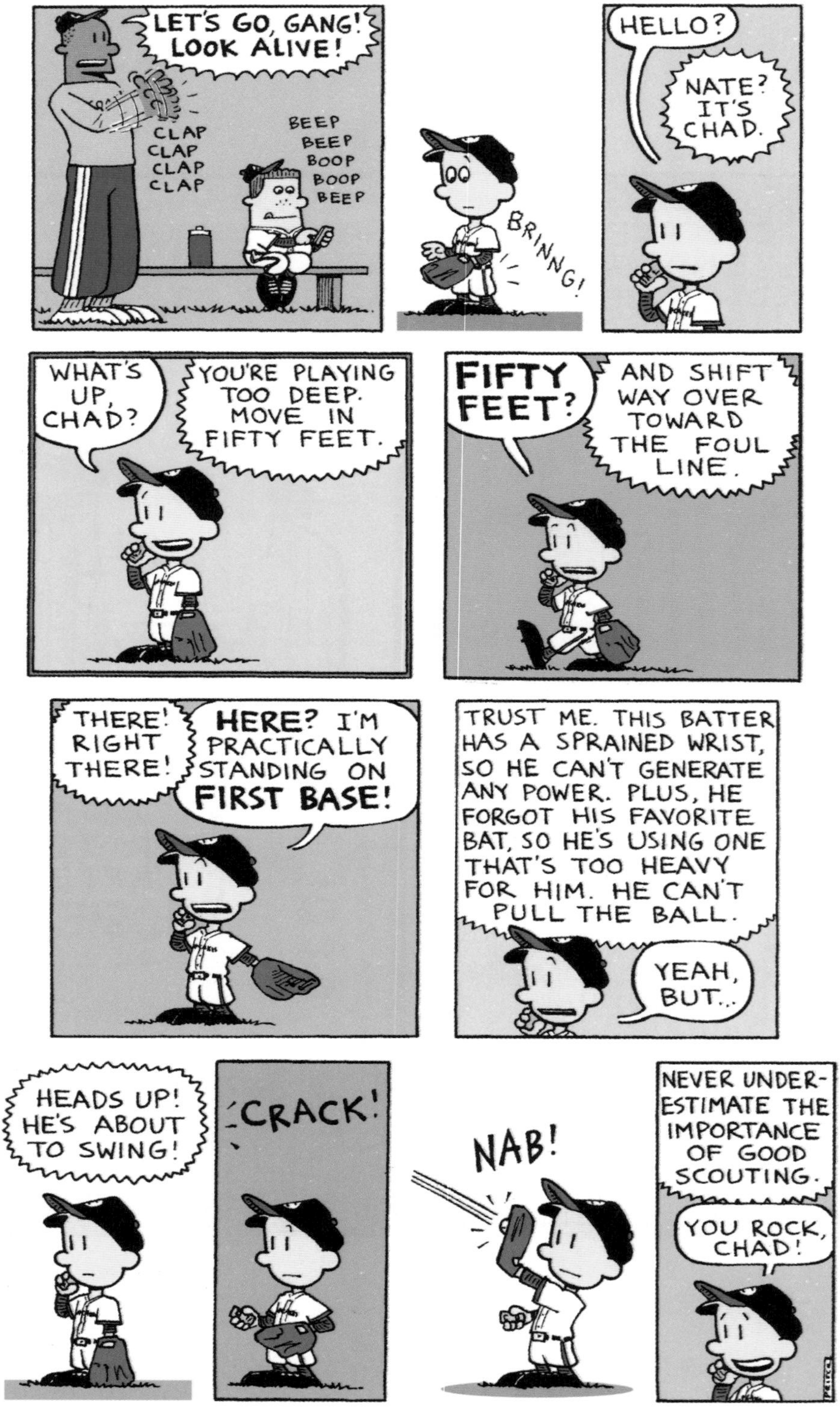
LET'S GO, GANG! LOOK ALIVE!
CLAP CLAP CLAP CLAP
BEEP BEEP BOOP BOOP BEEP
BRINNG!
HELLO?
NATE? IT'S CHAD.
WHAT'S UP, CHAD?
YOU'RE PLAYING TOO DEEP. MOVE IN FIFTY FEET.
FIFTY FEET?
AND SHIFT WAY OVER TOWARD THE FOUL LINE.
THERE! RIGHT THERE!
HERE? I'M PRACTICALLY STANDING ON FIRST BASE!
TRUST ME. THIS BATTER HAS A SPRAINED WRIST, SO HE CAN'T GENERATE ANY POWER. PLUS, HE FORGOT HIS FAVORITE BAT, SO HE'S USING ONE THAT'S TOO HEAVY FOR HIM. HE CAN'T PULL THE BALL.
YEAH, BUT...
HEADS UP! HE'S ABOUT TO SWING!
CRACK!
NAB!
NEVER UNDER-ESTIMATE THE IMPORTANCE OF GOOD SCOUTING.
YOU ROCK, CHAD!

MUNCH
MUNCH
MUNCH
MUNCH
MUNCH
HUNNY BURSTS
WHOA!
! !
HUNNY BURSTS
WHOA! WHOA!
WHOA! WHOA!
WHOA!
HUNNY BURSTS
IS THIS JUST YOUR REGULAR BREAKFAST SUGAR BUZZ, OR ARE YOU HAVING SOME SORT OF SPASM?
OA! WHOA!
OA! WHOA!
HUNNY

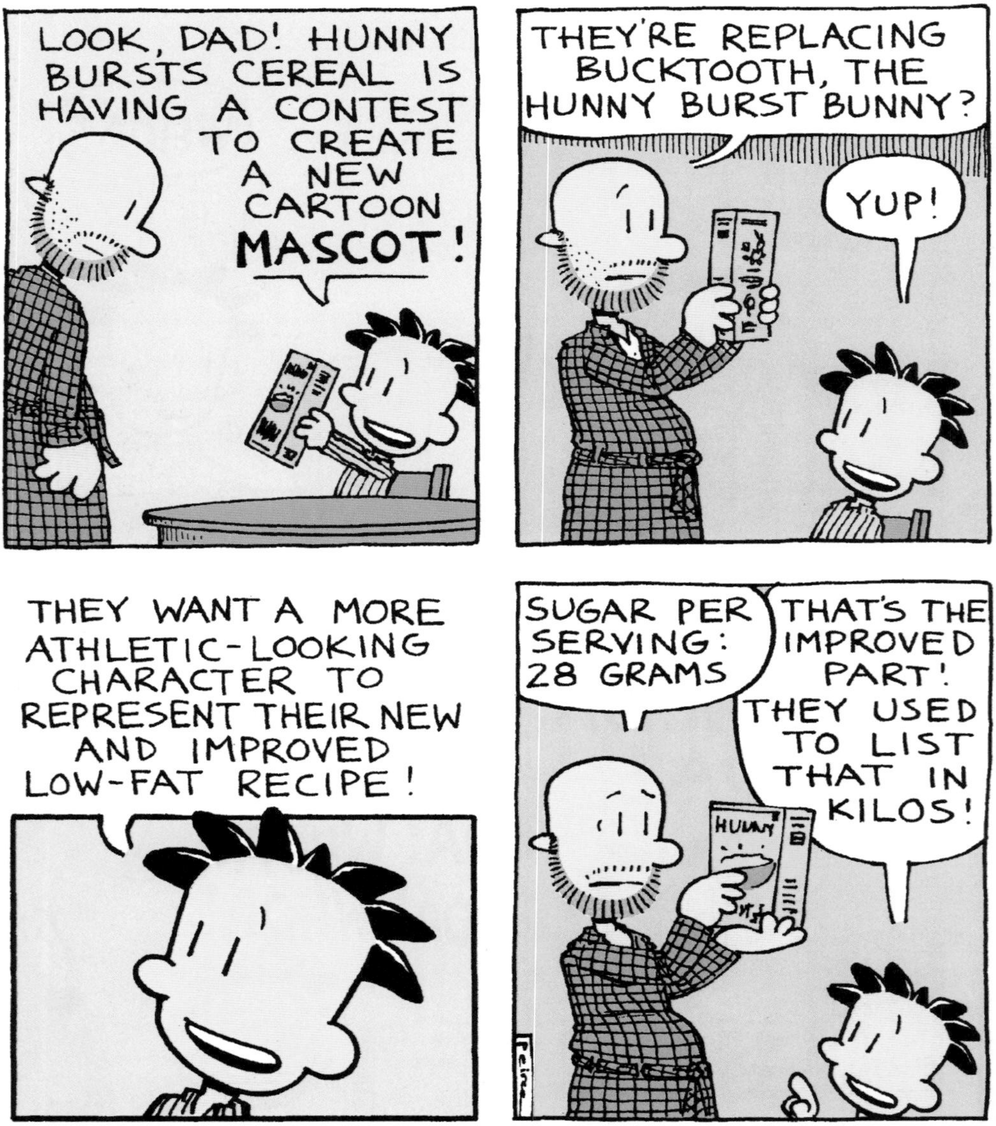
LOOK, DAD! HUNNY BURSTS CEREAL IS HAVING A CONTEST TO CREATE A NEW CARTOON MASCOT!
THEY'RE REPLACING BUCKTOOTH, THE HUNNY BURST BUNNY?
YUP!
THEY WANT A MORE ATHLETIC-LOOKING CHARACTER TO REPRESENT THEIR NEW AND IMPROVED LOW-FAT RECIPE!
SUGAR PER SERVING: 28 GRAMS
THAT'S THE IMPROVED PART! THEY USED TO LIST THAT IN KILOS!

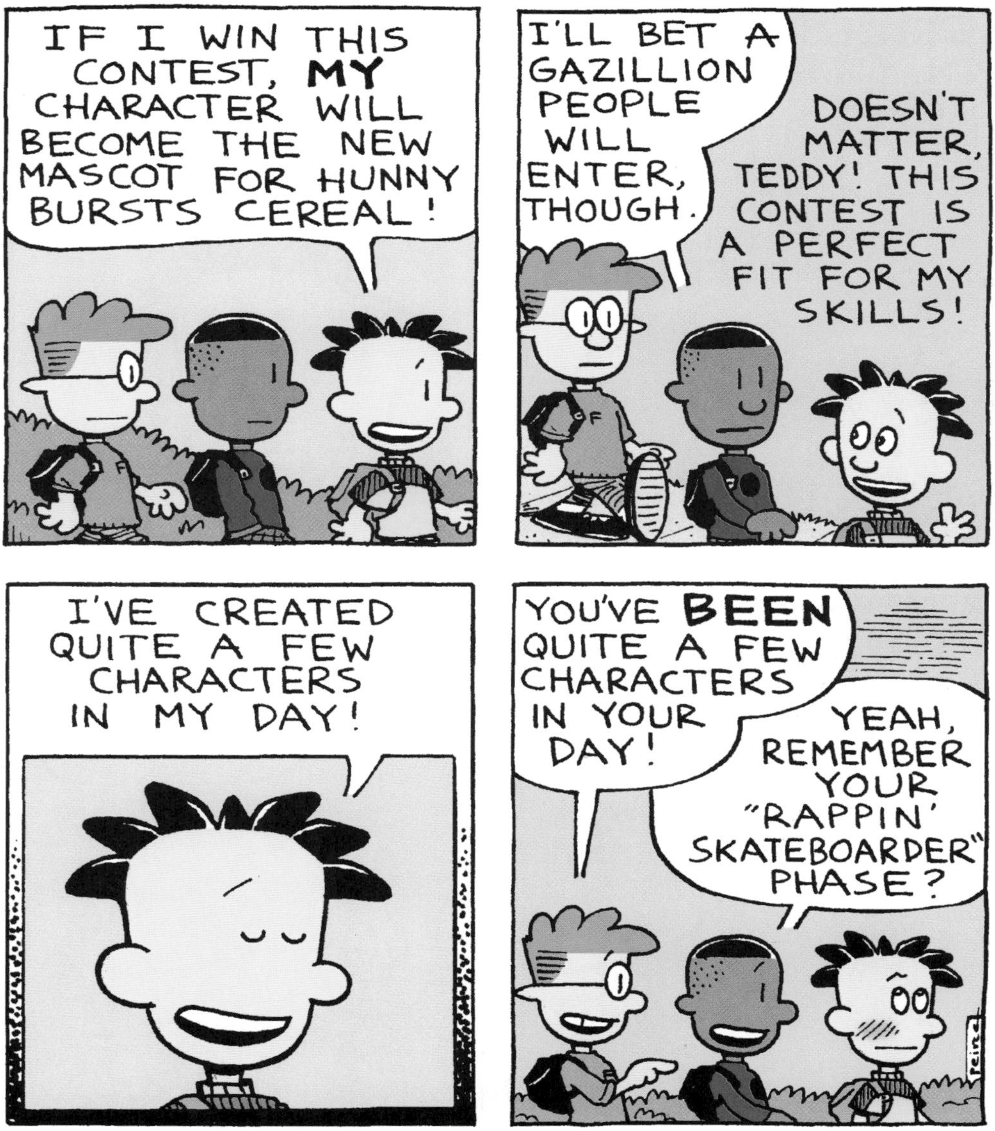
IF I WIN THIS CONTEST, **MY** CHARACTER WILL BECOME THE NEW MASCOT FOR HUNNY BURSTS CEREAL!
I'LL BET A GAZILLION PEOPLE WILL ENTER, THOUGH.
DOESN'T MATTER, TEDDY! THIS CONTEST IS A PERFECT FIT FOR MY SKILLS!
I'VE CREATED QUITE A FEW CHARACTERS IN MY DAY!
YOU'VE **BEEN** QUITE A FEW CHARACTERS IN YOUR DAY!
YEAH, REMEMBER YOUR "RAPPIN' SKATEBOARDER" PHASE?
Peirce

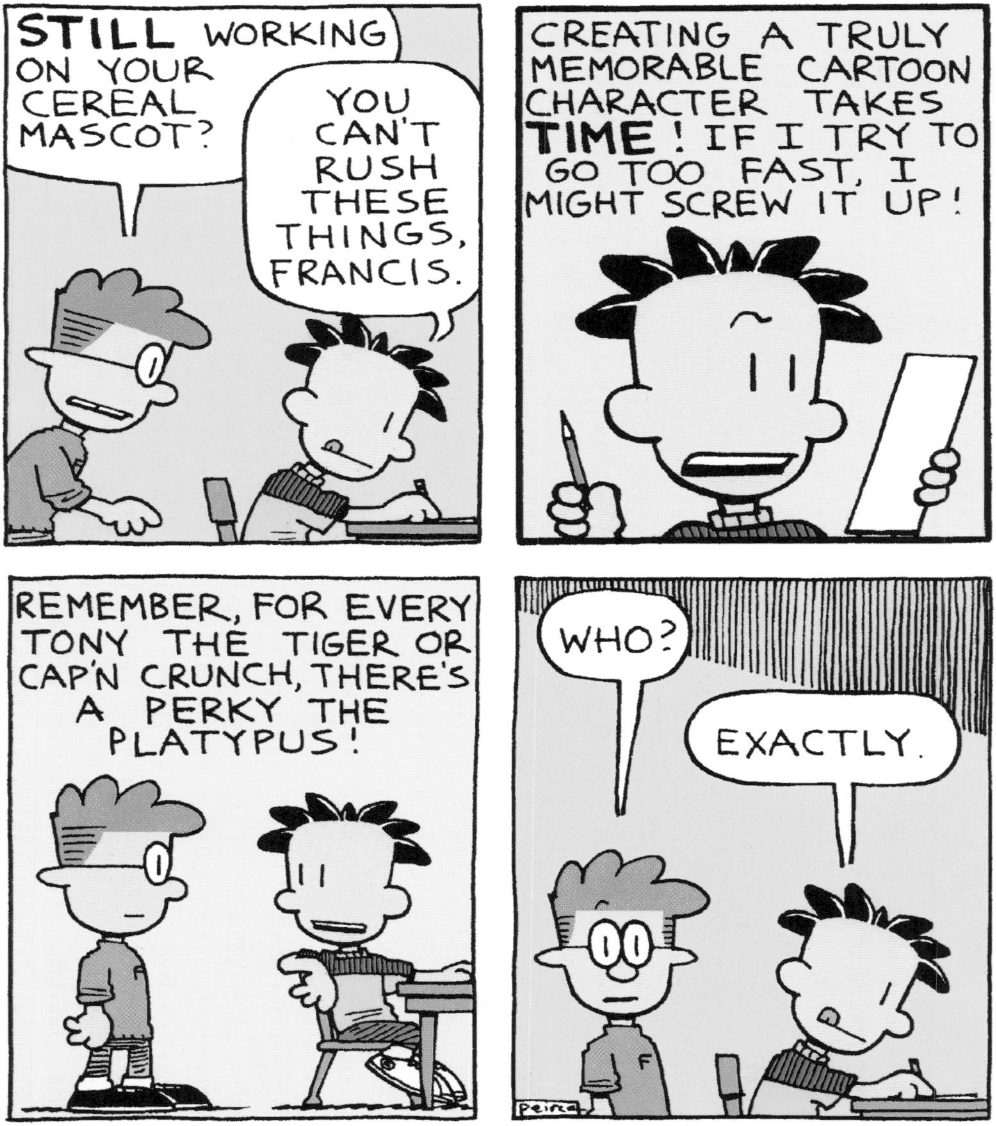
STILL WORKING ON YOUR CEREAL MASCOT?
YOU CAN'T RUSH THESE THINGS, FRANCIS.
CREATING A TRULY MEMORABLE CARTOON CHARACTER TAKES TIME! IF I TRY TO GO TOO FAST, I MIGHT SCREW IT UP!
REMEMBER, FOR EVERY TONY THE TIGER OR CAP'N CRUNCH, THERE'S A PERKY THE PLATYPUS!
WHO?
EXACTLY.
Peirce

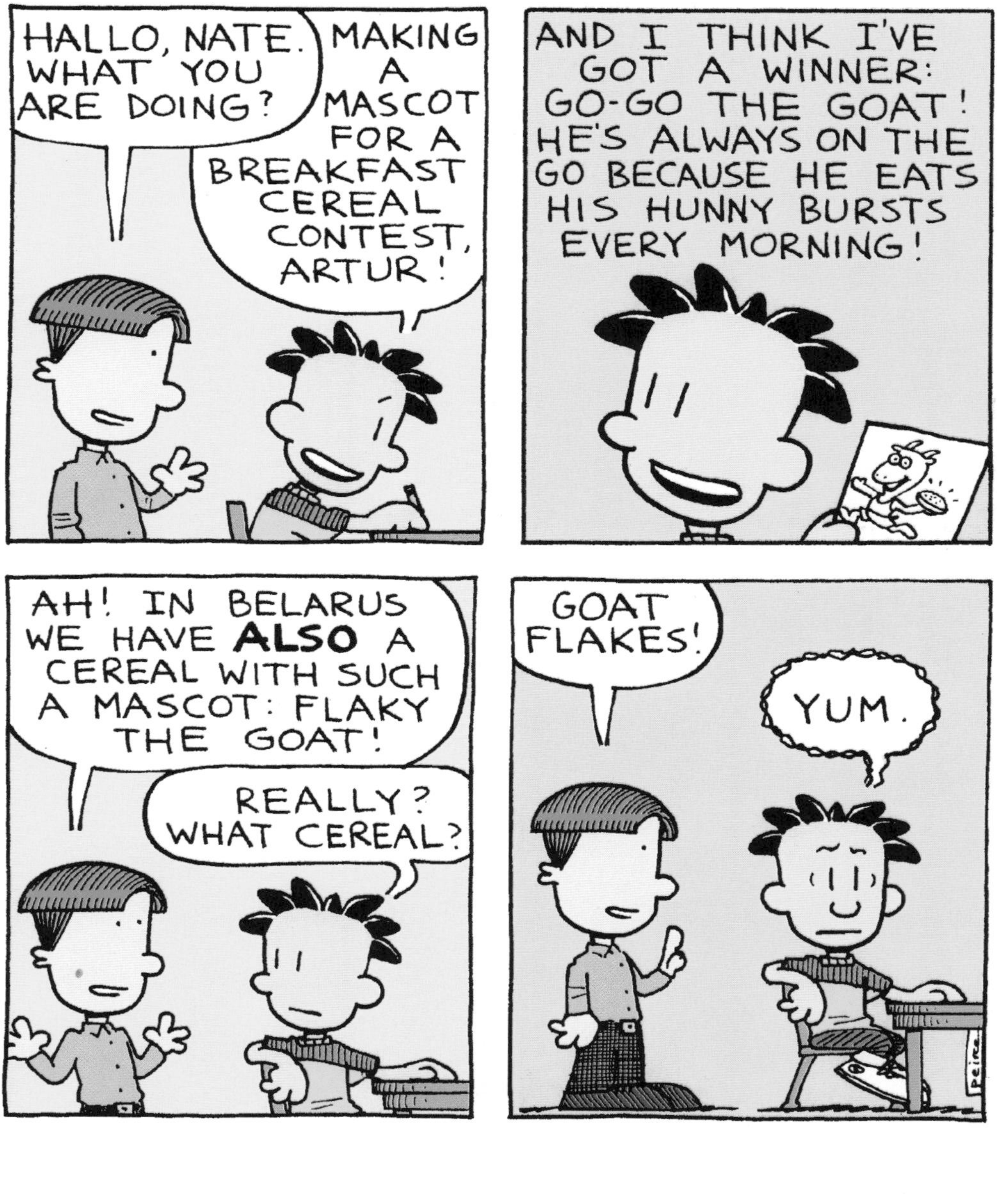
HALLO, NATE. WHAT YOU ARE DOING?
MAKING A MASCOT FOR A BREAKFAST CEREAL CONTEST, ARTUR!
AND I THINK I'VE GOT A WINNER: GO-GO THE GOAT! HE'S ALWAYS ON THE GO BECAUSE HE EATS HIS HUNNY BURSTS EVERY MORNING!
AH! IN BELARUS WE HAVE **ALSO** A CEREAL WITH SUCH A MASCOT: FLAKY THE GOAT!
REALLY? WHAT CEREAL?
GOAT FLAKES!
YUM.
peirce

FEAST YOUR EYES ON GO-GO THE GOAT, FRANCIS! ONCE I WIN THIS CONTEST, HE'LL BE ON EVERY BOX OF HUNNY BURSTS FROM COAST TO COAST!

I'M GOING TO BE **FAMOUS**!

UH...WON'T IT BE GO-GO THE GOAT WHO'S FAMOUS AND NOT YOU?

I MEAN, DOES ANYONE KNOW WHO CREATED TOUCAN SAM?

MANUEL R. VEGA

DUH.

SOMETIMES I FORGET WHO I'M TALKING TO.

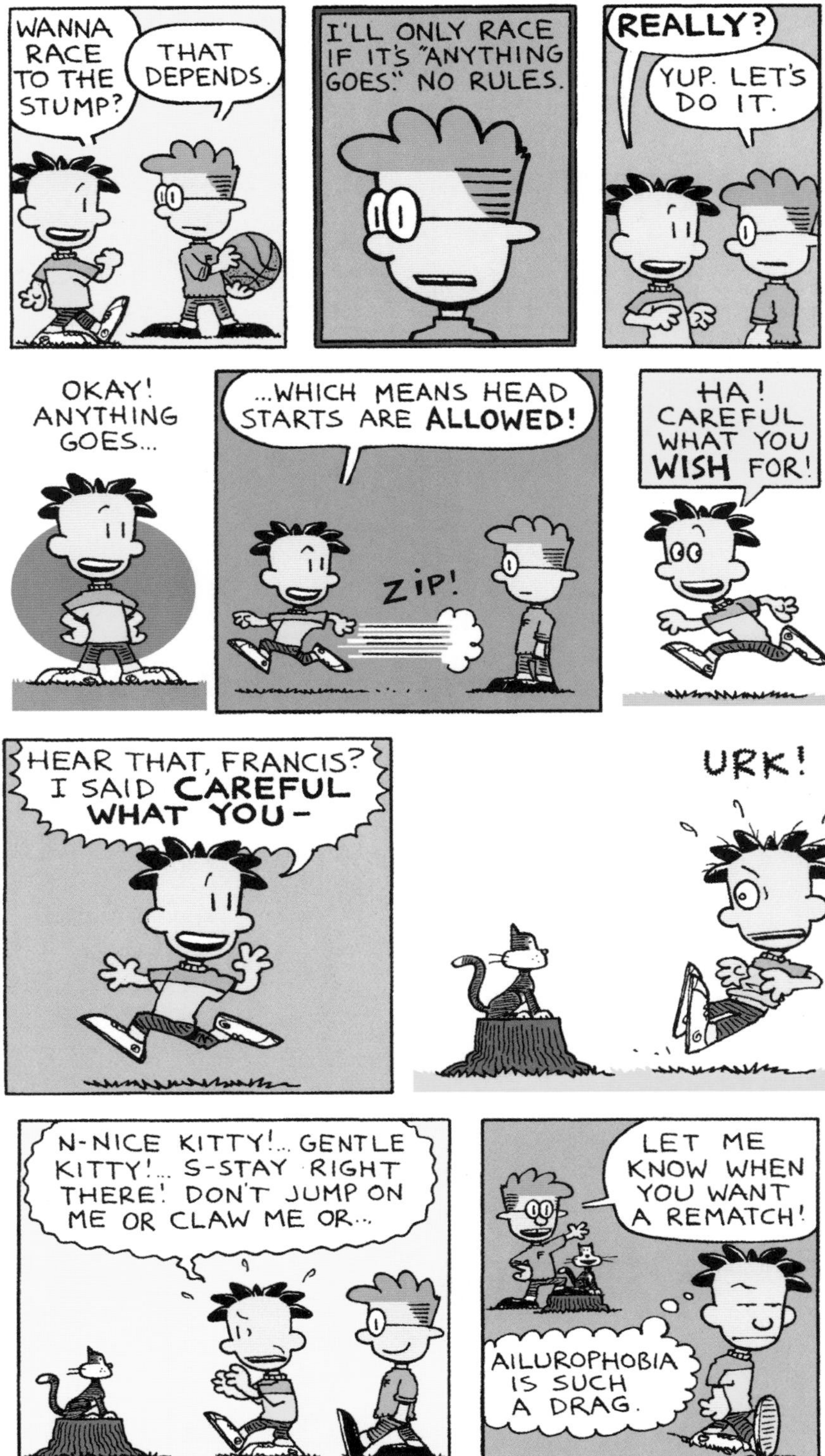

WANNA RACE TO THE STUMP?
THAT DEPENDS.
I'LL ONLY RACE IF IT'S "ANYTHING GOES." NO RULES.
REALLY?
YUP. LET'S DO IT.
OKAY! ANYTHING GOES...
...WHICH MEANS HEAD STARTS ARE ALLOWED!
ZIP!
HA! CAREFUL WHAT YOU WISH FOR!
HEAR THAT, FRANCIS? I SAID CAREFUL WHAT YOU-
URK!
N-NICE KITTY!... GENTLE KITTY!... S-STAY RIGHT THERE! DON'T JUMP ON ME OR CLAW ME OR...
LET ME KNOW WHEN YOU WANT A REMATCH!
AILUROPHOBIA IS SUCH A DRAG.
Peirce

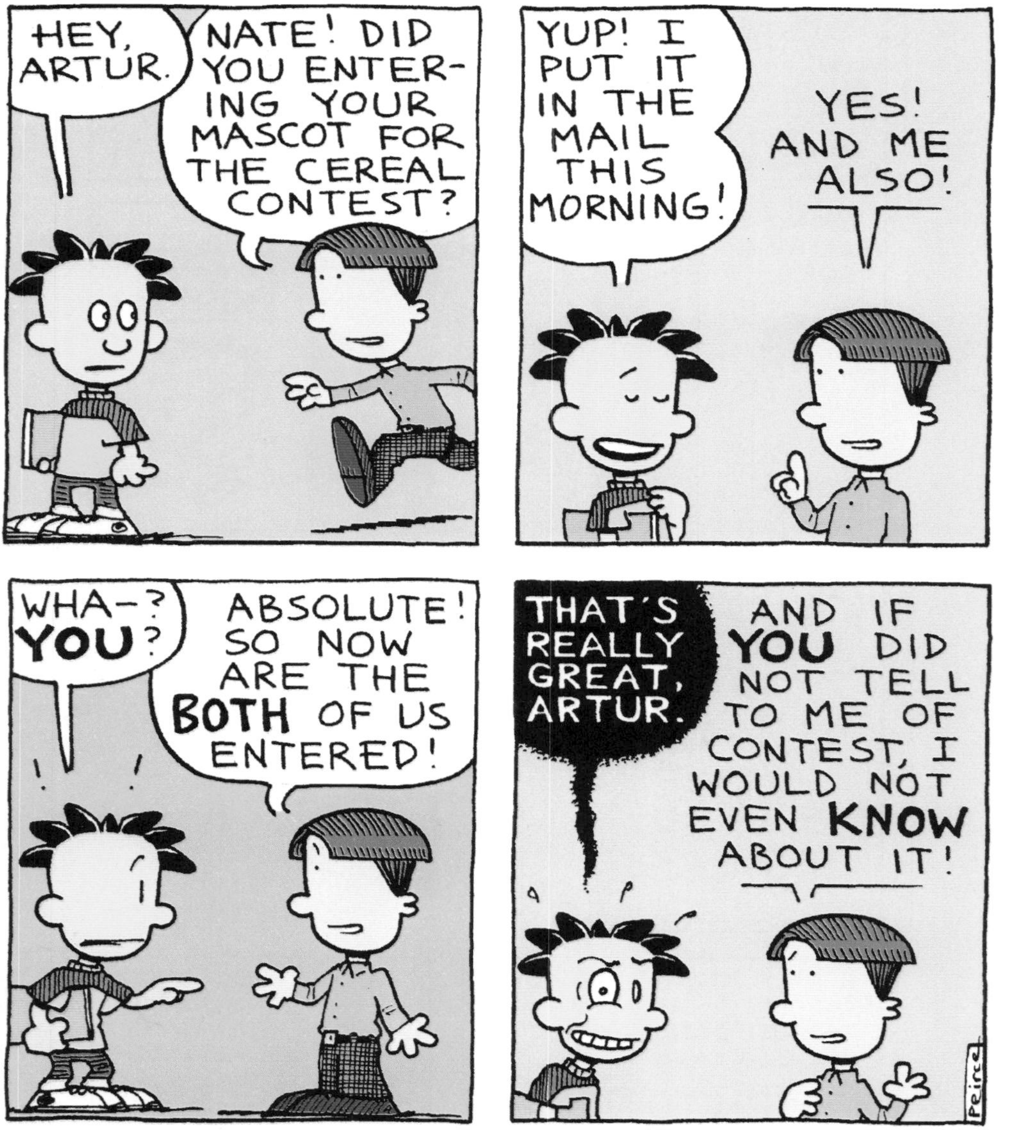
HEY, ARTUR.
NATE! DID YOU ENTERING YOUR MASCOT FOR THE CEREAL CONTEST?
YUP! I PUT IT IN THE MAIL THIS MORNING!
YES! AND ME ALSO!
WHA-? YOU?
ABSOLUTE! SO NOW ARE THE BOTH OF US ENTERED!
THAT'S REALLY GREAT, ARTUR.
AND IF YOU DID NOT TELL TO ME OF CONTEST, I WOULD NOT EVEN KNOW ABOUT IT!
Peirce

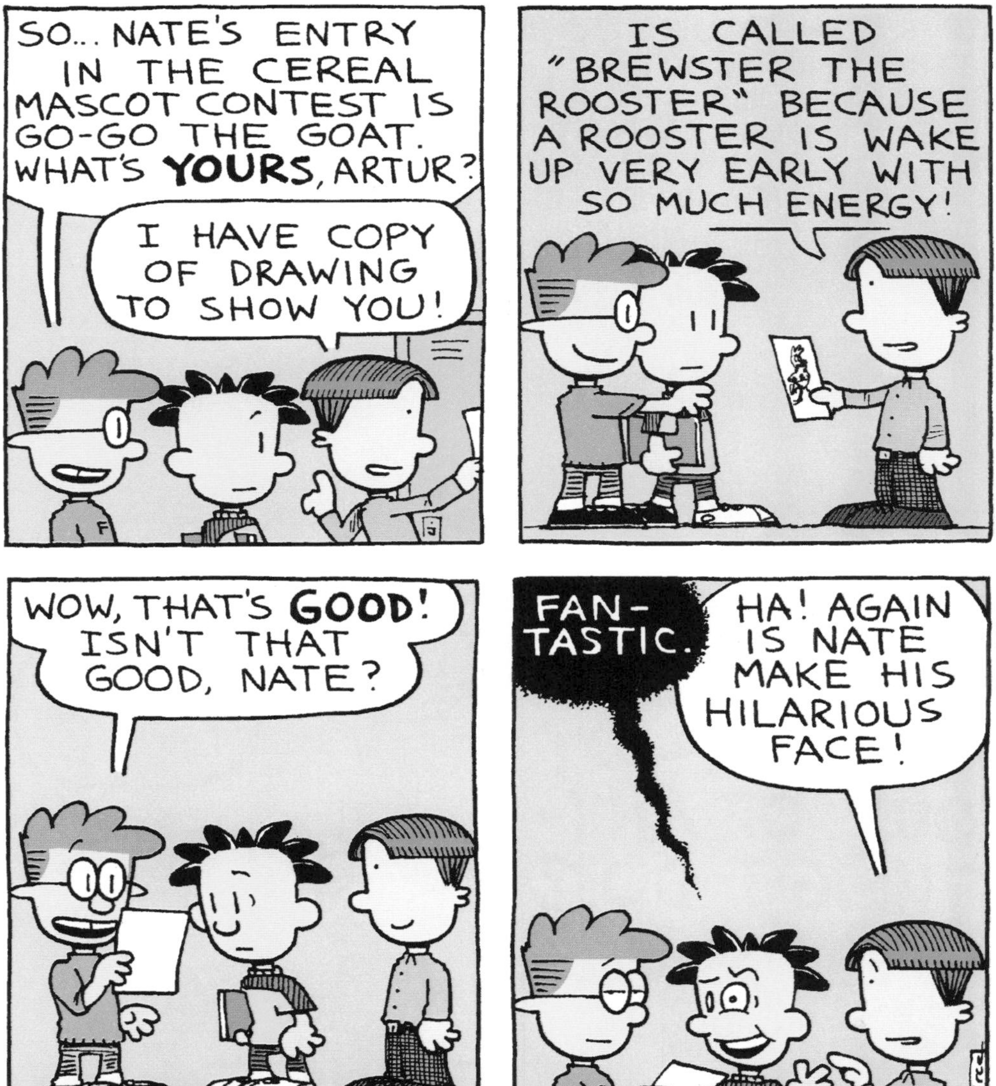
SO... NATE'S ENTRY IN THE CEREAL MASCOT CONTEST IS GO-GO THE GOAT. WHAT'S **YOURS**, ARTUR?
I HAVE COPY OF DRAWING TO SHOW YOU!
IS CALLED "BREWSTER THE ROOSTER" BECAUSE A ROOSTER IS WAKE UP VERY EARLY WITH SO MUCH ENERGY!
WOW, THAT'S **GOOD**! ISN'T THAT GOOD, NATE?
FAN-TASTIC.
HA! AGAIN IS NATE MAKE HIS HILARIOUS FACE!
PEIRCE

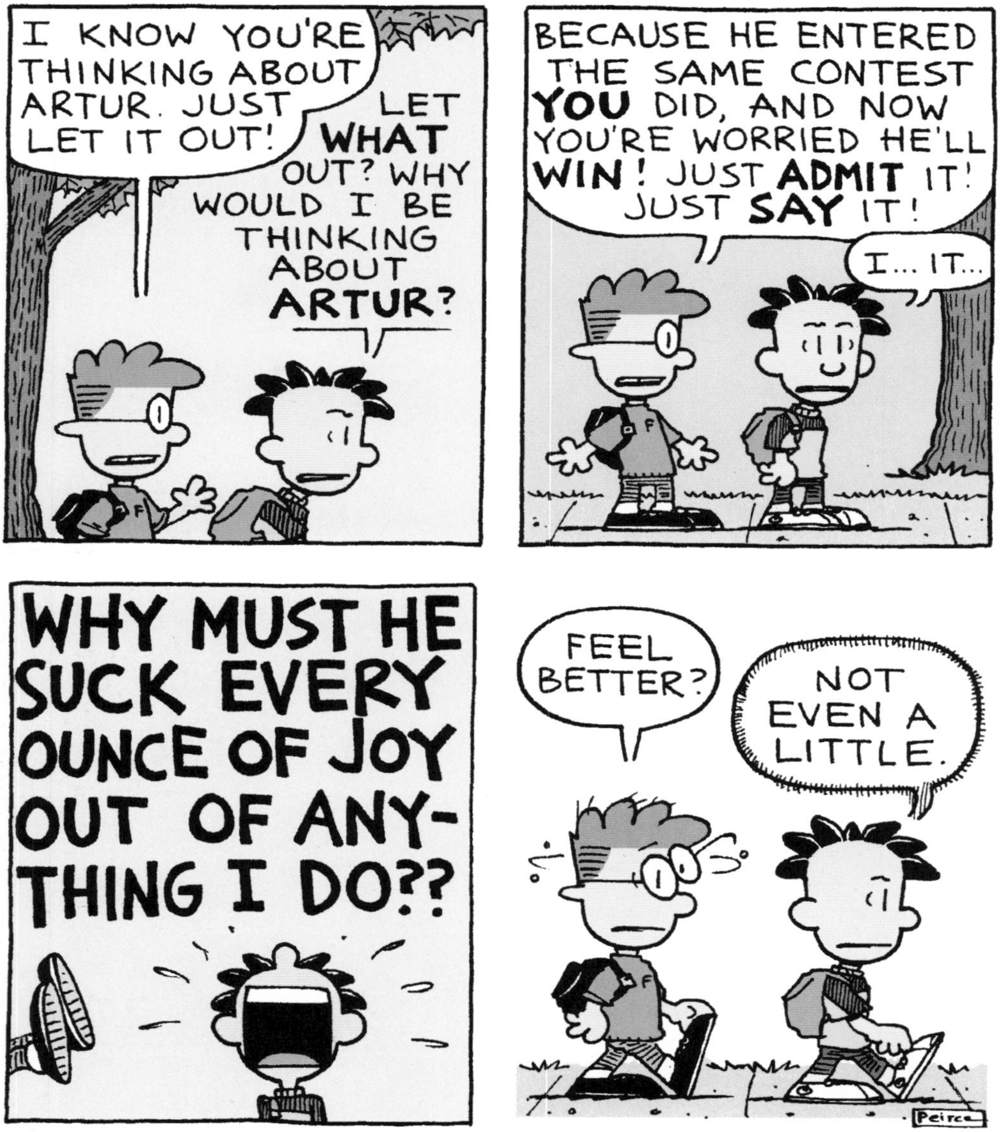
I KNOW YOU'RE THINKING ABOUT ARTUR. JUST LET IT OUT!
LET WHAT OUT? WHY WOULD I BE THINKING ABOUT ARTUR?
BECAUSE HE ENTERED THE SAME CONTEST YOU DID, AND NOW YOU'RE WORRIED HE'LL WIN! JUST ADMIT IT! JUST SAY IT!
I... IT...
WHY MUST HE SUCK EVERY OUNCE OF JOY OUT OF ANY-THING I DO??
FEEL BETTER?
NOT EVEN A LITTLE.
Peirce

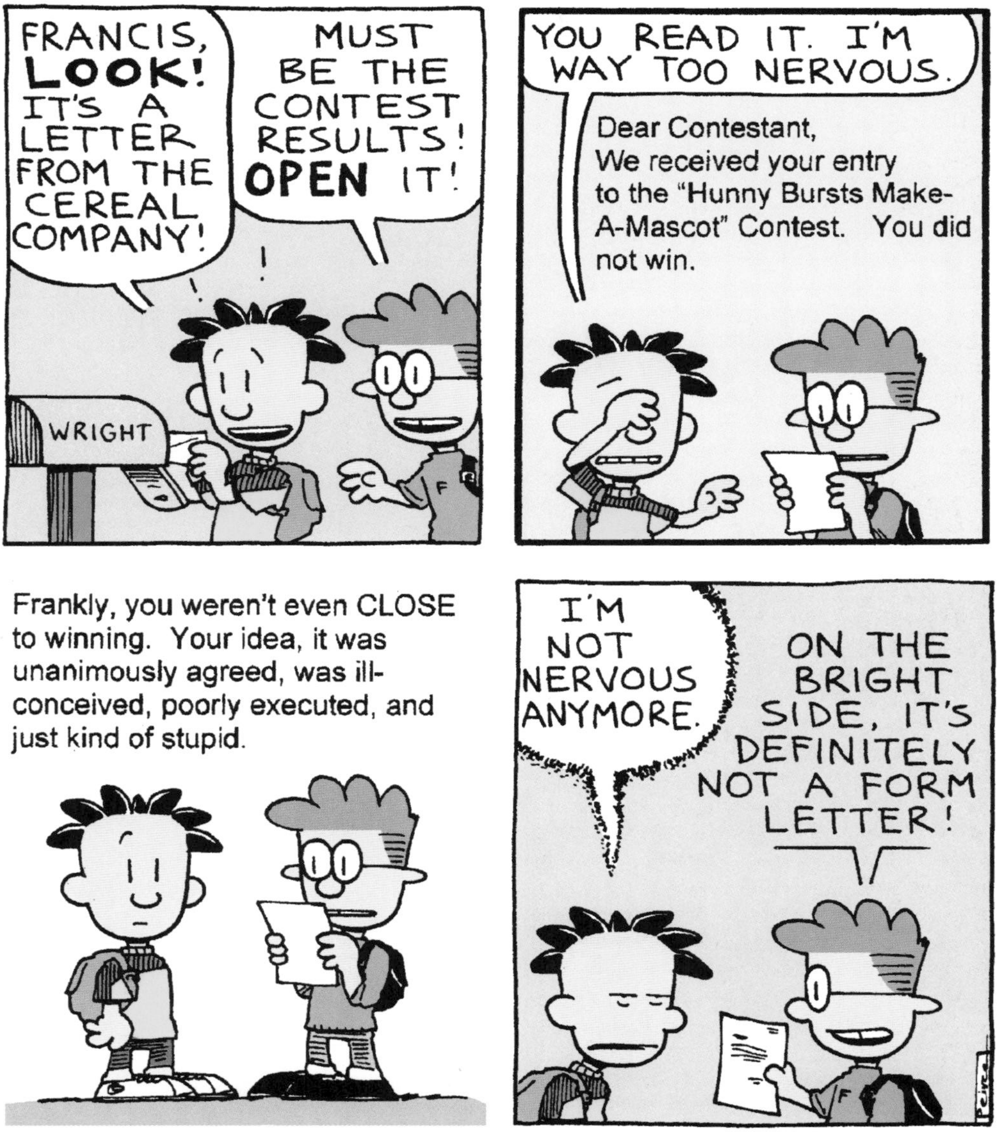
FRANCIS, **LOOK!** IT'S A LETTER FROM THE CEREAL COMPANY!
MUST BE THE CONTEST RESULTS! **OPEN** IT!
WRIGHT
YOU READ IT. I'M WAY TOO NERVOUS.
Dear Contestant,
We received your entry to the "Hunny Bursts Make-A-Mascot" Contest. You did not win.
Frankly, you weren't even CLOSE to winning. Your idea, it was unanimously agreed, was ill-conceived, poorly executed, and just kind of stupid.
I'M NOT NERVOUS ANYMORE.
ON THE BRIGHT SIDE, IT'S DEFINITELY NOT A FORM LETTER!
Peirce

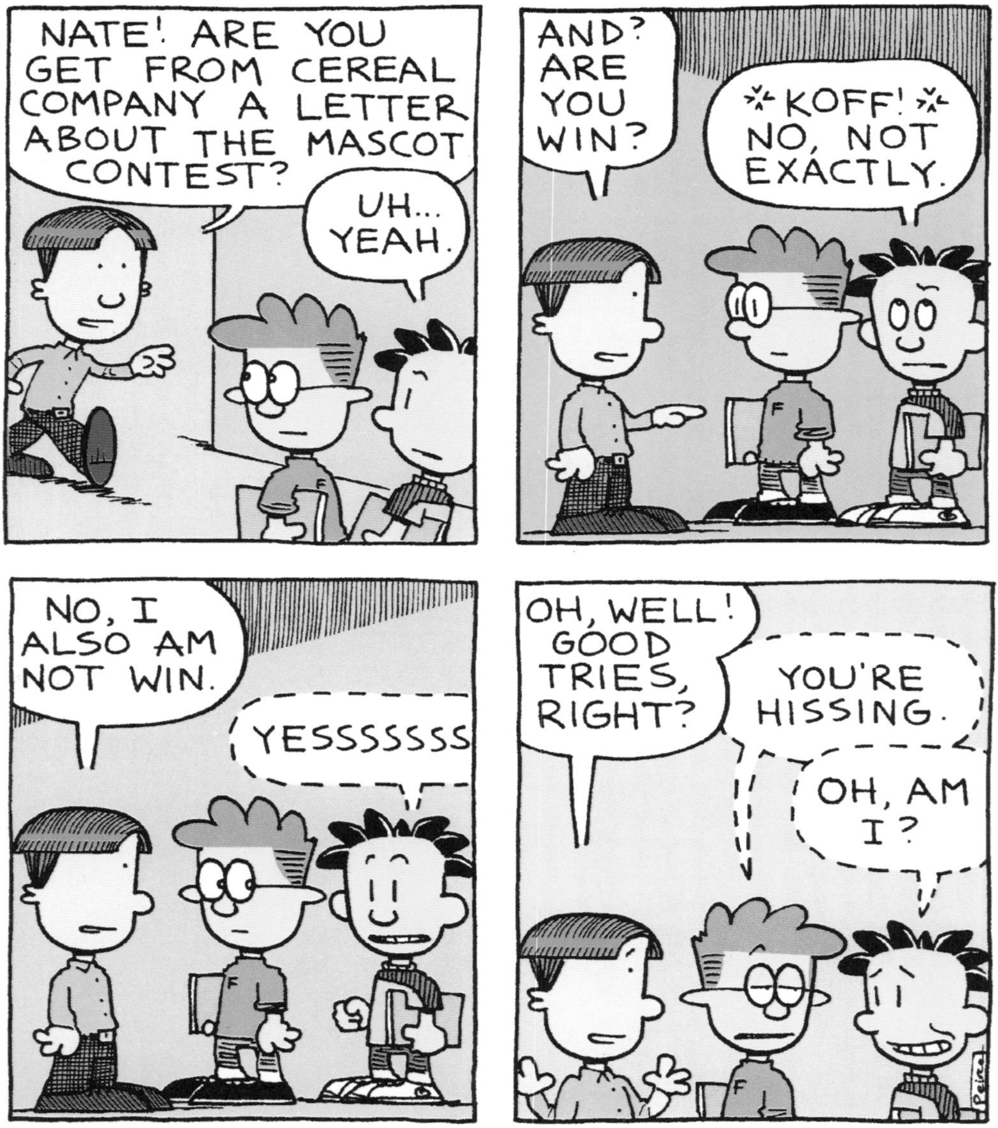
NATE! ARE YOU GET FROM CEREAL COMPANY A LETTER ABOUT THE MASCOT CONTEST?
UH... YEAH.
AND? ARE YOU WIN?
KOFF! NO, NOT EXACTLY.
NO, I ALSO AM NOT WIN.
YESSSSSSS
OH, WELL! GOOD TRIES, RIGHT?
YOU'RE HISSING.
OH, AM I?
Peirce

NATE, YOU TURNED THAT MASCOT CONTEST INTO A TONG WAR BETWEEN YOU AND ARTUR! WHY DO YOU ALWAYS COMPARE YOURSELF TO HIM?
I JUST **DO**, THAT'S ALL!
EVERYBODY COMPARES THEMSELVES TO SOMEONE ELSE! I MEASURE MYSELF AGAINST ARTUR, YOU MEASURE YOURSELF AGAINST GINA...
TEDDY, WHO DO **YOU** MEASURE YOURSELF AGAINST?
JAY-Z
I THINK JAY-Z'S WINNING.
IT'S A MARATHON, NOT A SPRINT.
Peirce

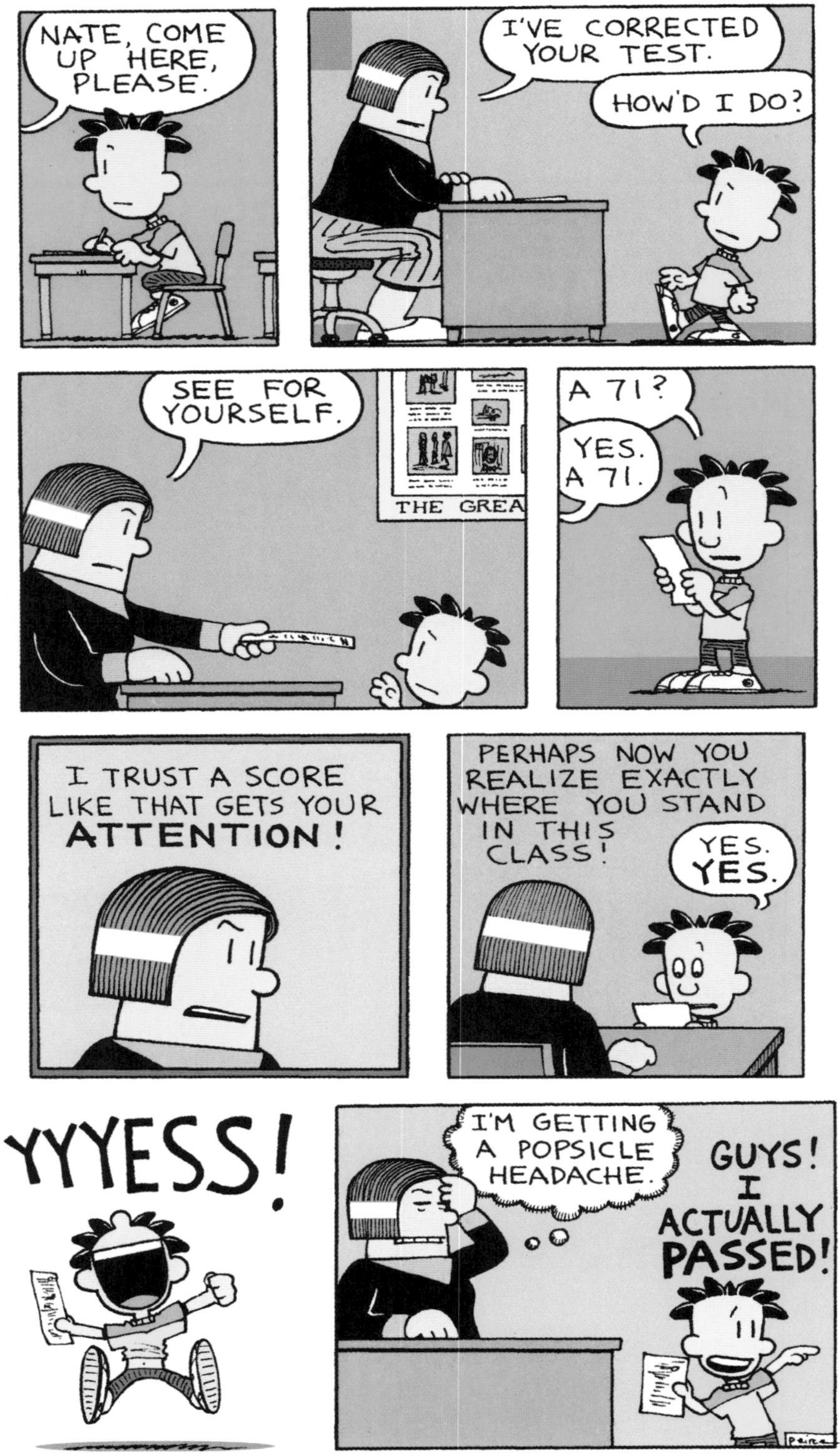
NATE, COME UP HERE, PLEASE.
I'VE CORRECTED YOUR TEST.
HOW'D I DO?
SEE FOR YOURSELF.
THE GREA
A 71?
YES. A 71.
I TRUST A SCORE LIKE THAT GETS YOUR **ATTENTION**!
PERHAPS NOW YOU REALIZE EXACTLY WHERE YOU STAND IN THIS CLASS!
YES. **YES**.
YYYESS!
I'M GETTING A POPSICLE HEADACHE.
GUYS! I ACTUALLY PASSED!

HOW'S THE PITCHING ARM, TEDDY?
GOOD! I'M READY!
I HOPE WE STOMP THESE GUYS!
WONDER WHO THEIR PITCHER IS?
WE'LL SOON FIND OUT!
RAC
LIT
LEA
I...
DON'T...
BELIEVE IT!
Peirce

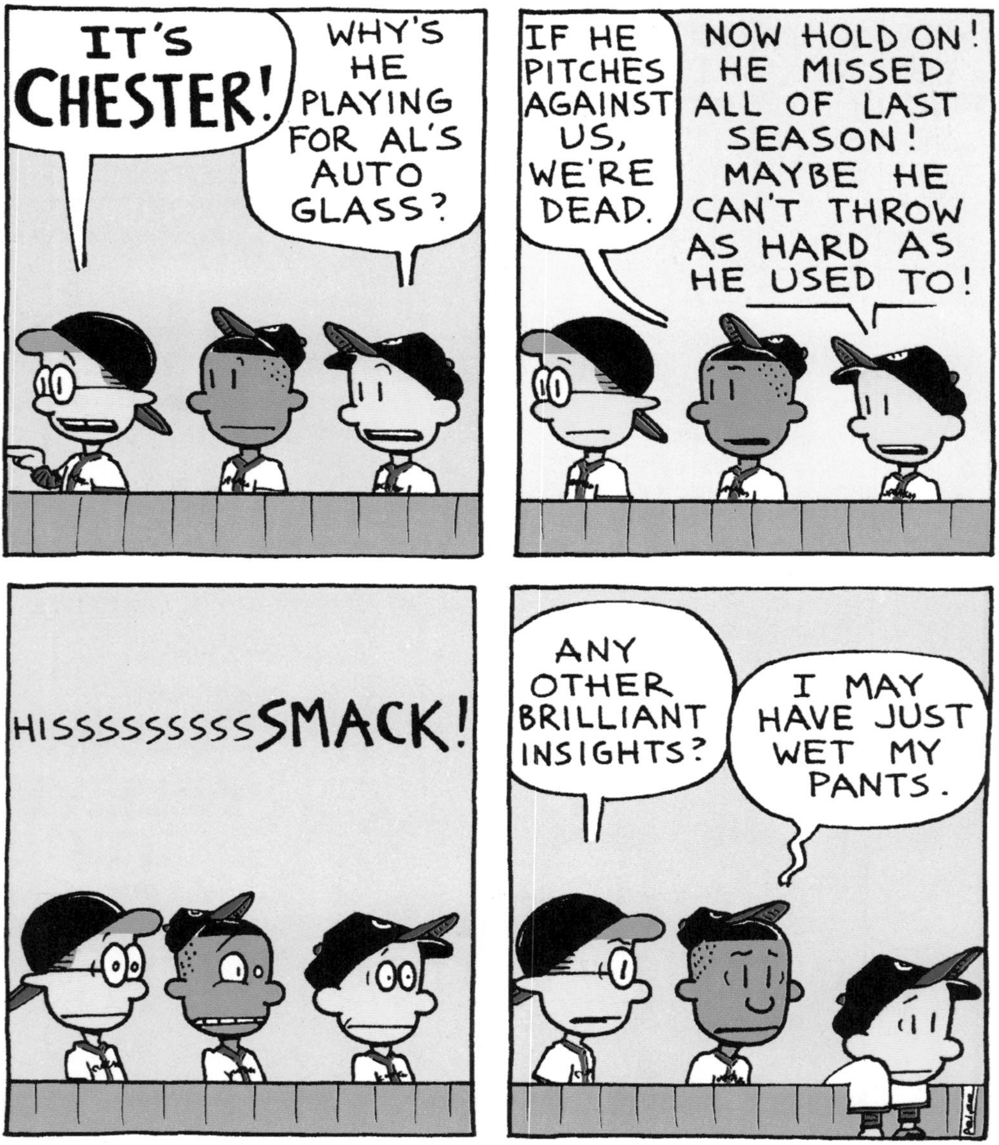
IT'S CHESTER!
WHY'S HE PLAYING FOR AL'S AUTO GLASS?
IF HE PITCHES AGAINST US, WE'RE DEAD.
NOW HOLD ON! HE MISSED ALL OF LAST SEASON! MAYBE HE CAN'T THROW AS HARD AS HE USED TO!
HISSSSSSSSSSMACK!
ANY OTHER BRILLIANT INSIGHTS?
I MAY HAVE JUST WET MY PANTS.

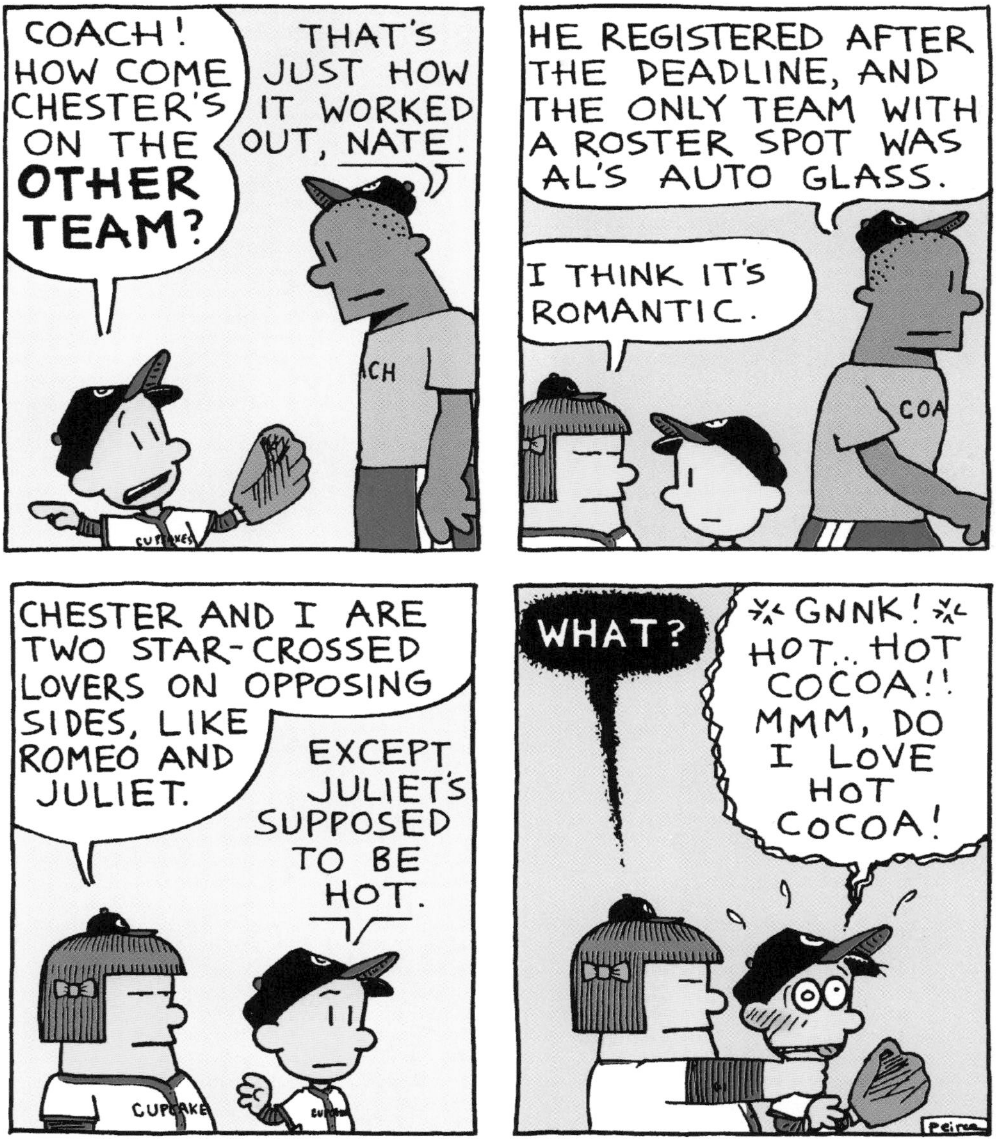
COACH! HOW COME CHESTER'S ON THE **OTHER TEAM**?
THAT'S JUST HOW IT WORKED OUT, NATE.
HE REGISTERED AFTER THE DEADLINE, AND THE ONLY TEAM WITH A ROSTER SPOT WAS AL'S AUTO GLASS.
I THINK IT'S ROMANTIC.
CHESTER AND I ARE TWO STAR-CROSSED LOVERS ON OPPOSING SIDES, LIKE ROMEO AND JULIET.
EXCEPT JULIET'S SUPPOSED TO BE HOT.
WHAT?
GNNK! HOT.. HOT COCOA!! MMM, DO I LOVE HOT COCOA!
Peirce

OKAY, GANG, WE ALL KNOW THAT CHESTER CAN THROW HARD, BUT HE **DOES** HAVE A WEAKNESS!
COACH
HE'S **WILD!** HALF THE TIME, HE HAS NO CLUE WHERE THE BALL IS GOING!
COACH
SO HE MIGHT **WALK** YOU!
COACH
WHAT GREAT NEWS.
...OR HE MIGHT **CRUSH OUR SKULLS!**
I'M NOT BATTING LEAD-OFF.
CH

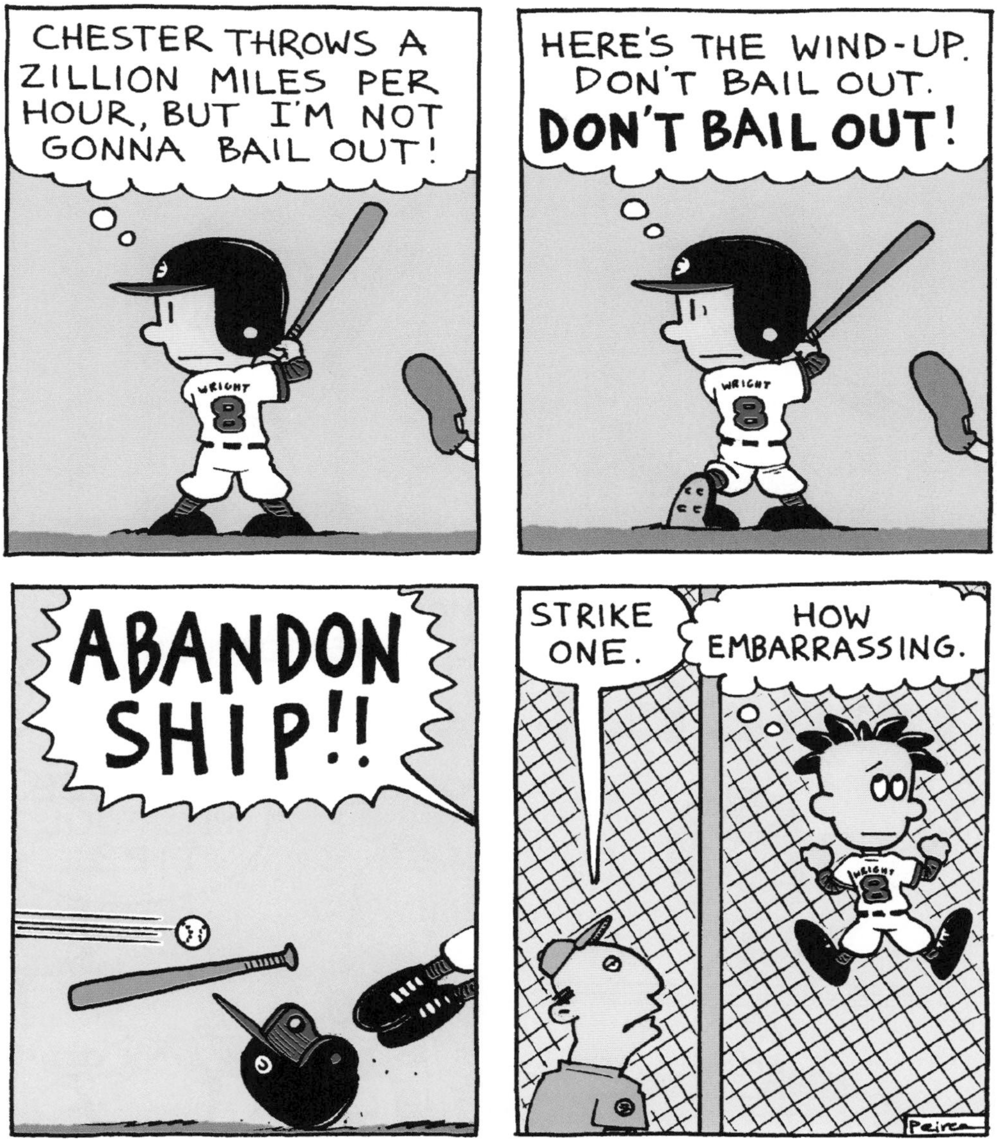
CHESTER THROWS A ZILLION MILES PER HOUR, BUT I'M NOT GONNA BAIL OUT!
WRIGHT 8
HERE'S THE WIND-UP. DON'T BAIL OUT. DON'T BAIL OUT!
WRIGHT 8
ABANDON SHIP!!
STRIKE ONE.
HOW EMBARRASSING.
WRIGHT 8
Peirce

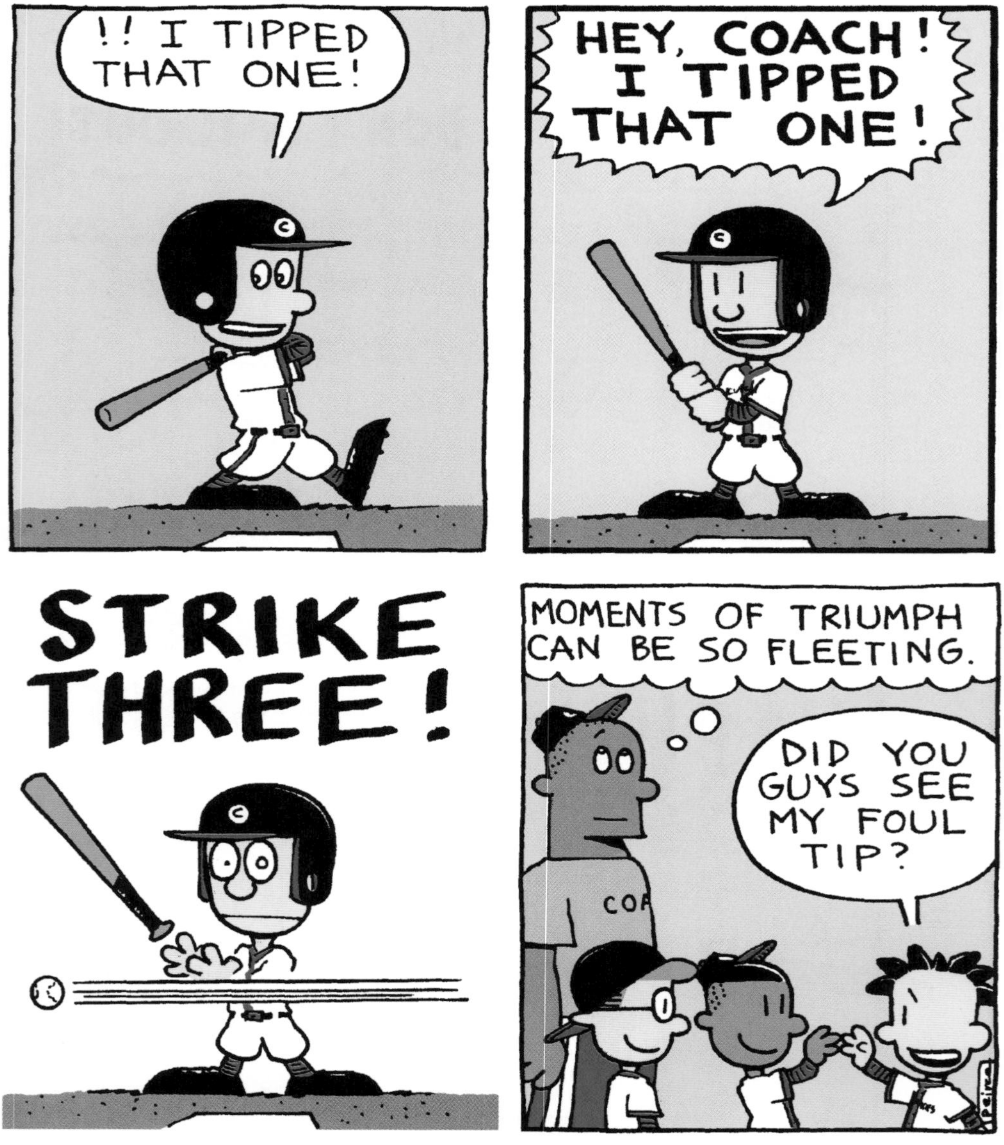
!! I TIPPED THAT ONE!
HEY, COACH! I TIPPED THAT ONE!
STRIKE THREE!
MOMENTS OF TRIUMPH CAN BE SO FLEETING.
DID YOU GUYS SEE MY FOUL TIP?

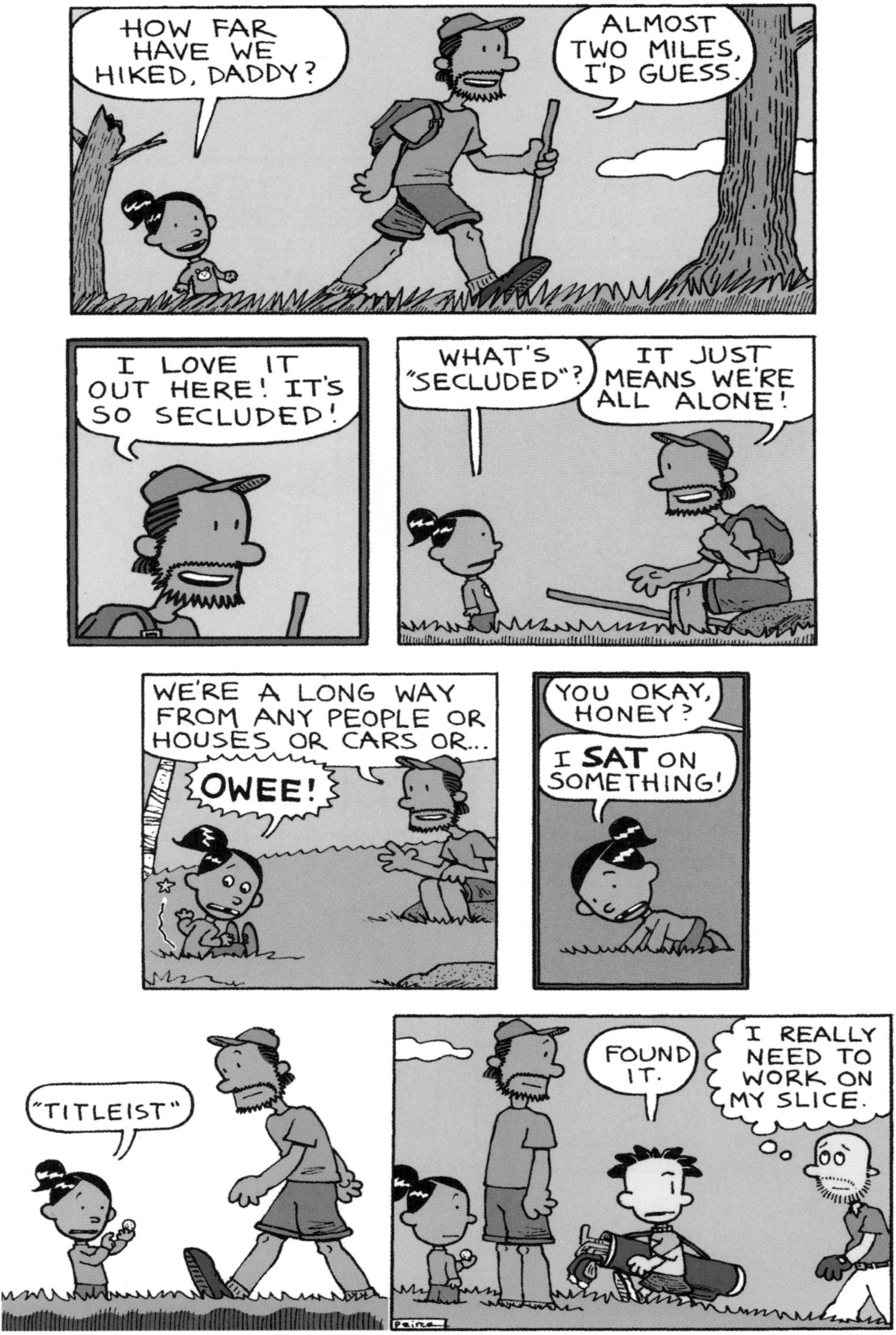
HOW FAR HAVE WE HIKED, DADDY?
ALMOST TWO MILES, I'D GUESS.
I LOVE IT OUT HERE! IT'S SO SECLUDED!
WHAT'S "SECLUDED"?
IT JUST MEANS WE'RE ALL ALONE!
WE'RE A LONG WAY FROM ANY PEOPLE OR HOUSES OR CARS OR...
OWEE!
YOU OKAY, HONEY?
I **SAT** ON SOMETHING!
"TITLEIST"
FOUND IT.
I REALLY NEED TO WORK ON MY SLICE.

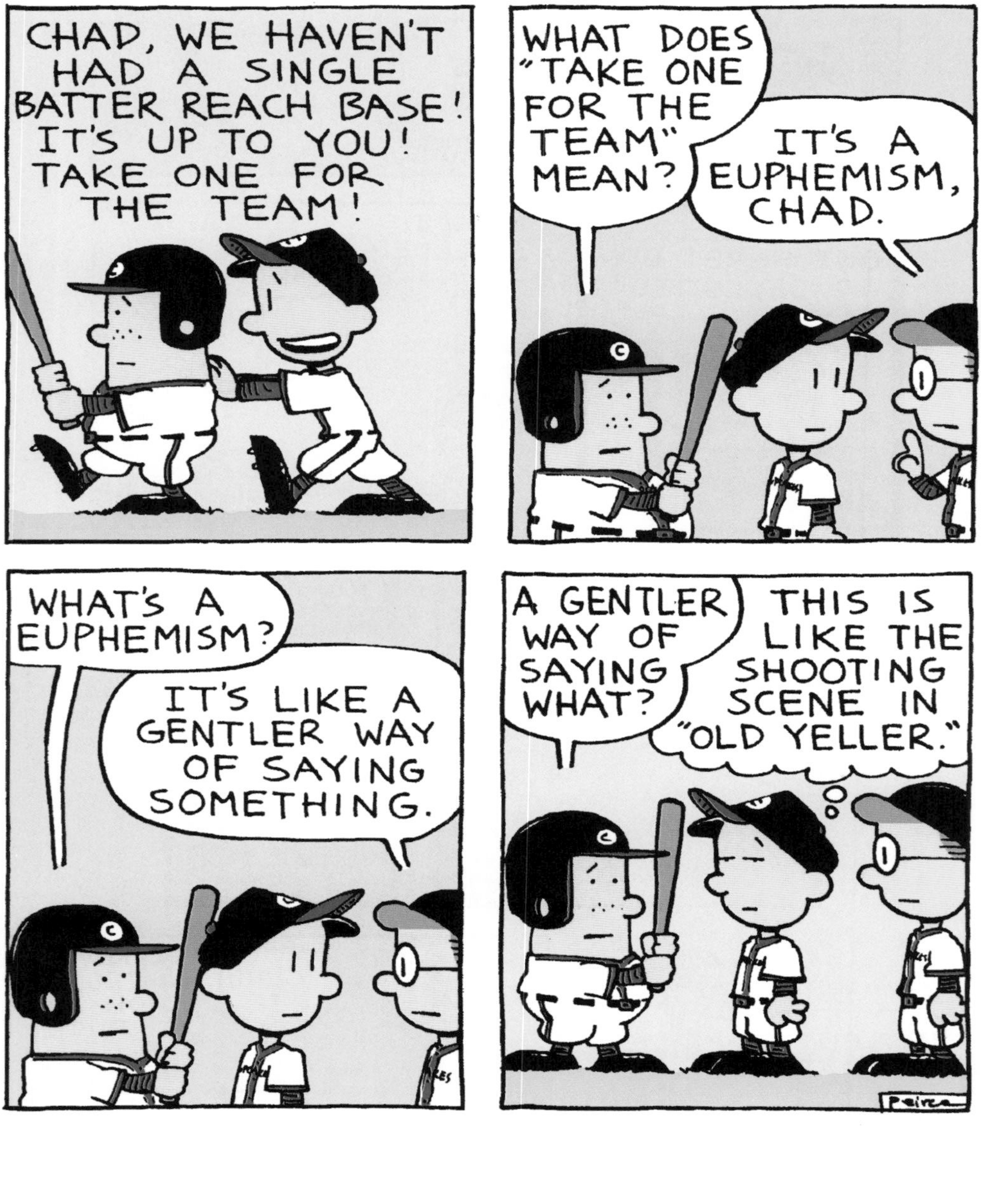
CHAD, WE HAVEN'T HAD A SINGLE BATTER REACH BASE! IT'S UP TO YOU! TAKE ONE FOR THE TEAM!
WHAT DOES "TAKE ONE FOR THE TEAM" MEAN?
IT'S A EUPHEMISM, CHAD.
WHAT'S A EUPHEMISM?
IT'S LIKE A GENTLER WAY OF SAYING SOMETHING.
A GENTLER WAY OF SAYING WHAT?
THIS IS LIKE THE SHOOTING SCENE IN "OLD YELLER."
Peirce

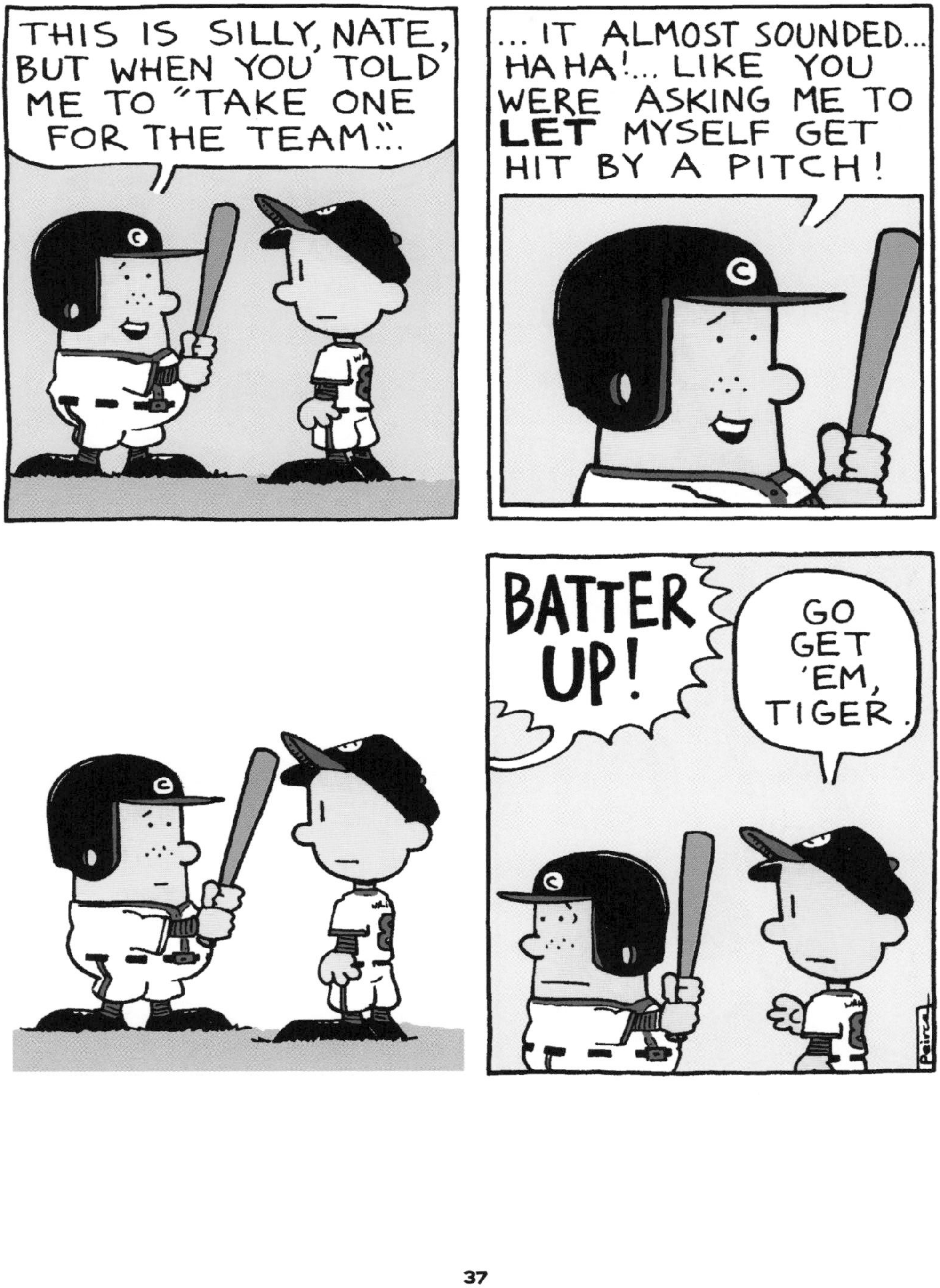
THIS IS SILLY, NATE, BUT WHEN YOU TOLD ME TO "TAKE ONE FOR THE TEAM"...
... IT ALMOST SOUNDED... HA HA!... LIKE YOU WERE ASKING ME TO **LET** MYSELF GET HIT BY A PITCH!
BATTER UP!
GO GET 'EM, TIGER.
Peirce

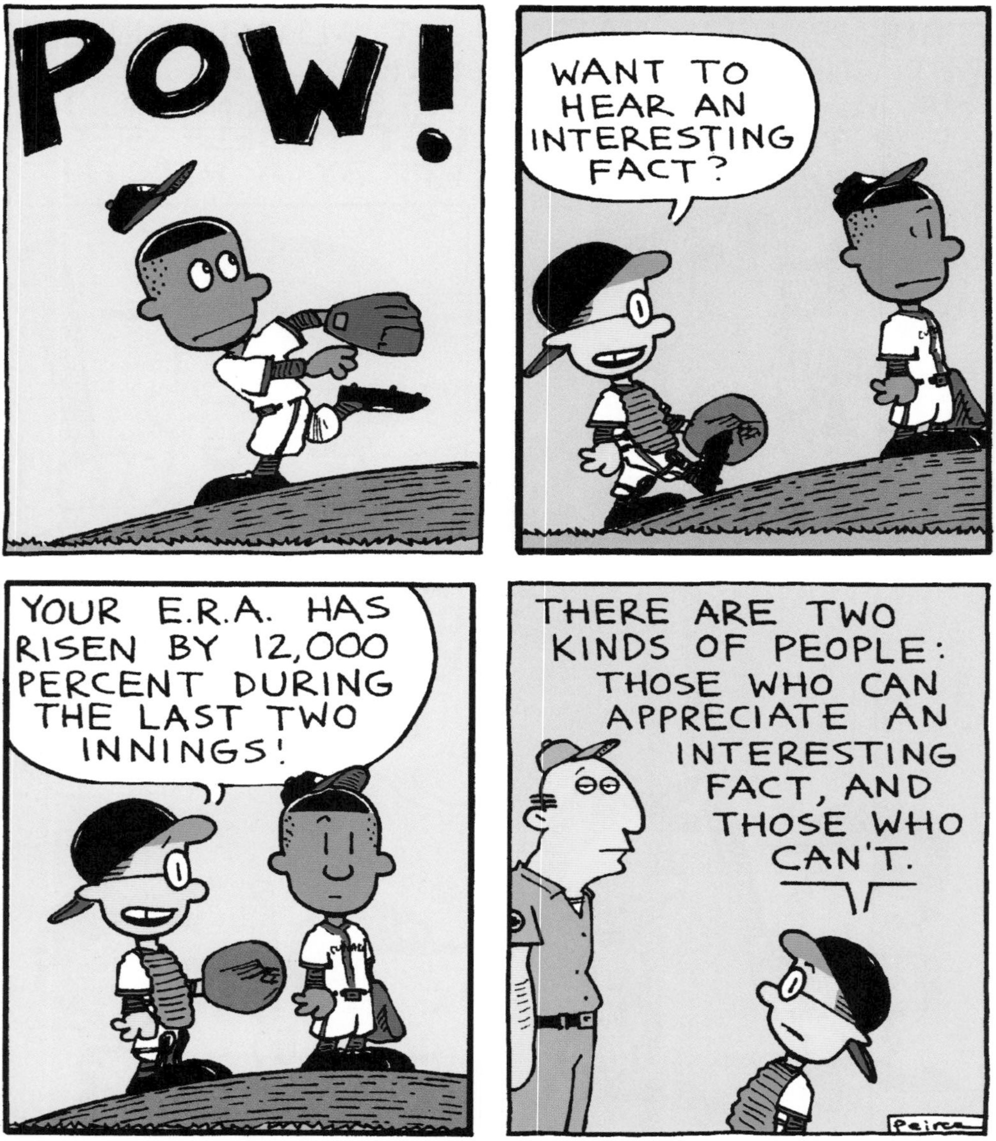
POW!
WANT TO HEAR AN INTERESTING FACT?
YOUR E.R.A. HAS RISEN BY 12,000 PERCENT DURING THE LAST TWO INNINGS!
THERE ARE TWO KINDS OF PEOPLE: THOSE WHO CAN APPRECIATE AN INTERESTING FACT, AND THOSE WHO CAN'T.
Peirce

I KNOW WHAT I'LL DO! I'LL **BUNT**!
THE ELEMENT OF SURPRISE! THAT'S WHAT WINS BALL GAMES!
CRUNCH!
...AND DESTROYS BATS.
I DIDN'T KNOW CARBON FIBER COULD BREAK LIKE THAT.

WOW! KIM! CHESTER EVEN STRUCK **YOU** OUT!
WHY WOULDN'T HE?
WELL... YOU'RE HIS GIRL-FRIEND.
HE RESPECTS ME TOO MUCH TO GO EASY ON ME.
AND HE KNOWS THAT IF HE **DOESN'T** RESPECT ME, I'LL DUMP HIM AND RESUME MY TORRID ROMANCE WITH **YOU**.
RESPECT IS GOOD.
I SENSE YOUR EXCITEMENT.
Peirce

THAT WAS RIDICULOUS! WE HAD NO CHANCE AGAINST CHESTER!
HE **WAS** PRETTY OVER-POWERING.
YEAH, BECAUSE HE'S **HUGE!**
WELL, YOU KNOW, PEOPLE MATURE AT DIFFERENT TIMES.
I WAS THE LAST BOY IN MY GRADE TO START SHAVING, AND LOOK AT ME **NOW!**
I'VE GOT HAIR IN PLACES I DON'T EVEN **KNOW** ABOUT!
CAN WE GO BACK TO TALKING ABOUT BASEBALL?
Peirce

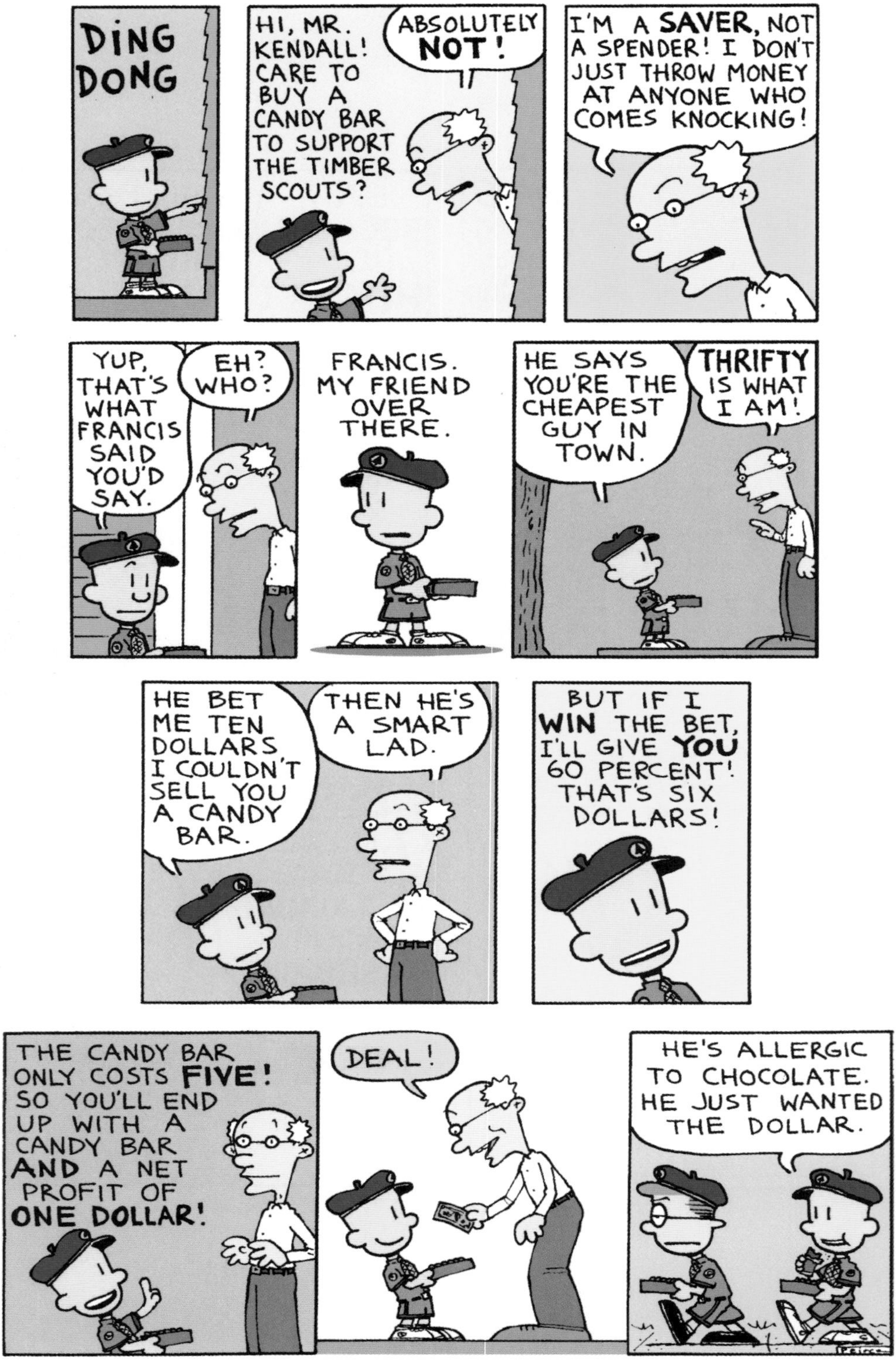
DING DONG
HI, MR. KENDALL! CARE TO BUY A CANDY BAR TO SUPPORT THE TIMBER SCOUTS?
ABSOLUTELY NOT!
I'M A SAVER, NOT A SPENDER! I DON'T JUST THROW MONEY AT ANYONE WHO COMES KNOCKING!
YUP, THAT'S WHAT FRANCIS SAID YOU'D SAY.
EH? WHO?
FRANCIS. MY FRIEND OVER THERE.
HE SAYS YOU'RE THE CHEAPEST GUY IN TOWN.
THRIFTY IS WHAT I AM!
HE BET ME TEN DOLLARS I COULDN'T SELL YOU A CANDY BAR.
THEN HE'S A SMART LAD.
BUT IF I WIN THE BET, I'LL GIVE YOU 60 PERCENT! THAT'S SIX DOLLARS!
THE CANDY BAR ONLY COSTS FIVE! SO YOU'LL END UP WITH A CANDY BAR AND A NET PROFIT OF ONE DOLLAR!
DEAL!
HE'S ALLERGIC TO CHOCOLATE. HE JUST WANTED THE DOLLAR.

MRS. GODFREY, WILL YOU TELL NATE TO STOP?
WHEN HE INHALES, HE HOLDS IT FOR A LONG TIME, THEN LETS IT OUT IN A LONG, LOUD EXHALE!
IT'S ANNOYING ME. IT MAKES IT HARD TO CONCENTRATE.
NATE, STOP BREATHING.
SO IT'S FINALLY COME TO THIS.

MRS. GODFREY, I **PROTEST**!
GINA'S COMPLAINED ABOUT THE WAY I GRIND MY TEETH, THE WAY I BOUNCE MY LEG... AND **NOW** SHE'S WHINING ABOUT MY **BREATHING**!
WHAT ARE YOU SAYING, NATE?
I'M SAYING I CAN'T HELP HOW I STINKIN' BREATHE!
SIIIIIIGH
PRINCI
Peirce

HAVE A SEAT, NATE.
HAVE A **SEAT**? I SHOULDN'T EVEN **BE** HERE!
GINA COMPLAINED ABOUT ME, AND OF **COURSE** MRS. GODFREY TOOK HER SIDE! ALL I WAS DOING WAS **BREATHING**!
THAT'S ALL?
YOU DIDN'T SCREAM AT MRS. GODFREY, "I CAN'T HELP HOW I STINKIN' BREATHE"?
SCREAM? WHAT? NO! I DIDN'T SCREAM!
I HEARD YOU FROM HERE.
IT MAY HAVE HAD A FAINTLY SCREAMISH QUALITY.

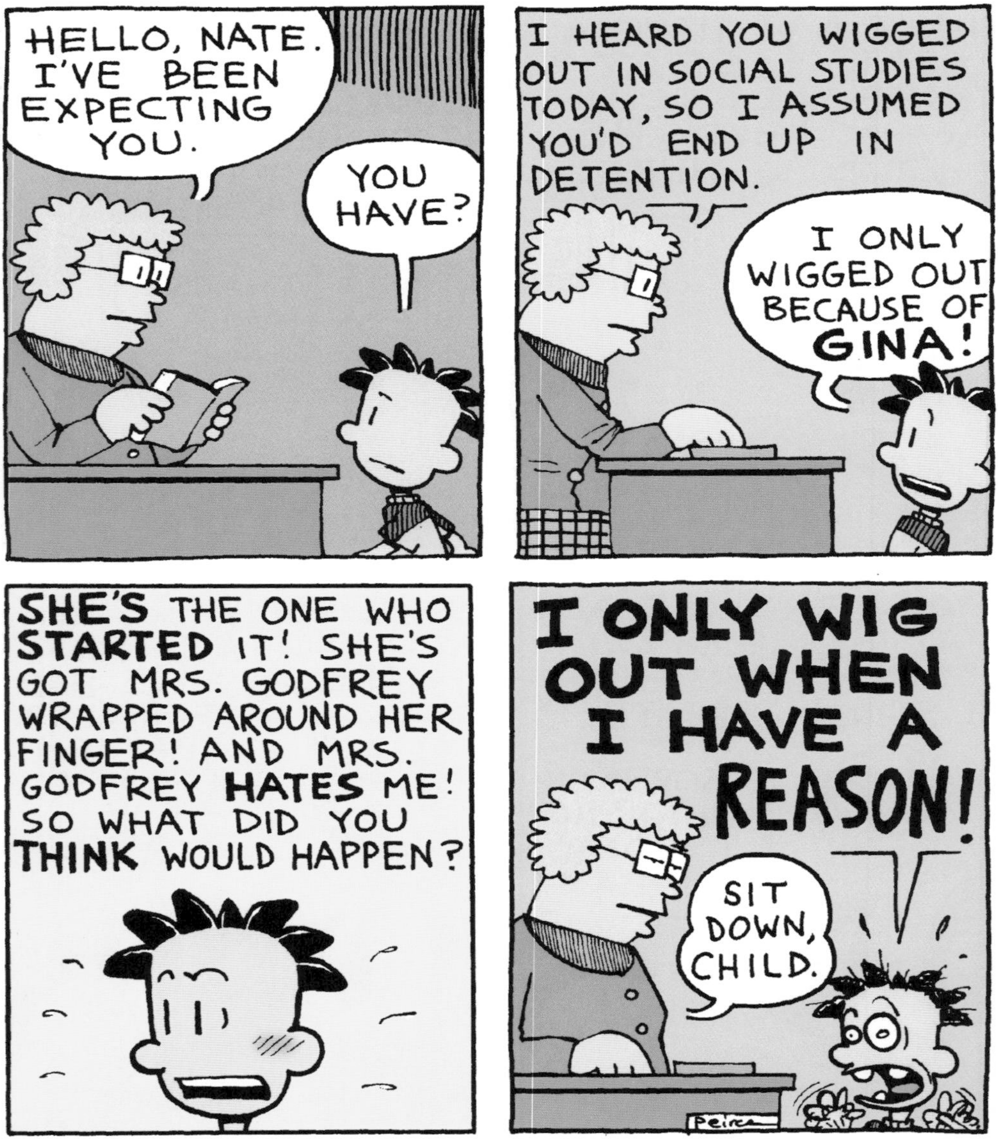
HELLO, NATE. I'VE BEEN EXPECTING YOU.
YOU HAVE?
I HEARD YOU WIGGED OUT IN SOCIAL STUDIES TODAY, SO I ASSUMED YOU'D END UP IN DETENTION.
I ONLY WIGGED OUT BECAUSE OF GINA!
SHE'S THE ONE WHO STARTED IT! SHE'S GOT MRS. GODFREY WRAPPED AROUND HER FINGER! AND MRS. GODFREY HATES ME! SO WHAT DID YOU THINK WOULD HAPPEN?
I ONLY WIG OUT WHEN I HAVE A REASON!
SIT DOWN, CHILD.
Peirce

NATE, YOU MUSN'T LET GINA IRRITATE YOU SO MUCH! THAT'S EXACTLY WHAT SHE **WANTS**!

SO WHAT DO I DO?

JUST LET IT ALL ROLL RIGHT OFF YOUR BACK! ACT AS IF NOTHING BOTHERS YOU! THAT'S WHAT **I** DO WHEN MY HUSBAND ACTS UP!

I JUST **IGNORE** IT WHEN HE DOES THINGS LIKE OVERFEEDING THE FISH, OR SPILLING BEER ON OUR BRAND-NEW SOFA...

... OR GIVING ME MADDEN NFL 25 FOR **VALENTINE'S DAY**!

CAN THIS MARRIAGE BE SAVED?

Peirce

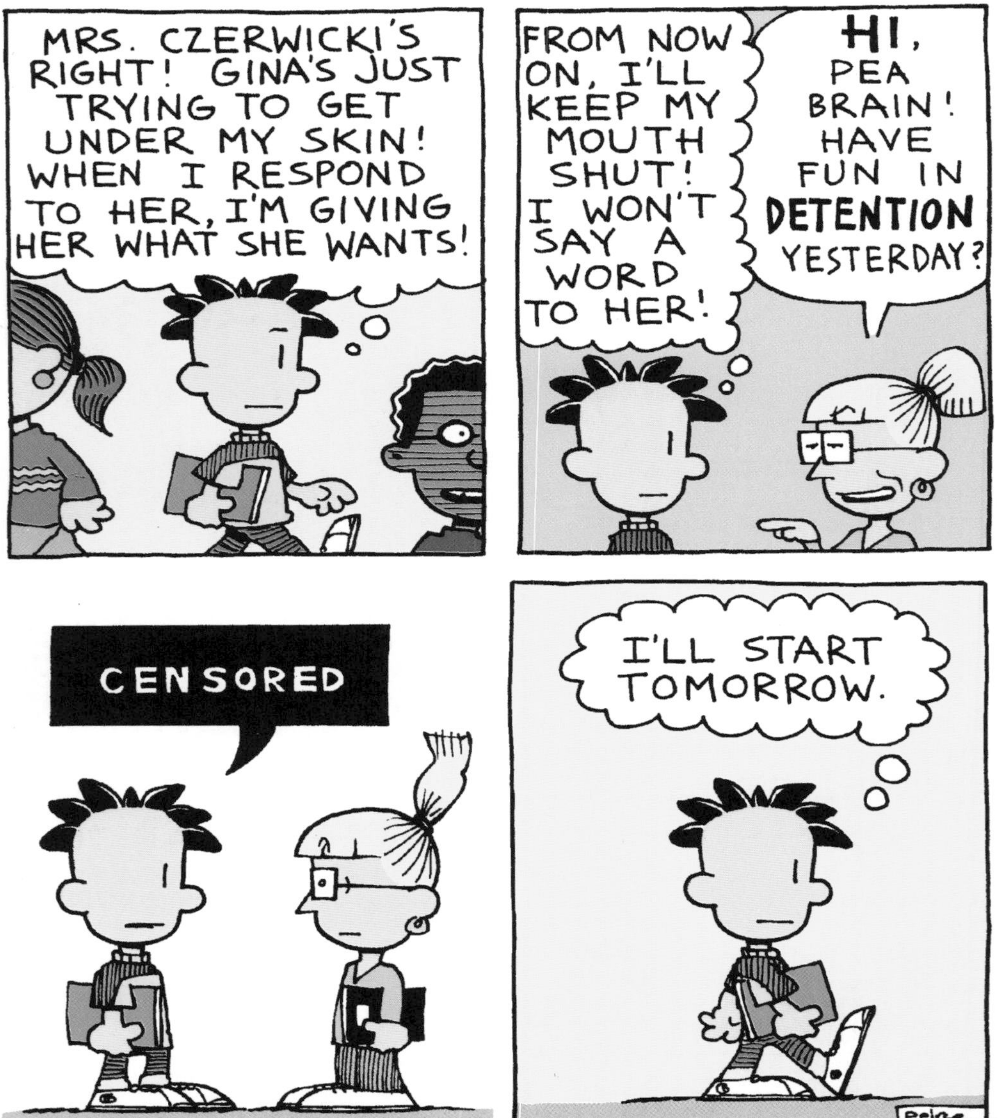
MRS. CZERWICKI'S RIGHT! GINA'S JUST TRYING TO GET UNDER MY SKIN! WHEN I RESPOND TO HER, I'M GIVING HER WHAT SHE WANTS!
FROM NOW ON, I'LL KEEP MY MOUTH SHUT! I WON'T SAY A WORD TO HER!
HI, PEA BRAIN! HAVE FUN IN DETENTION YESTERDAY?
CENSORED
I'LL START TOMORROW.
Peirce

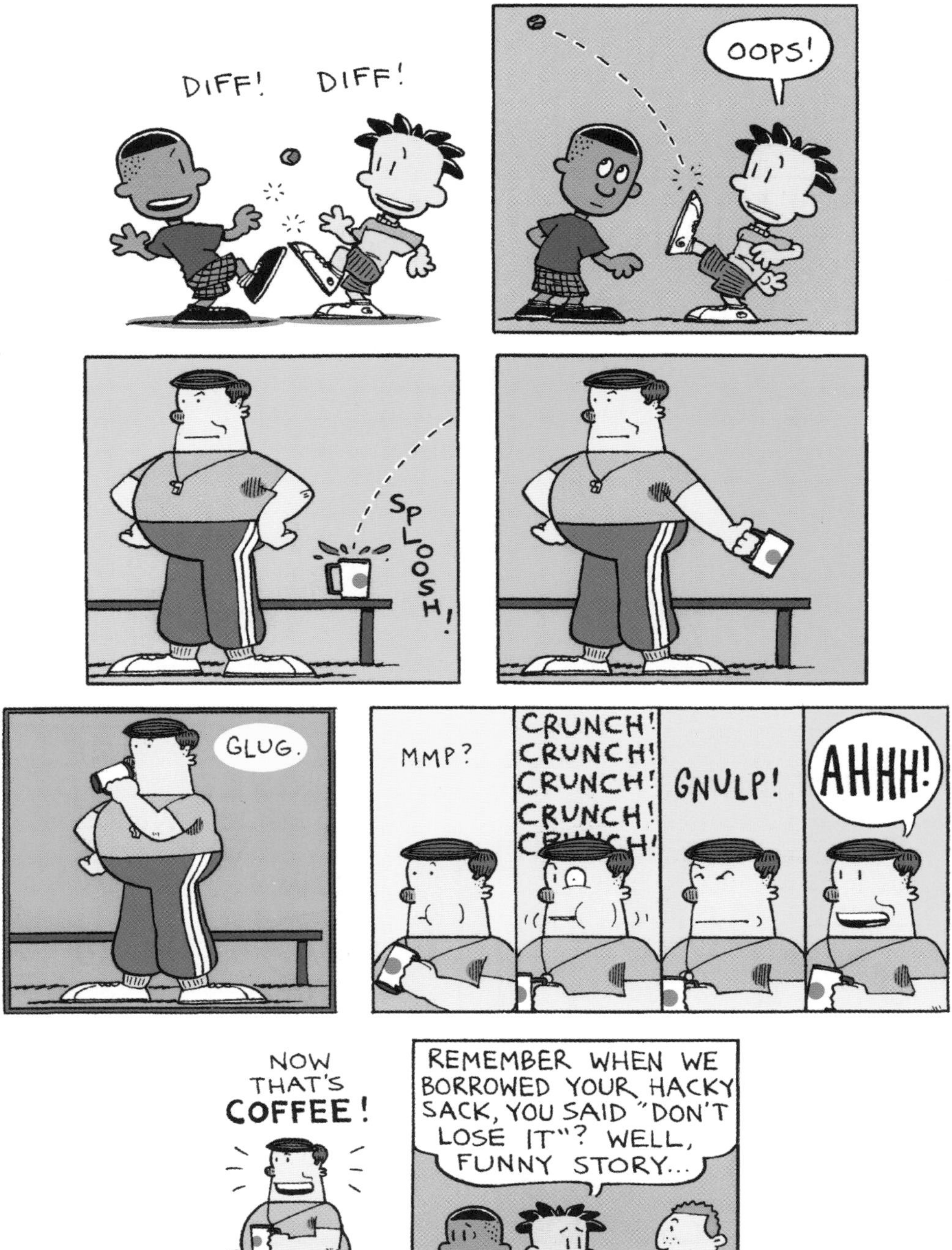
DIFF! DIFF!
OOPS!
SPLOOSH!
GLUG.
MMP?
CRUNCH! CRUNCH! CRUNCH! CRUNCH! CRUNCH!
GNULP!
AHHH!
NOW THAT'S **COFFEE**!
REMEMBER WHEN WE BORROWED YOUR HACKY SACK, YOU SAID "DON'T LOSE IT"? WELL, FUNNY STORY...
Peirce

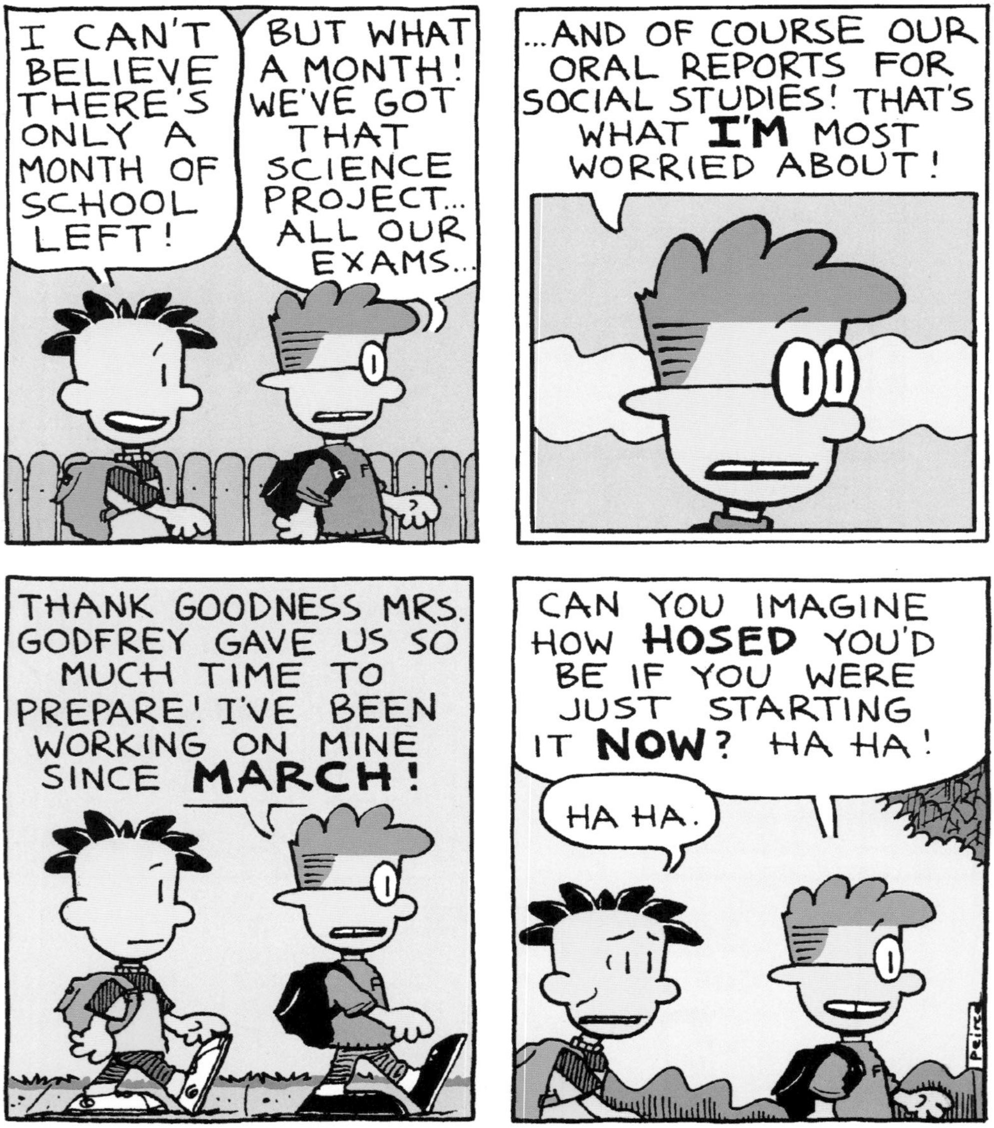
I CAN'T BELIEVE THERE'S ONLY A MONTH OF SCHOOL LEFT!
BUT WHAT A MONTH! WE'VE GOT THAT SCIENCE PROJECT... ALL OUR EXAMS...
...AND OF COURSE OUR ORAL REPORTS FOR SOCIAL STUDIES! THAT'S WHAT **I'M** MOST WORRIED ABOUT!
THANK GOODNESS MRS. GODFREY GAVE US SO MUCH TIME TO PREPARE! I'VE BEEN WORKING ON MINE SINCE **MARCH**!
CAN YOU IMAGINE HOW **HOSED** YOU'D BE IF YOU WERE JUST STARTING IT **NOW**? HA HA!
HA HA.
Peirce

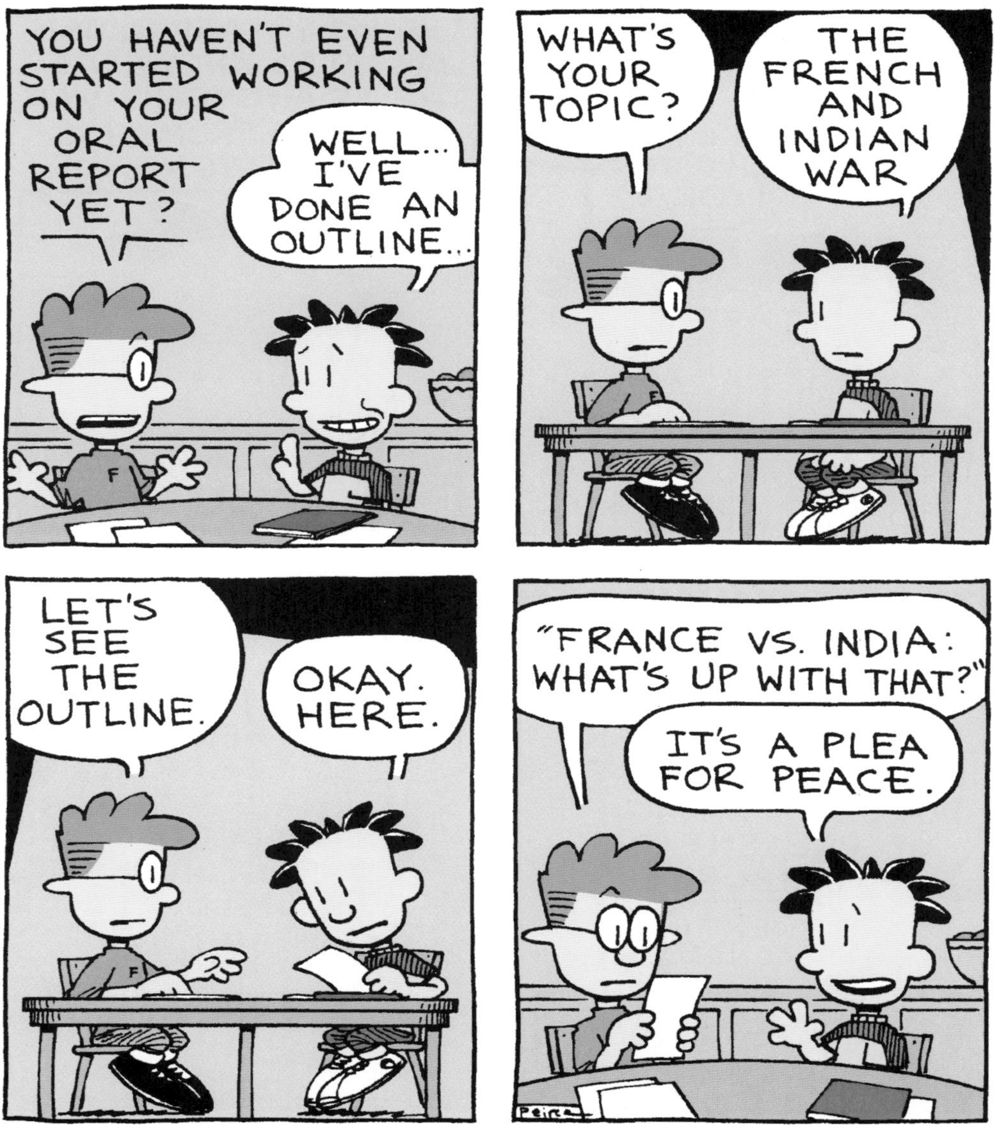
YOU HAVEN'T EVEN STARTED WORKING ON YOUR ORAL REPORT YET?
WELL... I'VE DONE AN OUTLINE...
WHAT'S YOUR TOPIC?
THE FRENCH AND INDIAN WAR
LET'S SEE THE OUTLINE.
OKAY. HERE.
"FRANCE VS. INDIA: WHAT'S UP WITH THAT?"
IT'S A PLEA FOR PEACE.
Peirce

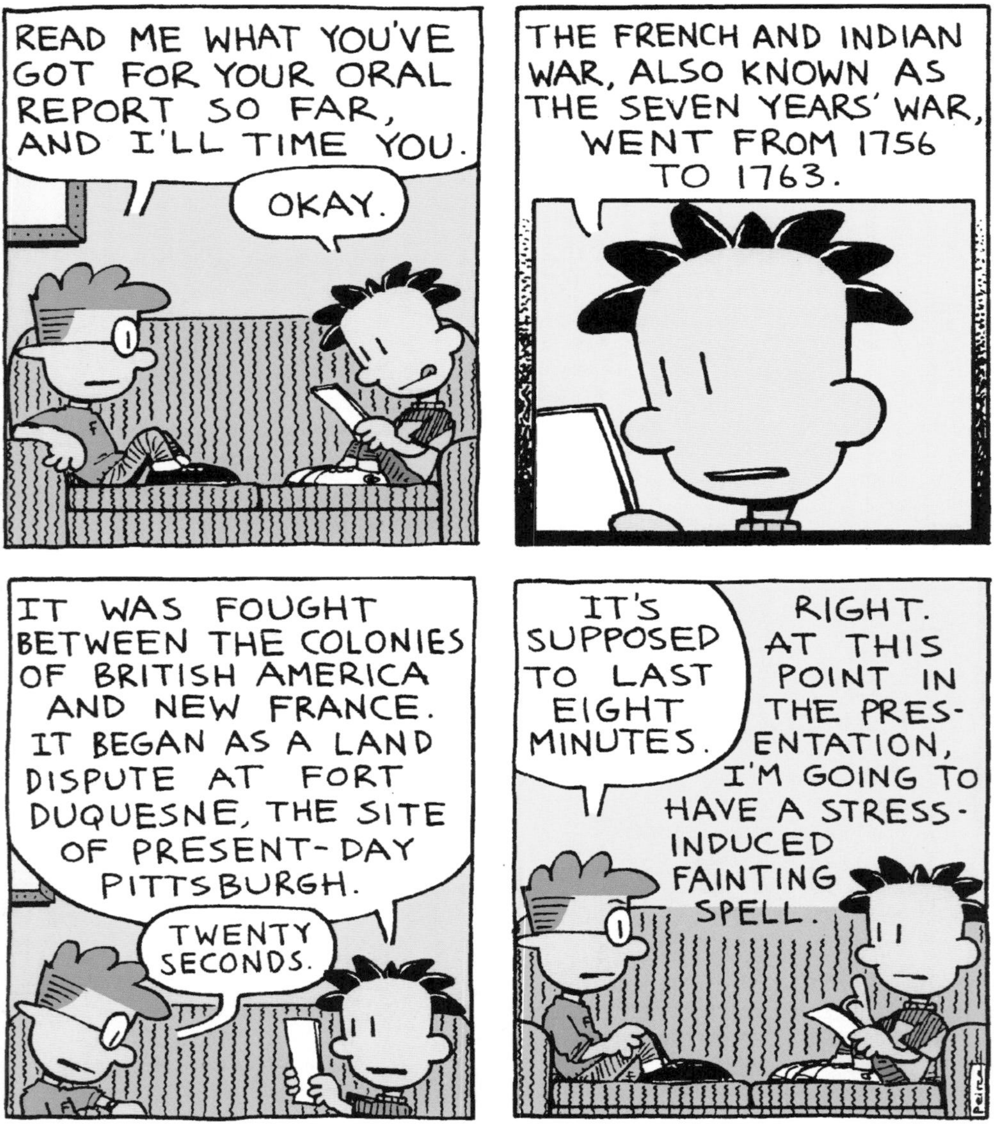
READ ME WHAT YOU'VE GOT FOR YOUR ORAL REPORT SO FAR, AND I'LL TIME YOU.
OKAY.
THE FRENCH AND INDIAN WAR, ALSO KNOWN AS THE SEVEN YEARS' WAR, WENT FROM 1756 TO 1763.
IT WAS FOUGHT BETWEEN THE COLONIES OF BRITISH AMERICA AND NEW FRANCE. IT BEGAN AS A LAND DISPUTE AT FORT DUQUESNE, THE SITE OF PRESENT-DAY PITTSBURGH.
TWENTY SECONDS.
IT'S SUPPOSED TO LAST EIGHT MINUTES.
RIGHT. AT THIS POINT IN THE PRESENTATION, I'M GOING TO HAVE A STRESS-INDUCED FAINTING SPELL.
Peirce

BEFORE I START MY REPORT, MRS. GODFREY, I'D LIKE TO REMIND YOU OF ABE LINCOLN'S GETTYSBURG ADDRESS.

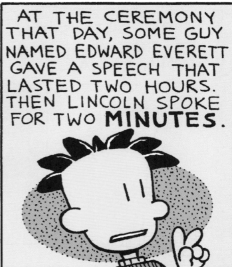

AT THE CEREMONY THAT DAY, SOME GUY NAMED EDWARD EVERETT GAVE A SPEECH THAT LASTED TWO HOURS. THEN LINCOLN SPOKE FOR TWO **MINUTES.**

NOBODY REMEMBERS WHAT THE FIRST DUDE SAID, WHILE LINCOLN'S VERY SHORT SPEECH HAS BECOME A TOTAL **CLASSIC.**

SPOKEN LIKE A KID WHOSE 8-MINUTE REPORT IS ABOUT 5 MINUTES SHORT.

SO, TO SUM UP: LENGTH ISN'T EVERY-THING. JUST SAYIN'.

MY REPORT IS ON THE FRENCH AND INDIAN WAR.
BUT BEFORE I BEGIN, PLEASE RISE AS POP MEGASTAR BEYONCÉ PERFORMS OUR NATIONAL ANTHEM.
KLIK
OHH WHOA WHOA SAAAAAY CAN YOU SEEEEEEEE...
THIS COUNTS TOWARD MY EIGHT MINUTES, RIGHT?
Peirce

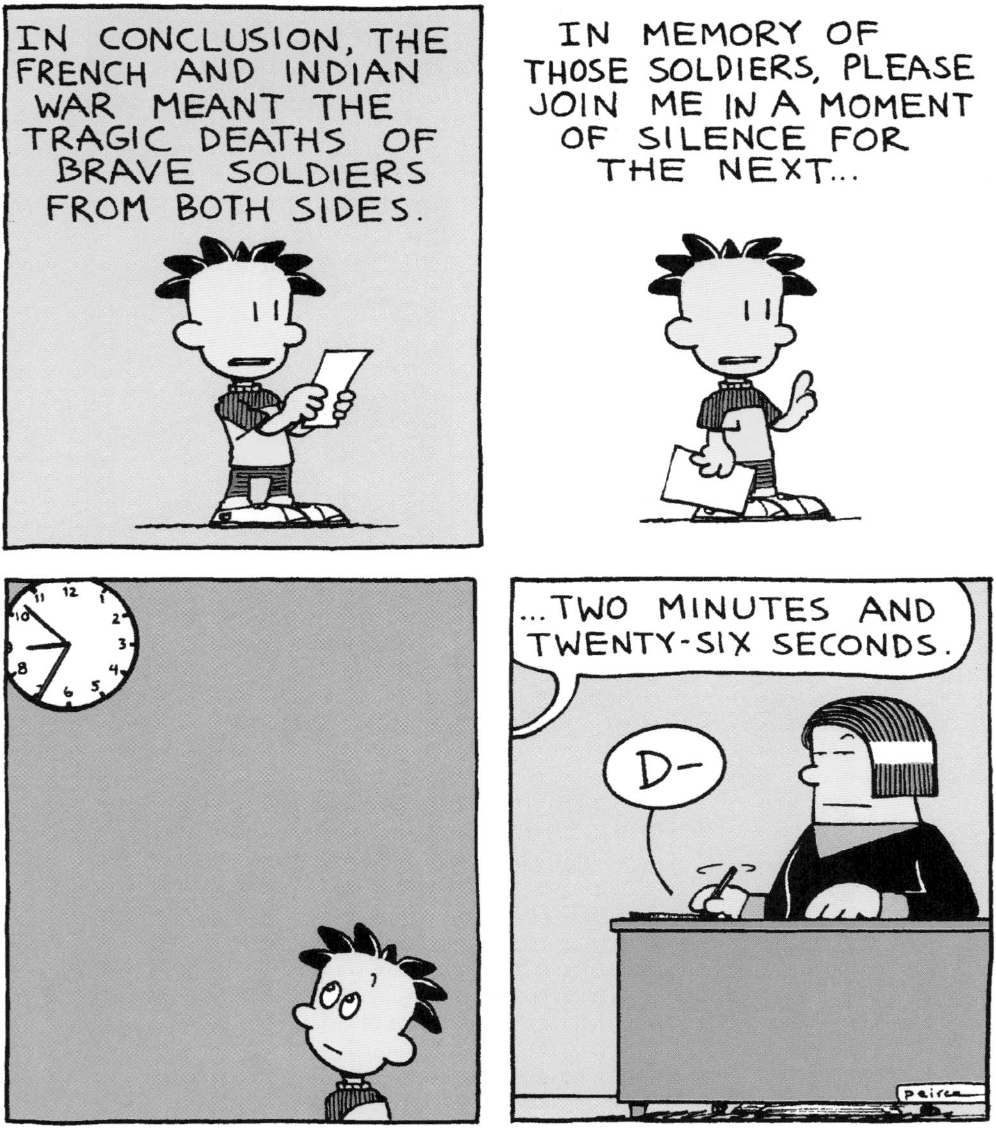
IN CONCLUSION, THE FRENCH AND INDIAN WAR MEANT THE TRAGIC DEATHS OF BRAVE SOLDIERS FROM BOTH SIDES.
IN MEMORY OF THOSE SOLDIERS, PLEASE JOIN ME IN A MOMENT OF SILENCE FOR THE NEXT...
...TWO MINUTES AND TWENTY-SIX SECONDS.
D-
peirce

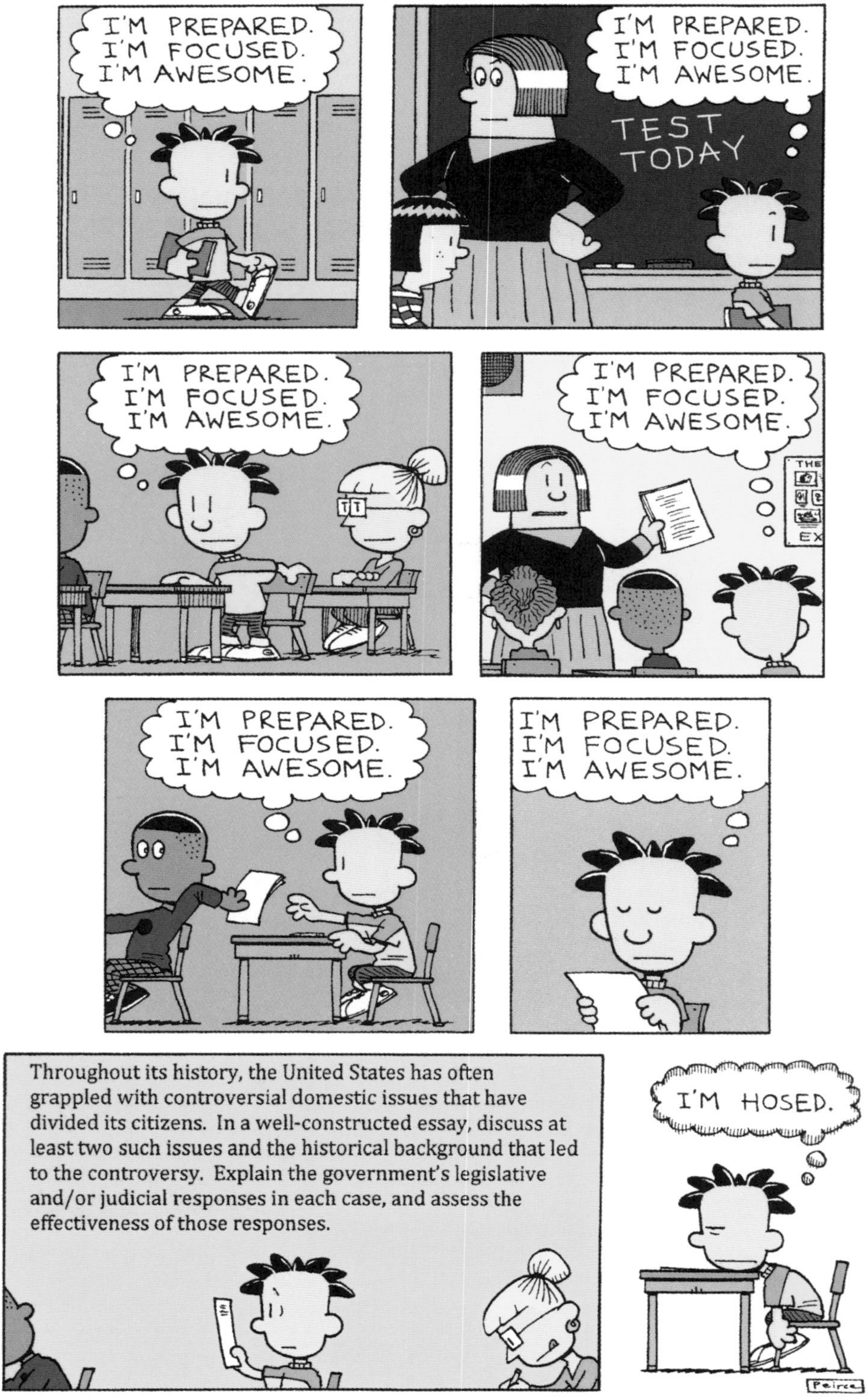
I'M PREPARED. I'M FOCUSED. I'M AWESOME.
I'M PREPARED. I'M FOCUSED. I'M AWESOME.
TEST TODAY
I'M PREPARED. I'M FOCUSED. I'M AWESOME.
I'M PREPARED. I'M FOCUSED. I'M AWESOME.
I'M PREPARED. I'M FOCUSED. I'M AWESOME.
I'M PREPARED. I'M FOCUSED. I'M AWESOME.
Throughout its history, the United States has often grappled with controversial domestic issues that have divided its citizens. In a well-constructed essay, discuss at least two such issues and the historical background that led to the controversy. Explain the government's legislative and/or judicial responses in each case, and assess the effectiveness of those responses.
I'M HOSED.
Peirce

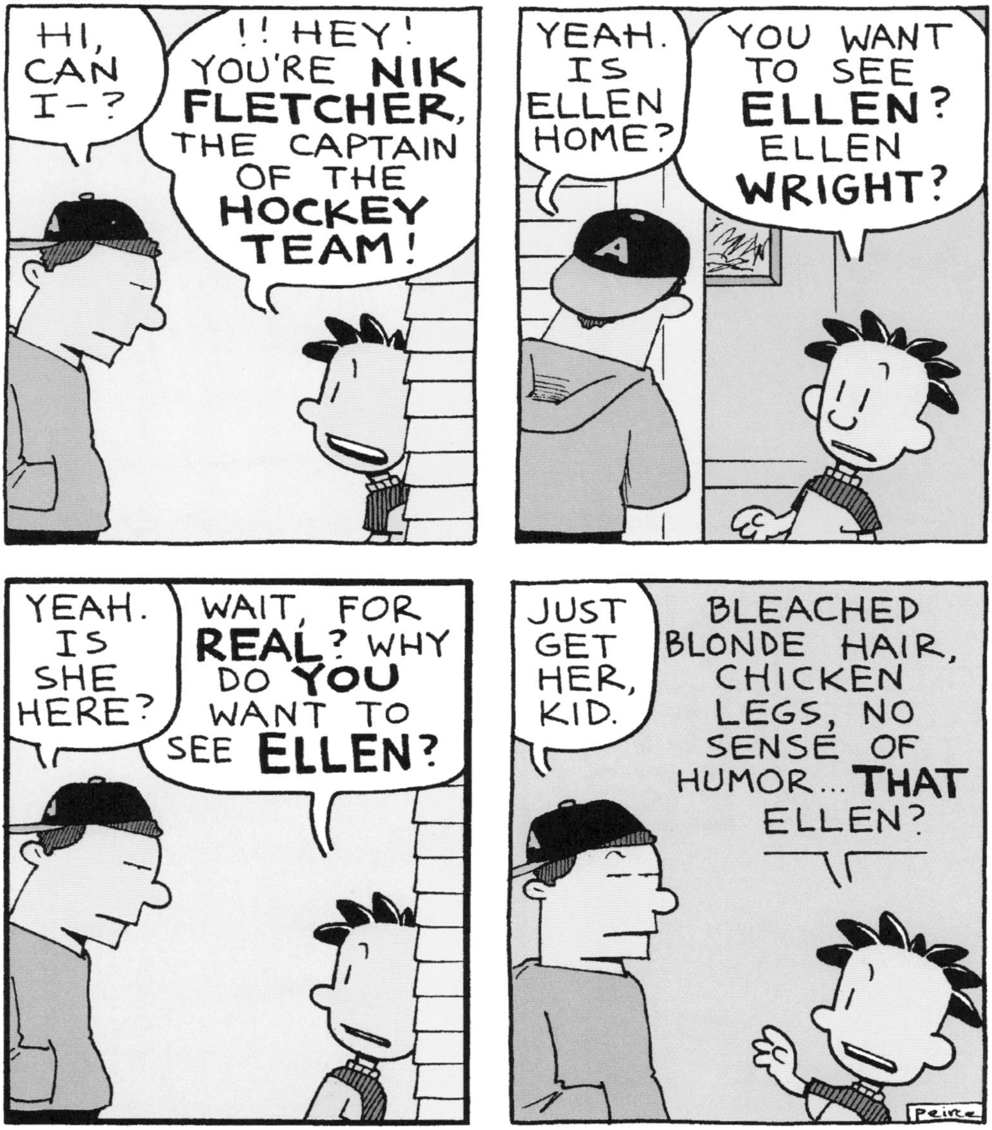
HI, CAN I-?
!! HEY! YOU'RE NIK FLETCHER, THE CAPTAIN OF THE HOCKEY TEAM!
YEAH. IS ELLEN HOME?
YOU WANT TO SEE ELLEN? ELLEN WRIGHT?
YEAH. IS SHE HERE?
WAIT, FOR REAL? WHY DO YOU WANT TO SEE ELLEN?
JUST GET HER, KID.
BLEACHED BLONDE HAIR, CHICKEN LEGS, NO SENSE OF HUMOR... THAT ELLEN?
Peirce

WOW! LOOK AT THIS! ALL IN ONE ROOM WE'VE GOT NIK, THE BEST HIGH SCHOOL HOCKEY PLAYER IN THE STATE...
WE'VE GOT **ME**, THE MOST TALENTED YOUNG CARTOONIST OF OUR TIME...
...AND WE'VE GOT ELLEN.
Peirce
WHAT'S WRONG WITH THIS PICTURE?
GO AWAY!

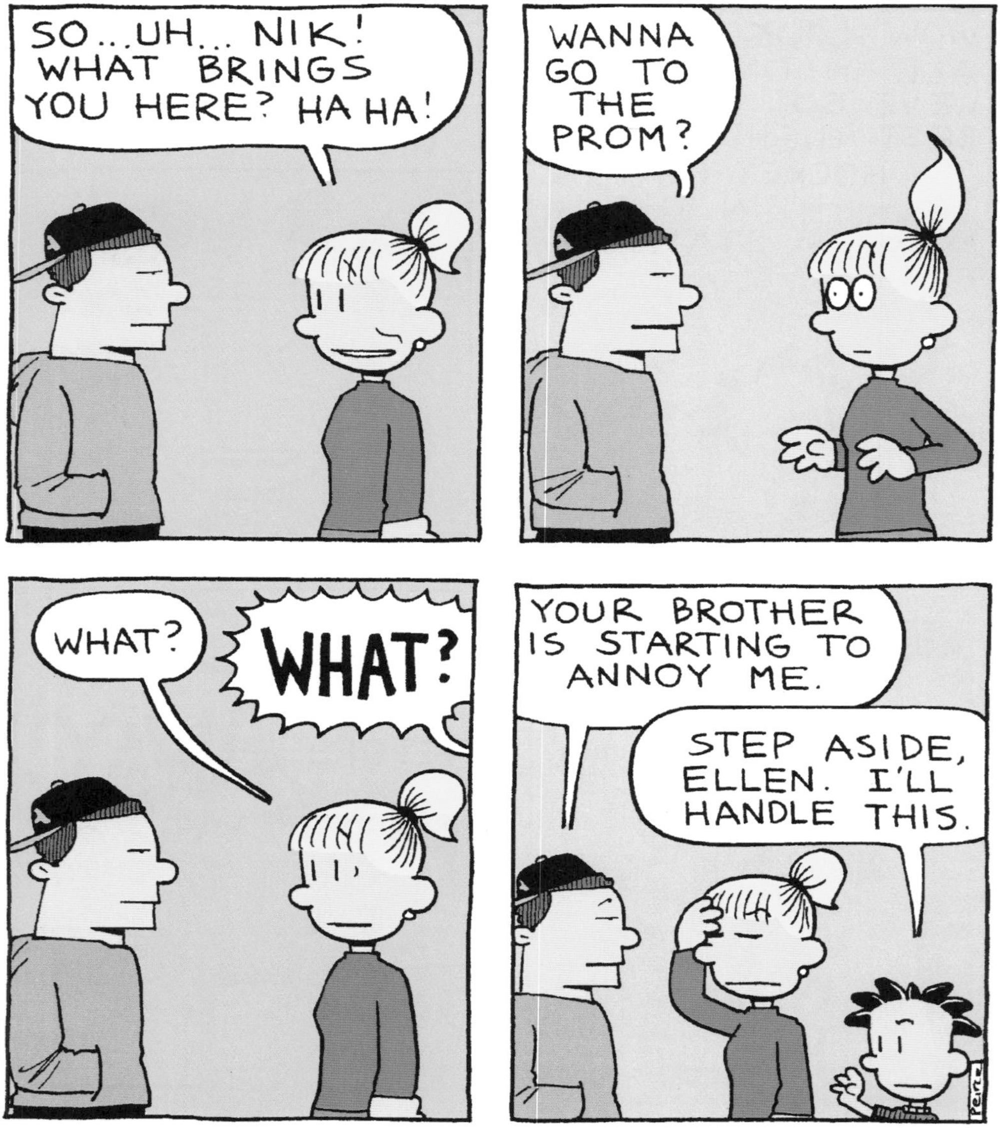
SO...UH... NIK! WHAT BRINGS YOU HERE? HA HA!
WANNA GO TO THE PROM?
WHAT?
WHAT?
YOUR BROTHER IS STARTING TO ANNOY ME.
STEP ASIDE, ELLEN. I'LL HANDLE THIS.
PEIRCE

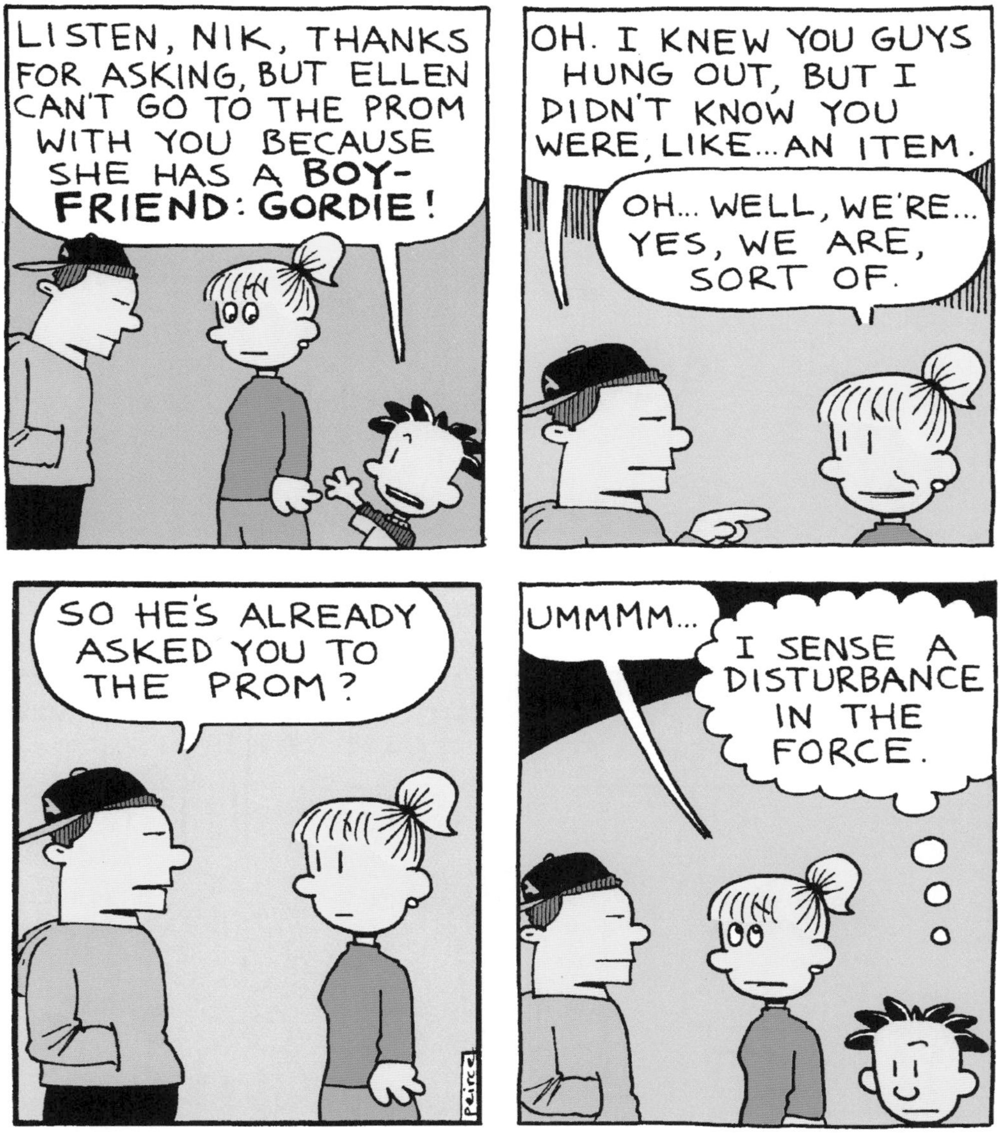
LISTEN, NIK, THANKS FOR ASKING, BUT ELLEN CAN'T GO TO THE PROM WITH YOU BECAUSE SHE HAS A **BOY-FRIEND: GORDIE**!
OH. I KNEW YOU GUYS HUNG OUT, BUT I DIDN'T KNOW YOU WERE, LIKE... AN ITEM.
OH... WELL, WE'RE... YES, WE ARE, SORT OF.
SO HE'S ALREADY ASKED YOU TO THE PROM?
Peirce
UMMMM...
I SENSE A DISTURBANCE IN THE FORCE.

HI, NATE!
GORDIE! GET IN HERE!
WHAT'S THIS ALL ABOUT? YOU SOUNDED SO WEIRD OVER THE PHONE!
YOUR **GIRLFRIEND**, THAT'S WHAT IT'S ABOUT!
BUT I JUST SAW ELLEN A FEW HOURS AGO AT **SCHOOL**! IF SOMETHING WAS URGENT, SHE WOULD'VE...
...TOLD ME.
URGENT ENOUGH FOR YOU?
Peirce

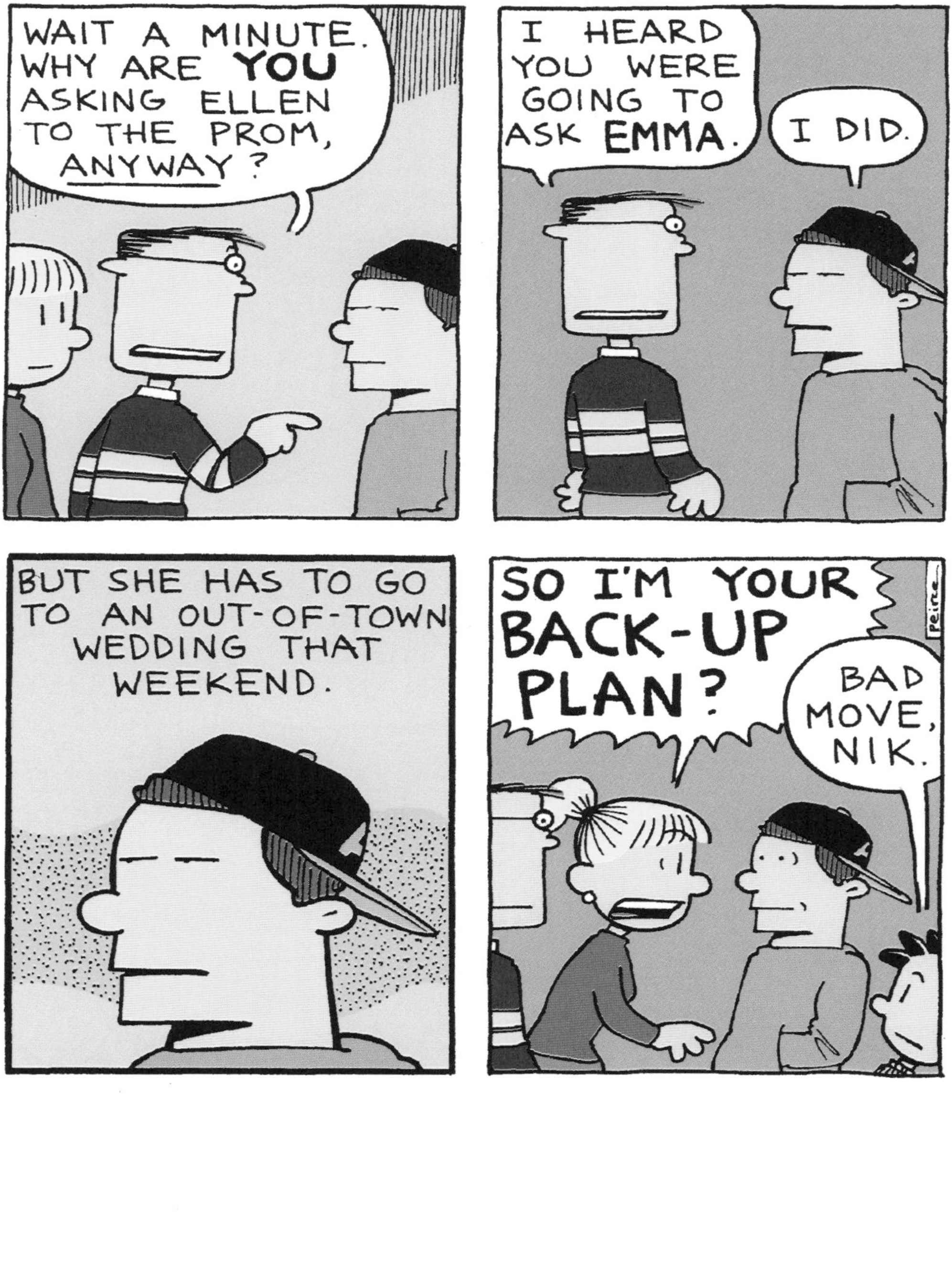
WAIT A MINUTE. WHY ARE **YOU** ASKING ELLEN TO THE PROM, ANYWAY?
I HEARD YOU WERE GOING TO ASK **EMMA**.
I DID.
BUT SHE HAS TO GO TO AN OUT-OF-TOWN WEDDING THAT WEEKEND.
SO I'M YOUR BACK-UP PLAN?
BAD MOVE, NIK.
peirce

YOU KNOW, NIK, I **THOUGHT** IT SEEMED ODD, YOU SHOWING UP OUT OF THE BLUE AND ASKING ME TO THE PROM!

OBVIOUSLY, YOU ONLY THOUGHT TO INVITE ME AFTER YOUR **FIRST** CHOICE BACKED OUT ON YOU!

PLUS, WHAT'S UP WITH HAVING NO "C" IN YOUR NAME? I MEAN... "**NIK**"?

I'LL TAKE IT FROM HERE, THANKS.

I'M JUST SAYIN'. IT'S A LITTLE SKETCHY.

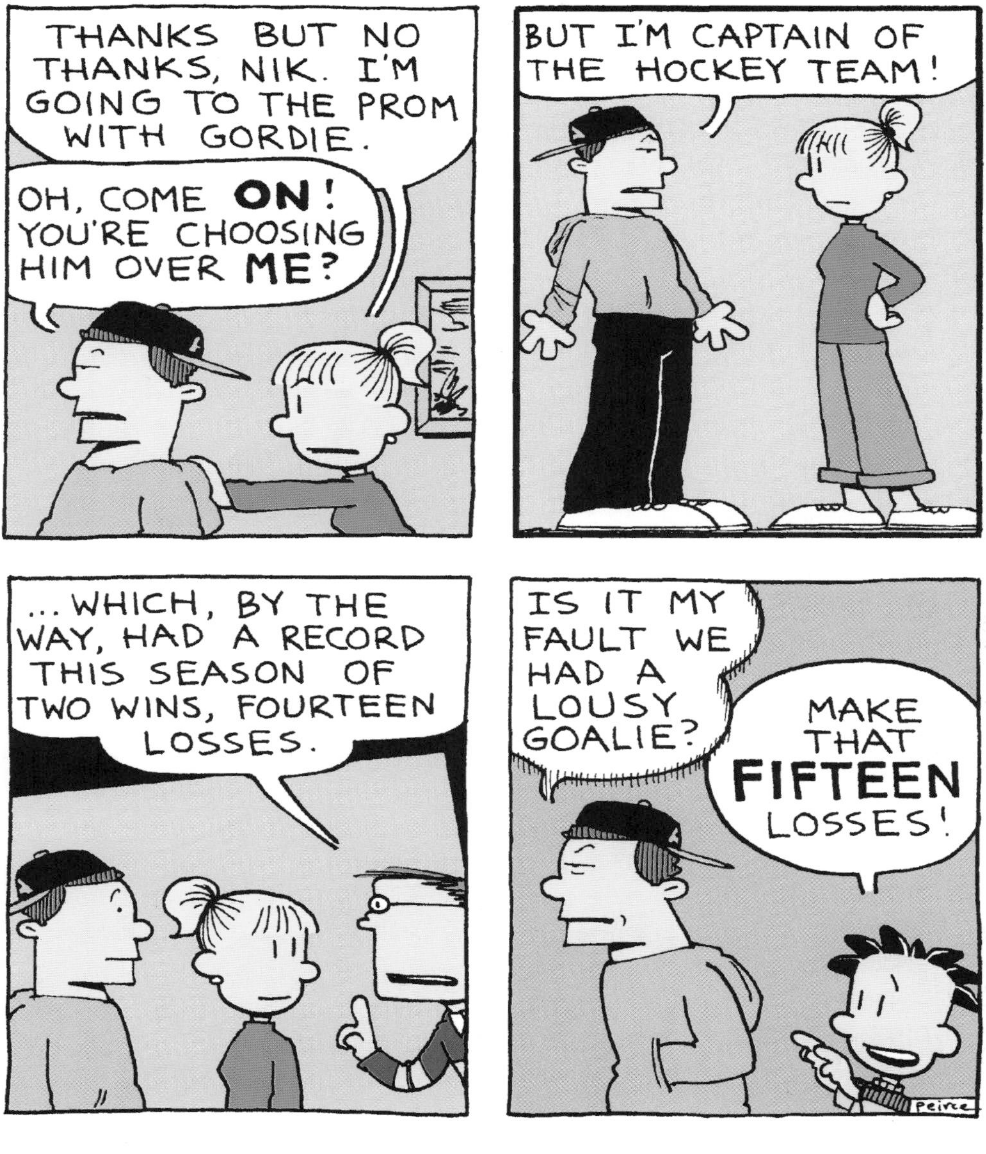
THANKS BUT NO THANKS, NIK. I'M GOING TO THE PROM WITH GORDIE.
OH, COME **ON**! YOU'RE CHOOSING HIM OVER **ME**?
BUT I'M CAPTAIN OF THE HOCKEY TEAM!
...WHICH, BY THE WAY, HAD A RECORD THIS SEASON OF TWO WINS, FOURTEEN LOSSES.
IS IT MY FAULT WE HAD A LOUSY GOALIE?
MAKE THAT **FIFTEEN** LOSSES!
Peirce

THANKS FOR TIPPING ME OFF ABOUT NIK, NATE. I OWE YOU.

AW, ELLEN NEVER WOULD'VE GONE TO THE PROM WITH THAT GUY.

HE DOESN'T HAVE YOUR SMARTS... HE DOESN'T HAVE YOUR CHARM...

HE DOESN'T HAVE YOUR JOB AT THE COMICS STORE.

RIGHT. THAT'S KEY.

LET'S GO BACK TO THE PART WHERE YOU SAID "I OWE YOU."

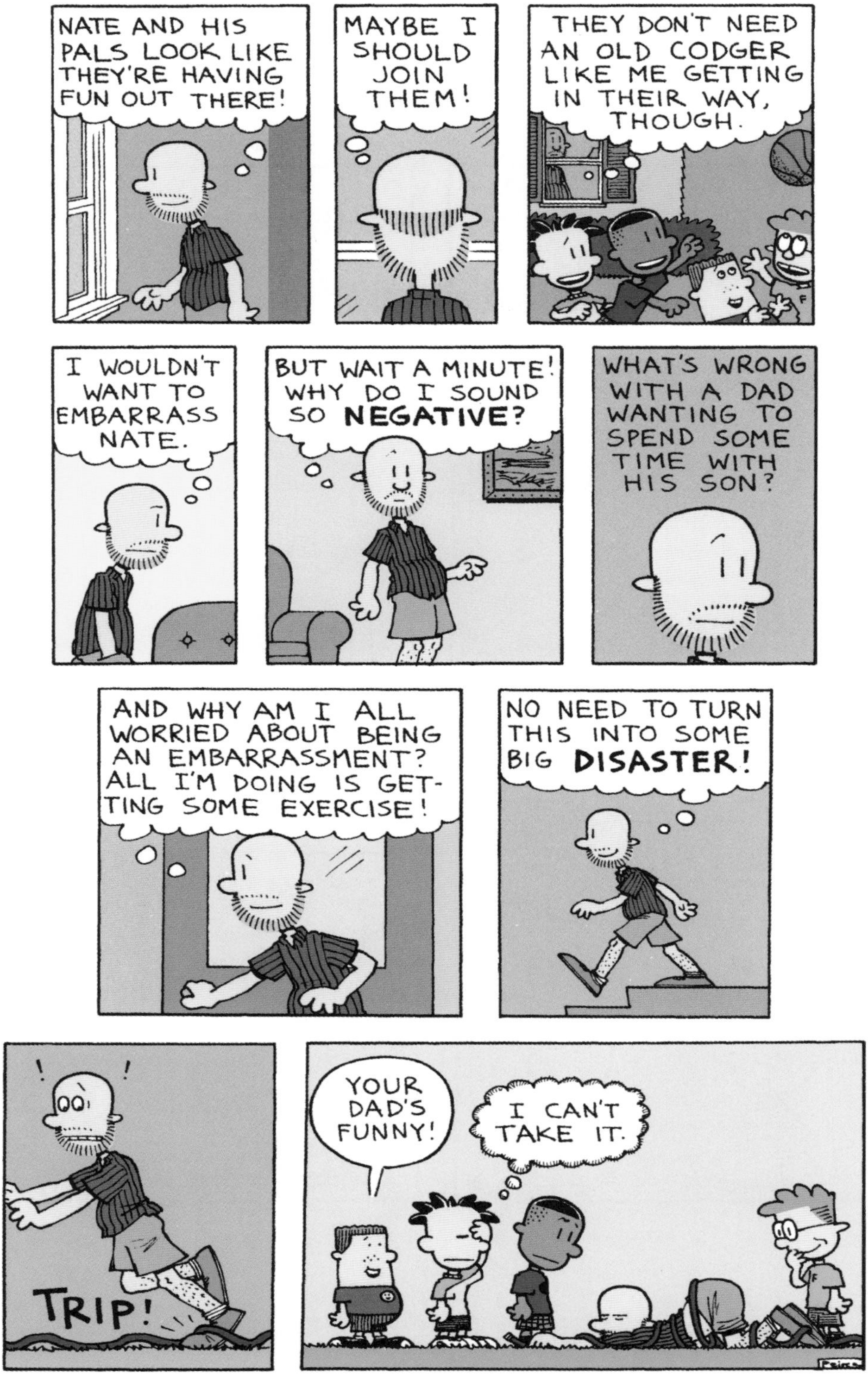
NATE AND HIS PALS LOOK LIKE THEY'RE HAVING FUN OUT THERE!
MAYBE I SHOULD JOIN THEM!
THEY DON'T NEED AN OLD CODGER LIKE ME GETTING IN THEIR WAY, THOUGH.
I WOULDN'T WANT TO EMBARRASS NATE.
BUT WAIT A MINUTE! WHY DO I SOUND SO **NEGATIVE**?
WHAT'S WRONG WITH A DAD WANTING TO SPEND SOME TIME WITH HIS SON?
AND WHY AM I ALL WORRIED ABOUT BEING AN EMBARRASSMENT? ALL I'M DOING IS GETTING SOME EXERCISE!
NO NEED TO TURN THIS INTO SOME BIG **DISASTER**!
! !
TRIP!
YOUR DAD'S FUNNY!
I CAN'T TAKE IT.

FRANCIS, I CAN'T BELIEVE YOU'VE NEVER WONDERED ABOUT WHAT **PRISON** IS LIKE!
WHY **WOULD** I?
BECAUSE IT'S JUST ONE OF THOSE THINGS **EVERYONE** THINKS ABOUT, THAT'S ALL!
IT'S LIKE ASKING YOURSELF WHAT WOULD BE THE WORST WAY TO DIE!
AND THE ANSWER, AS WE ALL KNOW, IS SLIDING DOWN A BANISTER MADE OF RAZOR BLADES.
YES.
EW.

THERE ARE CERTAIN UNIVERSAL QUESTIONS. EVERYONE WONDERS IF THEY'D SURVIVE IN PRISON. EVERYONE WONDERS WHERE YOU GO AFTER YOU DIE.

EVERYONE WONDERS WHAT IT WOULD BE LIKE TO SWIM NAKED IN A POOL FULL OF JUNIOR MINTS!

...DON'T THEY?

CHAD, CHAD, CHAD.

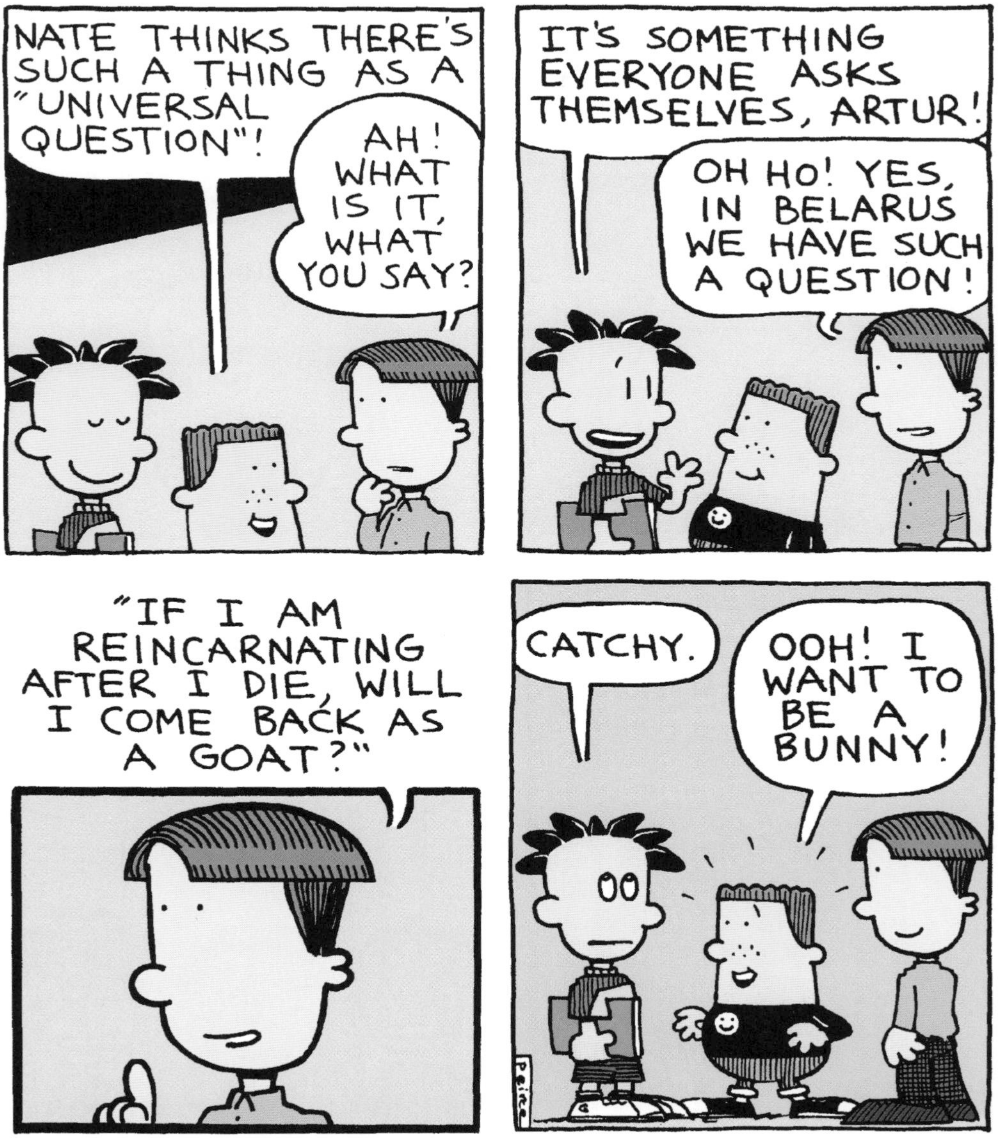
NATE THINKS THERE'S SUCH A THING AS A "UNIVERSAL QUESTION"!
AH! WHAT IS IT, WHAT YOU SAY?
IT'S SOMETHING EVERYONE ASKS THEMSELVES, ARTUR!
OH HO! YES, IN BELARUS WE HAVE SUCH A QUESTION!
"IF I AM REINCARNATING AFTER I DIE, WILL I COME BACK AS A GOAT?"
CATCHY.
OOH! I WANT TO BE A BUNNY!
PEIRCE

IF YOU WERE REINCARNATED, WHAT ANIMAL WOULD YOU COME BACK AS?
I'D BE A HYBRID! I'D COMBINE THE SPEED OF A CHEETAH AND THE STRENGTH OF A RHINO!
A CHEETAH AND A RHINO?
THAT'S A CHEETO!
YOU'RE RETURNING TO EARTH AS A SNACK FOOD!
PEIRCE

MRS. GODFREY, SOME OF US HAVE BEEN TALKING ABOUT REIN-CARNATION!

IF YOU WERE REINCARNATED, WHAT WOULD YOU WANT TO COME BACK AS?

I'D COME BACK AS **MYSELF**, SO I COULD LIVE MY LIFE OVER AND OVER AGAIN. FOREVER.

I HAD HER PEGGED AS A WATER BUFFALO.

F-F-F-F-F-FOREVER.

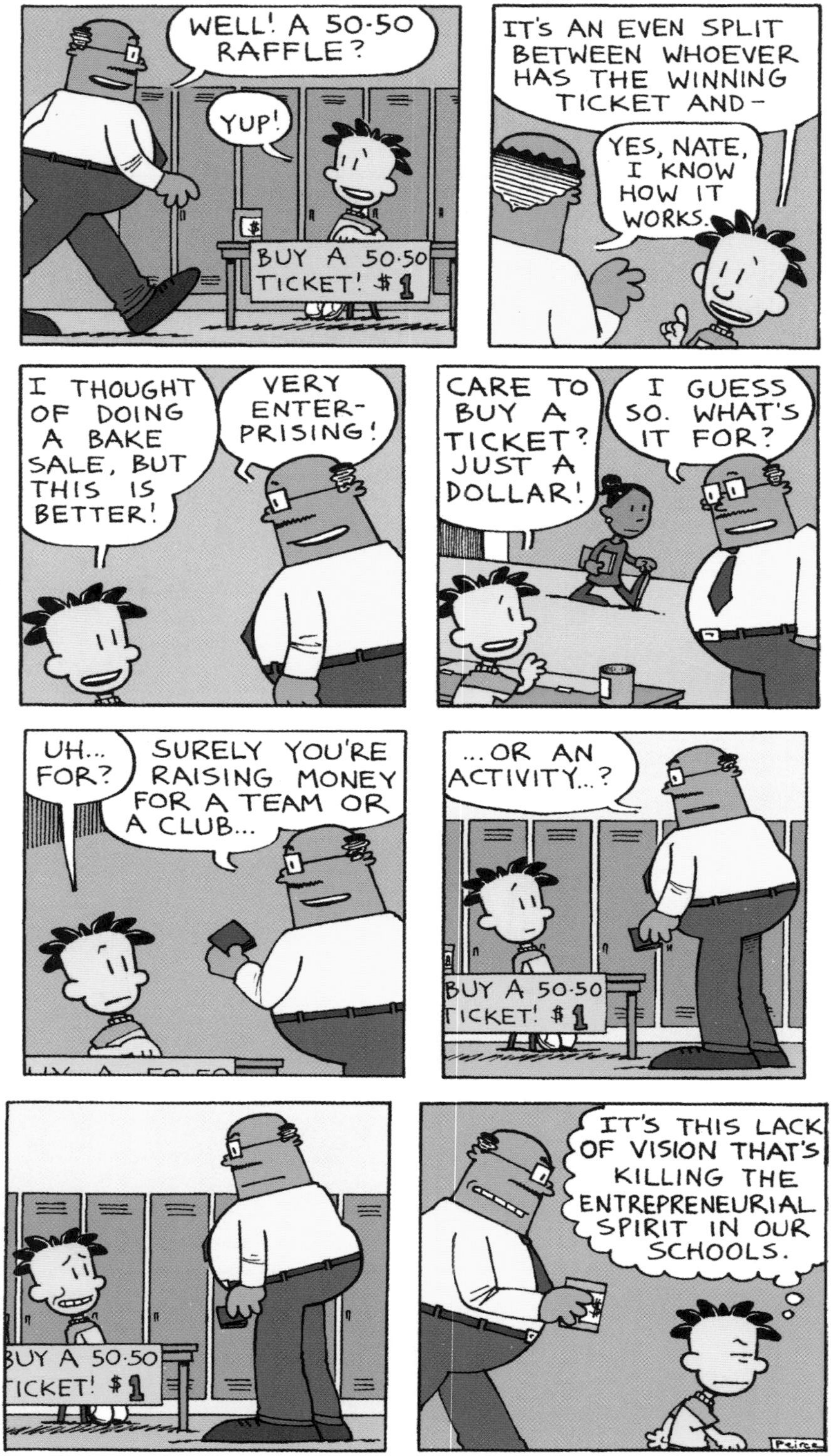
WELL! A 50-50 RAFFLE?
YUP!
BUY A 50-50 TICKET! $1
IT'S AN EVEN SPLIT BETWEEN WHOEVER HAS THE WINNING TICKET AND—
YES, NATE, I KNOW HOW IT WORKS.
I THOUGHT OF DOING A BAKE SALE, BUT THIS IS BETTER!
VERY ENTER-PRISING!
CARE TO BUY A TICKET? JUST A DOLLAR!
I GUESS SO. WHAT'S IT FOR?
UH... FOR?
SURELY YOU'RE RAISING MONEY FOR A TEAM OR A CLUB...
...OR AN ACTIVITY...?
BUY A 50-50 TICKET! $1
BUY A 50-50 TICKET! $1
IT'S THIS LACK OF VISION THAT'S KILLING THE ENTREPRENEURIAL SPIRIT IN OUR SCHOOLS.
Peirce

CLASS, MRS. GODFREY IS HAVING SOME MINOR SURGERY, AND SHE'LL BE OUT OF ACTION FOR THE REST OF THE YEAR!
THE GOOD NEWS IS: IT'S NOT SERIOUS, AND SHE'LL BE BACK IN THE CLASSROOM NEXT FALL!
THAT'S THE **GOOD** NEWS?
WHAT I MEANT TO SAY WAS: THAT **IS** GOOD NEWS!
KEEP WALKING.

MS. CLARKE, WHAT KIND OF SURGERY IS MRS. GODFREY HAVING?

I'M AFRAID I CAN'T TELL YOU THAT, NATE. IT'S CONFIDENTIAL.

AH. OKAY, SO I'LL HAVE TO GUESS.

I SUPPOSE COSMETIC FACIAL SURGERY WOULD BE TOO MUCH TO HOPE FOR?

SPEAKING OF SURGERY, SOME PEOPLE AROUND HERE COULD USE A HUMOR TRANSFUSION.

I HEARD WHAT MRS. GODFREY'S SURGERY WAS! SHE HAD HER GALL-BLADDER REMOVED!
WHAT'S THAT?
A GALLBLADDER IS WHERE YOUR BODY STORES BILE.
SO WITHOUT A GALL-BLADDER, WHAT WILL MRS. GODFREY DO WITH ALL HER BILE?
SHE'LL SPEW IT ALL OVER US!!
SUMMER VACATION IS GETTING HERE JUST IN TIME.

HERE. SIGN THIS "GET WELL SOON" CARD FOR MRS. GODFREY.

DREAM ON, GINA.

I'M NOT A BUTT-KISSING **TOADIE** LIKE **YOU**! I HAVE NO INTENTION OF SIGNING YOUR LAME LITTLE CARD!

GREAT IDEA, GENIUS. WHEN SHE SEES YOU'RE THE ONLY ONE WHO **DIDN'T** SIGN IT, SHE'LL STICK YOU IN **SUMMER SCHOOL!**

Feel better fast. Nate

ADD A SMILEY FACE.

I HATE MYSELF

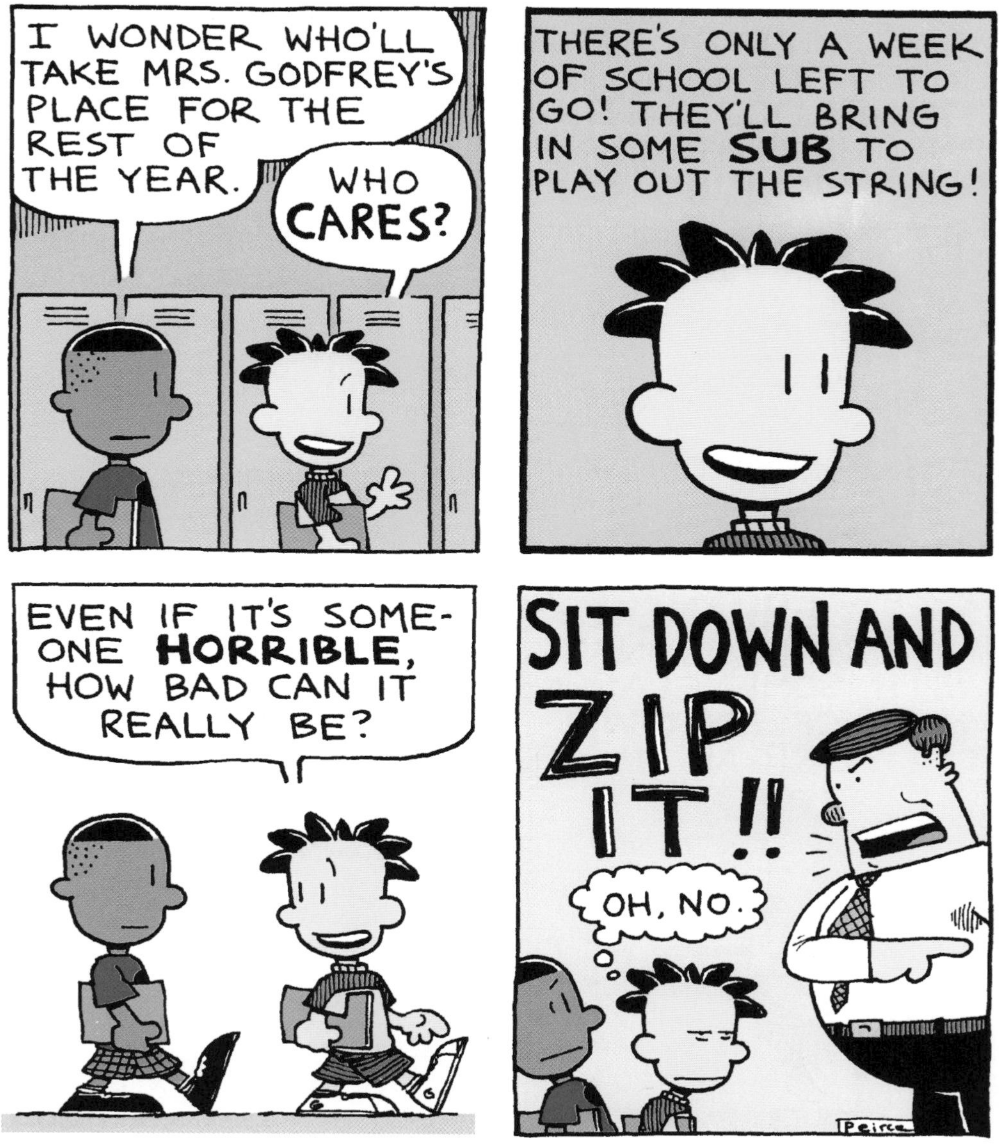
I WONDER WHO'LL TAKE MRS. GODFREY'S PLACE FOR THE REST OF THE YEAR.
WHO **CARES?**
THERE'S ONLY A WEEK OF SCHOOL LEFT TO GO! THEY'LL BRING IN SOME **SUB** TO PLAY OUT THE STRING!
EVEN IF IT'S SOME-ONE **HORRIBLE**, HOW BAD CAN IT REALLY BE?
SIT DOWN AND ZIP IT!!
OH, NO.
Peirce

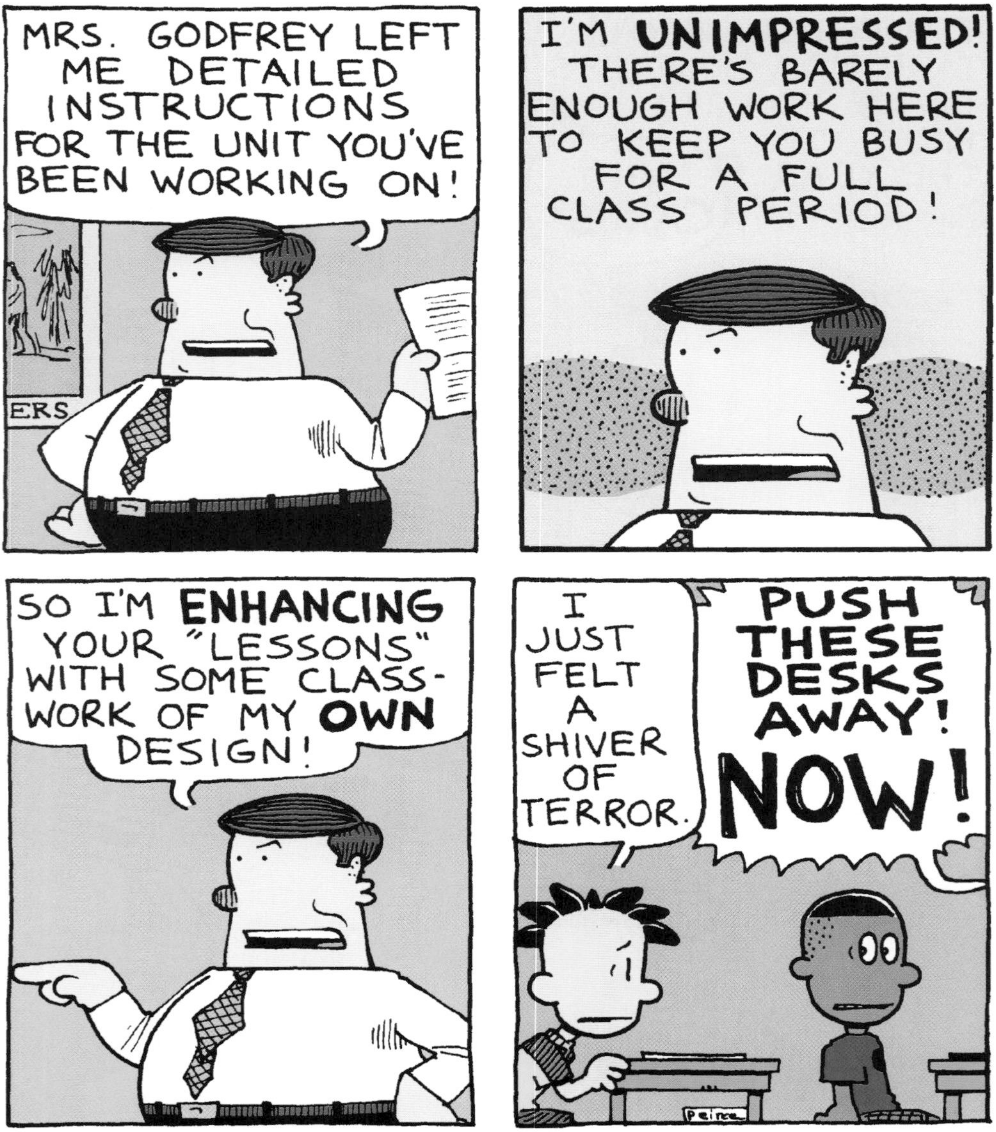
MRS. GODFREY LEFT ME DETAILED INSTRUCTIONS FOR THE UNIT YOU'VE BEEN WORKING ON!
ERS
I'M **UNIMPRESSED!** THERE'S BARELY ENOUGH WORK HERE TO KEEP YOU BUSY FOR A FULL CLASS PERIOD!
SO I'M **ENHANCING** YOUR "LESSONS" WITH SOME CLASS-WORK OF MY **OWN** DESIGN!
I JUST FELT A SHIVER OF TERROR.
PUSH THESE DESKS AWAY! NOW!
Peirce

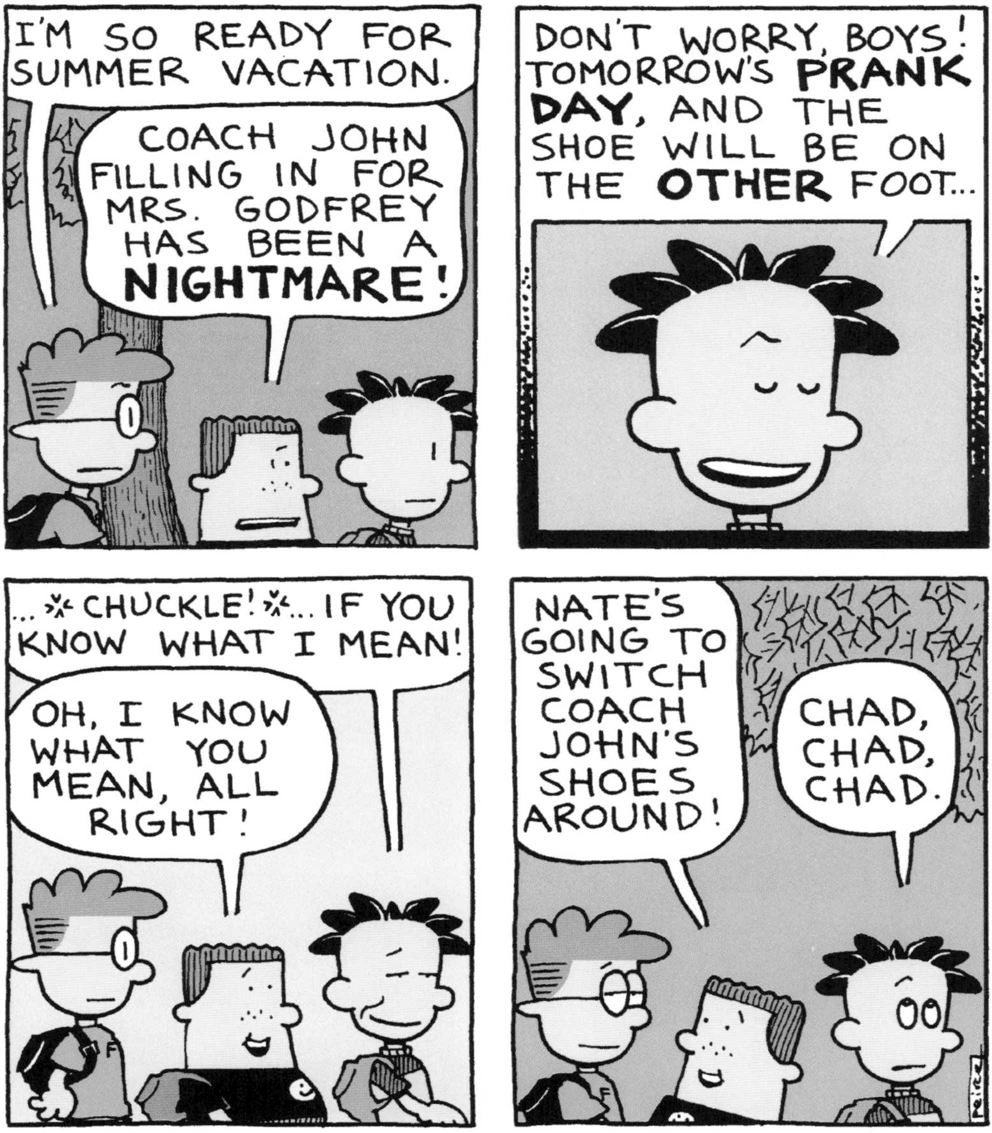
I'M SO READY FOR SUMMER VACATION.
COACH JOHN FILLING IN FOR MRS. GODFREY HAS BEEN A **NIGHTMARE**!
DON'T WORRY, BOYS! TOMORROW'S **PRANK DAY**, AND THE SHOE WILL BE ON THE **OTHER** FOOT...
...*CHUCKLE!*...IF YOU KNOW WHAT I MEAN!
OH, I KNOW WHAT YOU MEAN, ALL RIGHT!
NATE'S GOING TO SWITCH COACH JOHN'S SHOES AROUND!
CHAD, CHAD, CHAD.
PEIRCE

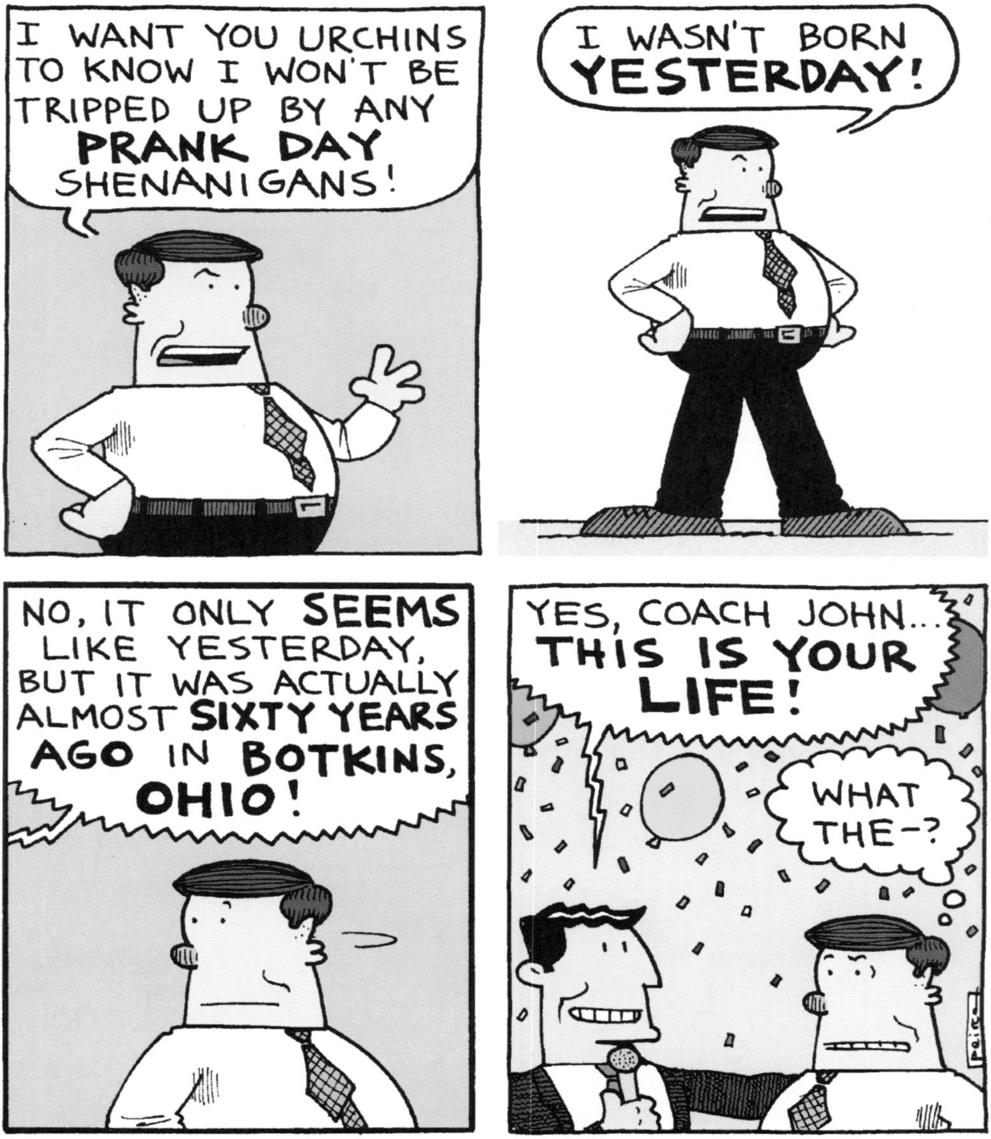
I WANT YOU URCHINS TO KNOW I WON'T BE TRIPPED UP BY ANY PRANK DAY SHENANIGANS!
I WASN'T BORN YESTERDAY!
NO, IT ONLY SEEMS LIKE YESTERDAY, BUT IT WAS ACTUALLY ALMOST SIXTY YEARS AGO IN BOTKINS, OHIO!
YES, COACH JOHN... THIS IS YOUR LIFE!
WHAT THE-?

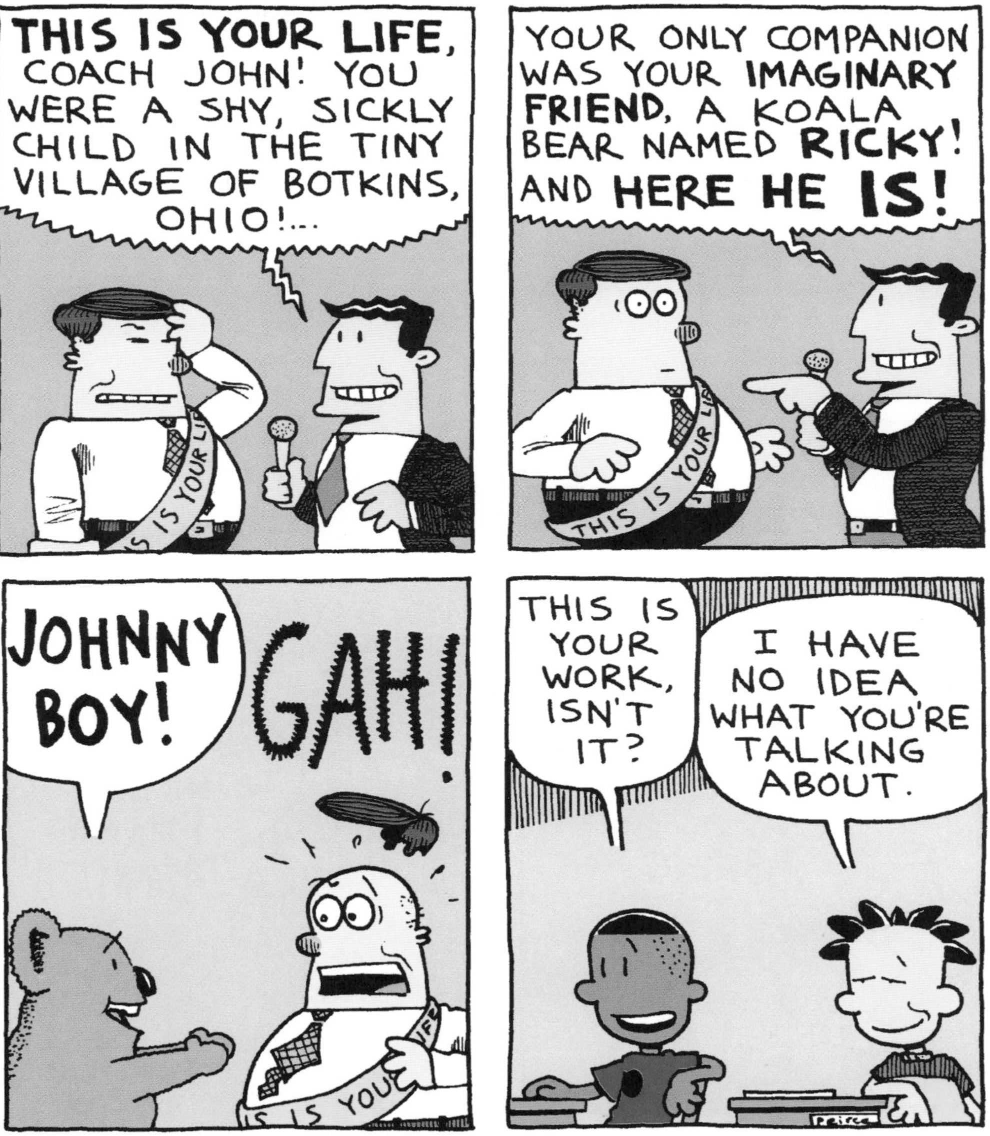

THIS IS YOUR LIFE, COACH JOHN! YOU WERE A SHY, SICKLY CHILD IN THE TINY VILLAGE OF BOTKINS, OHIO!...
THIS IS YOUR LI
YOUR ONLY COMPANION WAS YOUR IMAGINARY FRIEND, A KOALA BEAR NAMED RICKY! AND HERE HE IS!
THIS IS YOUR LI
JOHNNY BOY!
GAH!
IS IS YOUR LIFE
THIS IS YOUR WORK, ISN'T IT?
I HAVE NO IDEA WHAT YOU'RE TALKING ABOUT.

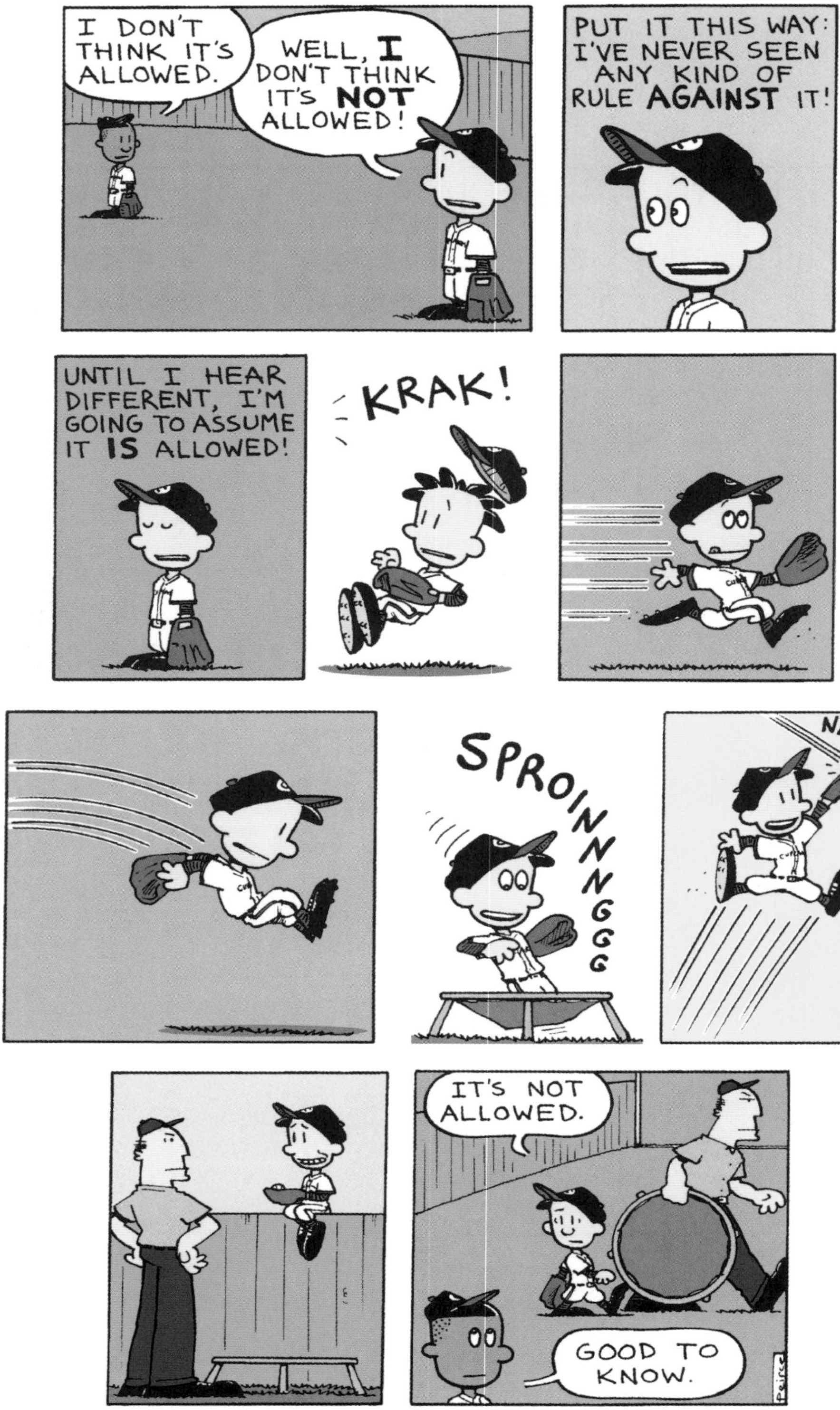

I DON'T THINK IT'S ALLOWED.
WELL, I DON'T THINK IT'S NOT ALLOWED!
PUT IT THIS WAY: I'VE NEVER SEEN ANY KIND OF RULE AGAINST IT!
UNTIL I HEAR DIFFERENT, I'M GOING TO ASSUME IT IS ALLOWED!
KRAK!
SPROINNNGGG
NAB!
IT'S NOT ALLOWED.
GOOD TO KNOW.
Peirce

JENNY, M'LADY! WILL YOU SIGN MY YEARBOOK?
OKAY
THERE.
HEY!
YOU DIDN'T WRITE A MESSAGE OR ANYTHING! YOU JUST PUT YOUR NAME!
THAT'S WHAT YOU ASKED FOR, SO THAT'S WHAT I GAVE YOU.
WHEN YOU REALLY LIKE SOMEBODY, THERE'S NOTHING WORSE THAN A NAKED SIGNATURE.
Peirce

JENNY, COME ON! YOU CAN'T JUST WRITE NOTHING IN MY YEARBOOK!
ALL RIGHT, ALL RIGHT!
HERE
"HAVE A NICE LIFE" ISN'T QUITE THE WARM, FUZZY MESSAGE I HAD IN MIND.
PEIRCE

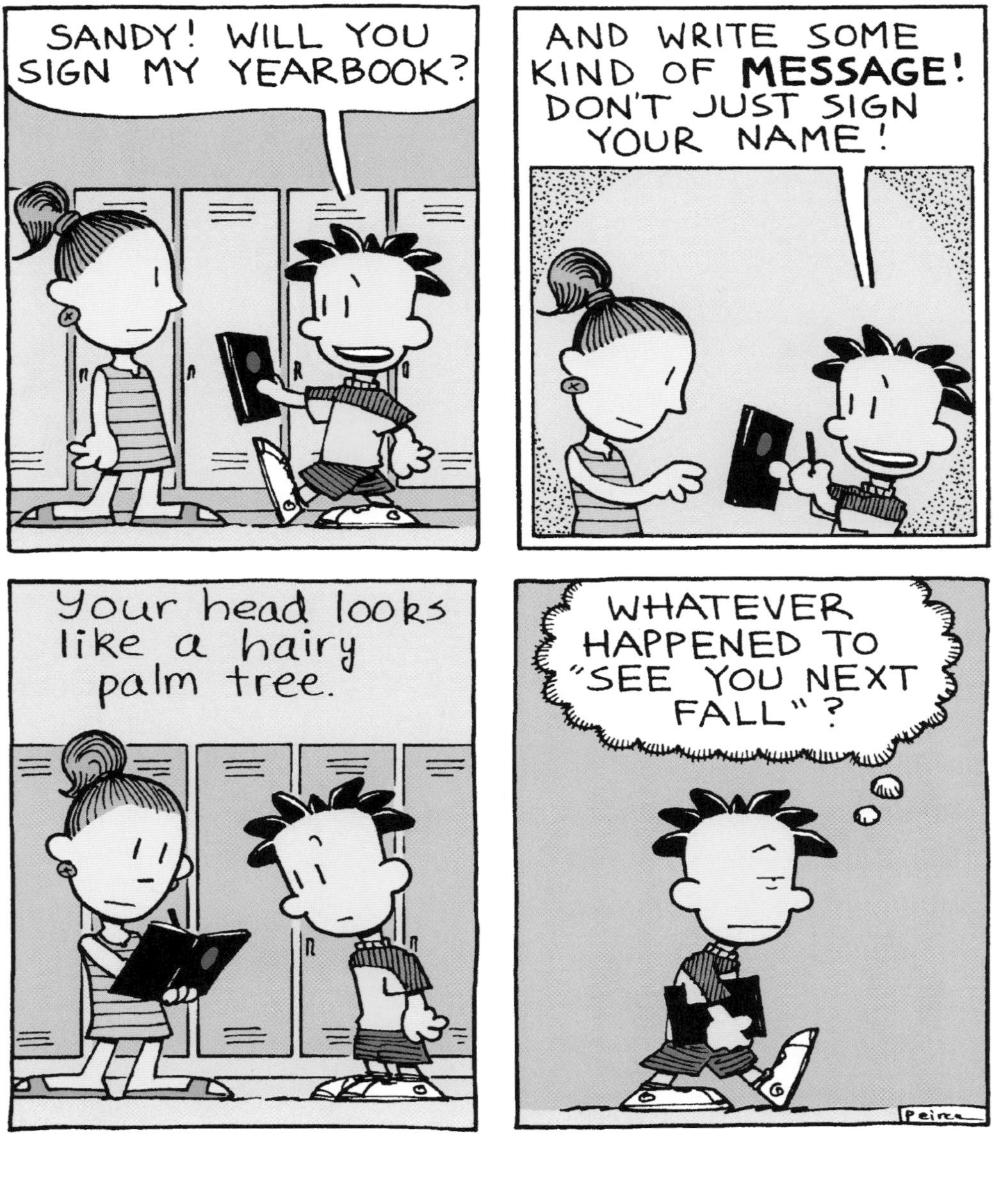
SANDY! WILL YOU SIGN MY YEARBOOK?
AND WRITE SOME KIND OF **MESSAGE**! DON'T JUST SIGN YOUR NAME!
Your head looks like a hairy palm tree.
WHATEVER HAPPENED TO "SEE YOU NEXT FALL"?
Peirce

THANKS FOR SIGNING MY YEARBOOK, CYNDI!
UH-HUH.
AHEM! I'D BE HAPPY TO SIGN **YOURS**, IF YOU WANT!
UMMM...
SORRY, THERE'S NO TIME! I'M LATE FOR MY... UH... MY PIANO LESSON!
BUT SHE PLAYS THE PICCOLO.
NOW I'M QUESTIONING THE SINCERITY OF HER "HAVE A GREAT SUMMER" AND SMILEY FACE.
Peirce

HEY. SIGN MY YEAR-BOOK.
K-KIM!
Y'KNOW, I'M NOT SURE I SHOULD. I... IT'S... UM...
YOU'RE WORRIED ABOUT MY INSANELY JEALOUS BOYFRIEND, CHESTER.
BUT YOU CAN RELAX. I TOLD HIM YOU MEAN NOTHING TO ME ANYMORE, SO EVEN IF HE SEES US TALKING, HE'LL BE FINE WITH IT.
URK!
OF COURSE, I COULD BE WRONG.
Peirce

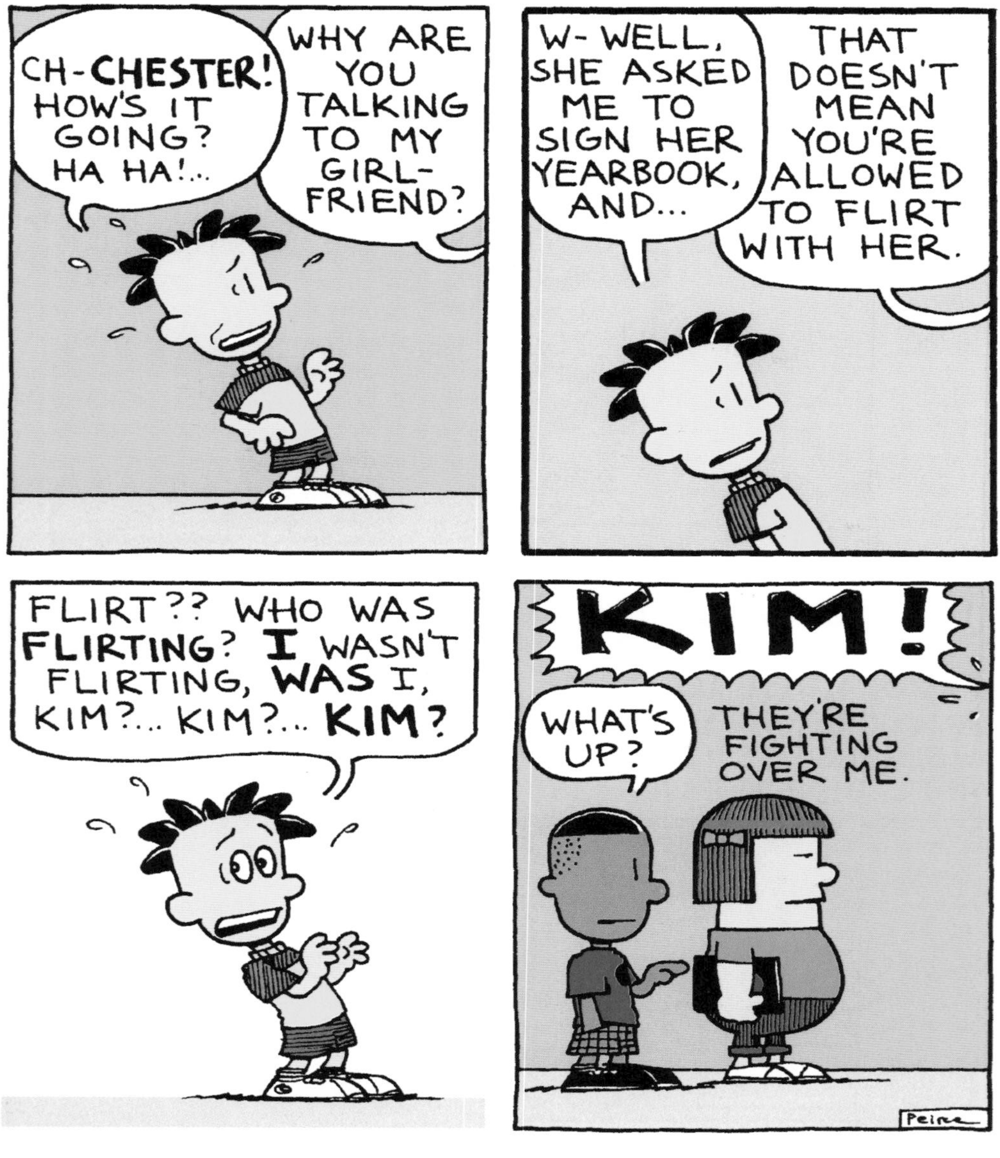
CH-**CHESTER!** HOW'S IT GOING? HA HA!...
WHY ARE YOU TALKING TO MY GIRL-FRIEND?
W-WELL, SHE ASKED ME TO SIGN HER YEARBOOK, AND...
THAT DOESN'T MEAN YOU'RE ALLOWED TO FLIRT WITH HER.
FLIRT?? WHO WAS **FLIRTING**? **I** WASN'T FLIRTING, **WAS** I, KIM?... KIM?... **KIM**?
KIM!
WHAT'S UP?
THEY'RE FIGHTING OVER ME.
Peirce

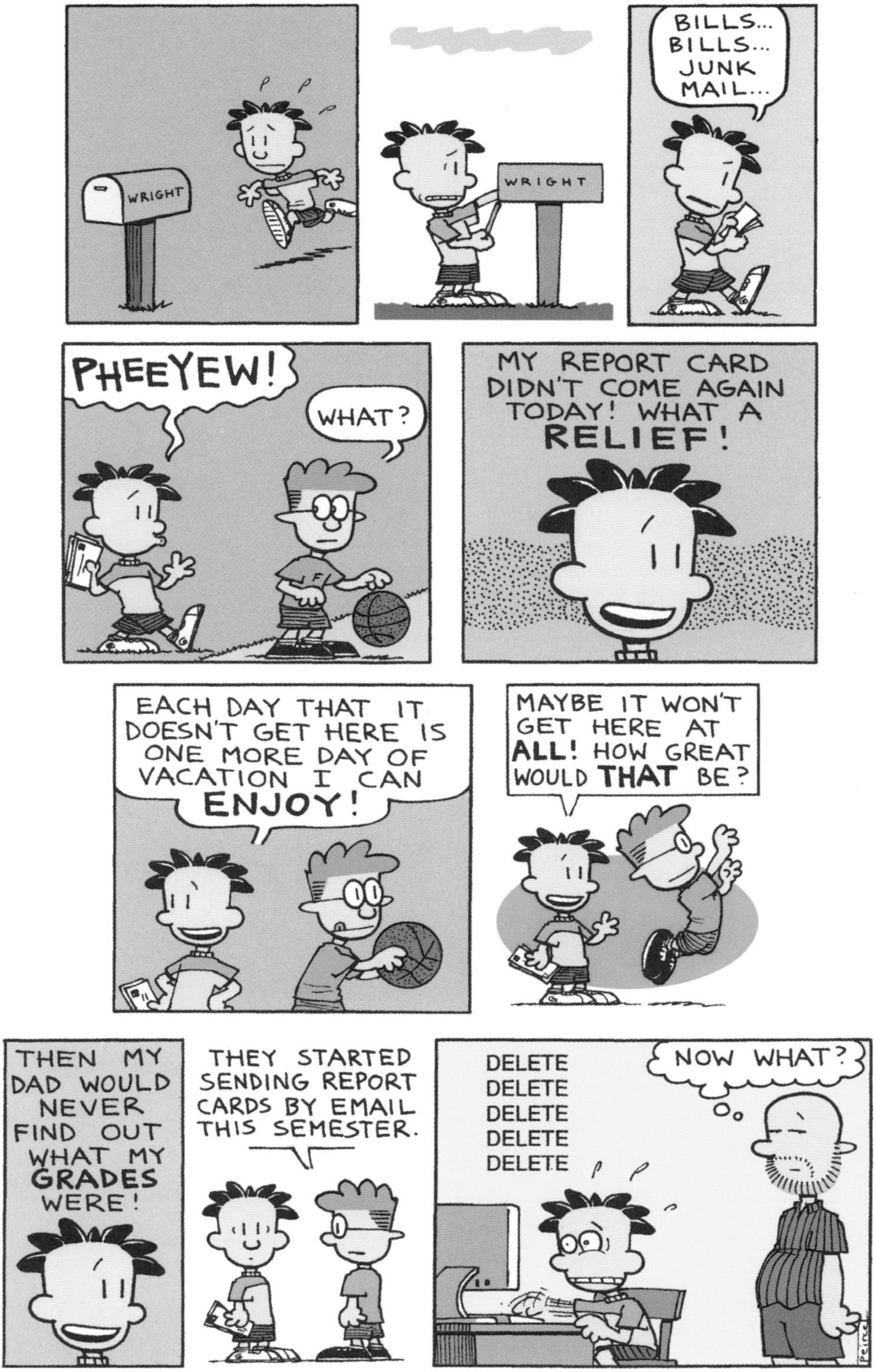
WRIGHT
WRIGHT
BILLS... BILLS... JUNK MAIL...
PHEEYEW!
WHAT?
MY REPORT CARD DIDN'T COME AGAIN TODAY! WHAT A **RELIEF**!
EACH DAY THAT IT DOESN'T GET HERE IS ONE MORE DAY OF VACATION I CAN **ENJOY**!
MAYBE IT WON'T GET HERE AT **ALL**! HOW GREAT WOULD **THAT** BE?
THEN MY DAD WOULD NEVER FIND OUT WHAT MY **GRADES** WERE!
THEY STARTED SENDING REPORT CARDS BY EMAIL THIS SEMESTER.
DELETE
DELETE
DELETE
DELETE
DELETE
NOW WHAT?

AH! NATE! ELLEN! MY BELOVED KINSPERSONS!
HI, UNCLE TED.
WHAT JOLLITY WE'LL HAVE FOR THE NEXT FEW DAYS!
ER... ACTUALLY, I WAS INVITED TO STAY WITH MY FRIEND AMY WHILE DAD'S GONE.
AH! THEN IT WILL BE JUST YOUNG NATE AND MYSELF!
LET THE MALE BONDING **BEGIN**!
I HATE YOU.

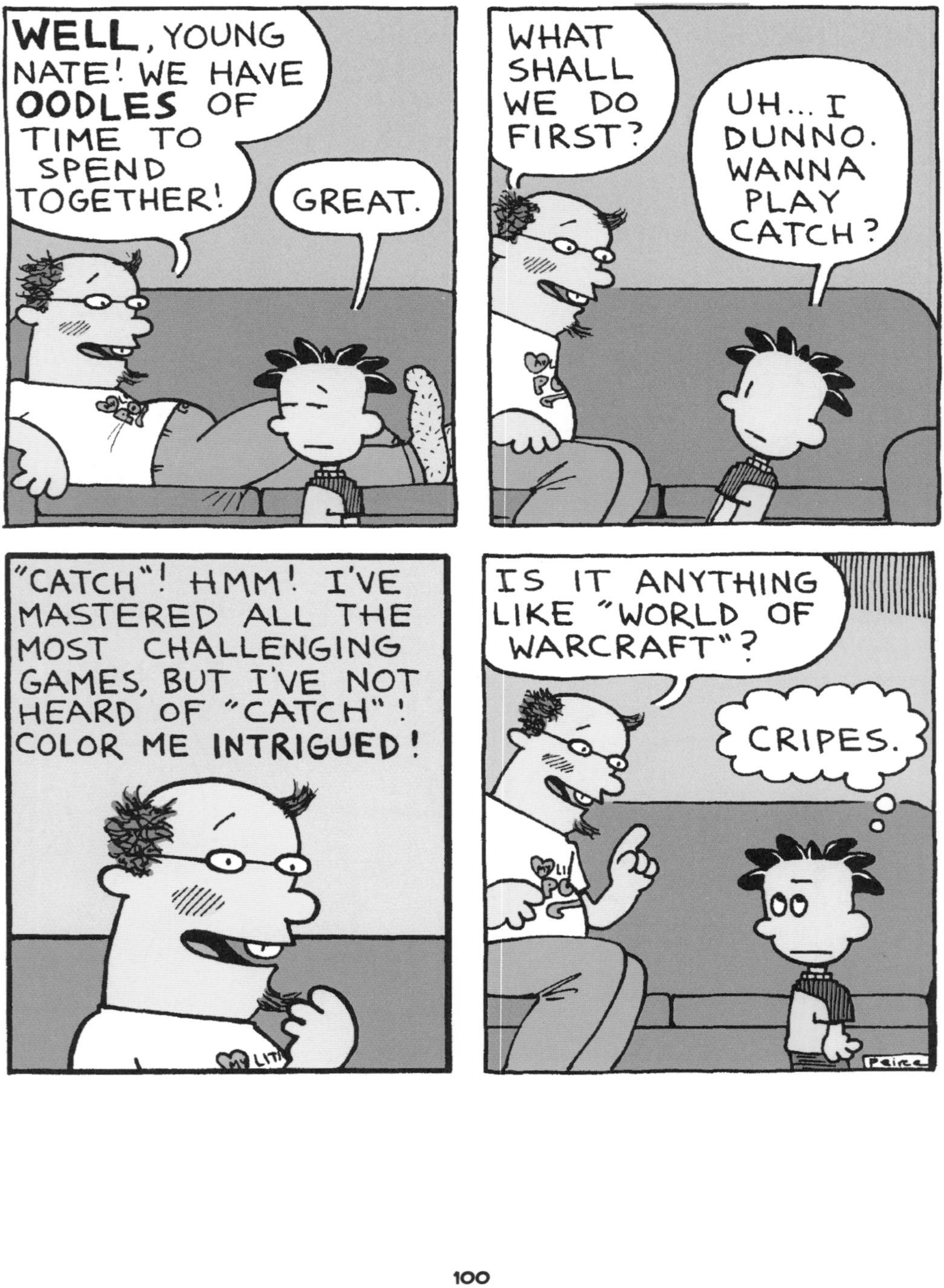

WELL, YOUNG NATE! WE HAVE OODLES OF TIME TO SPEND TOGETHER!
GREAT.
WHAT SHALL WE DO FIRST?
UH... I DUNNO. WANNA PLAY CATCH?
"CATCH"! HMM! I'VE MASTERED ALL THE MOST CHALLENGING GAMES, BUT I'VE NOT HEARD OF "CATCH"! COLOR ME INTRIGUED!
IS IT ANYTHING LIKE "WORLD OF WARCRAFT"?
CRIPES.
Peirce

EGAD! PLAYING "CATCH" IS EXHAUSTING! I'M UTTERLY **FAMISHED**!
WELL, IT'S ALMOST SUPPERTIME.
SUPPER! INDEED! A **CAPITAL** IDEA!
WHAT WILL YOU BE PREPARING?
AN ESCAPE PLAN.
JUST AN FYI: I LIKE MY TATER TOTS EXTRA CRISPY!
peirce

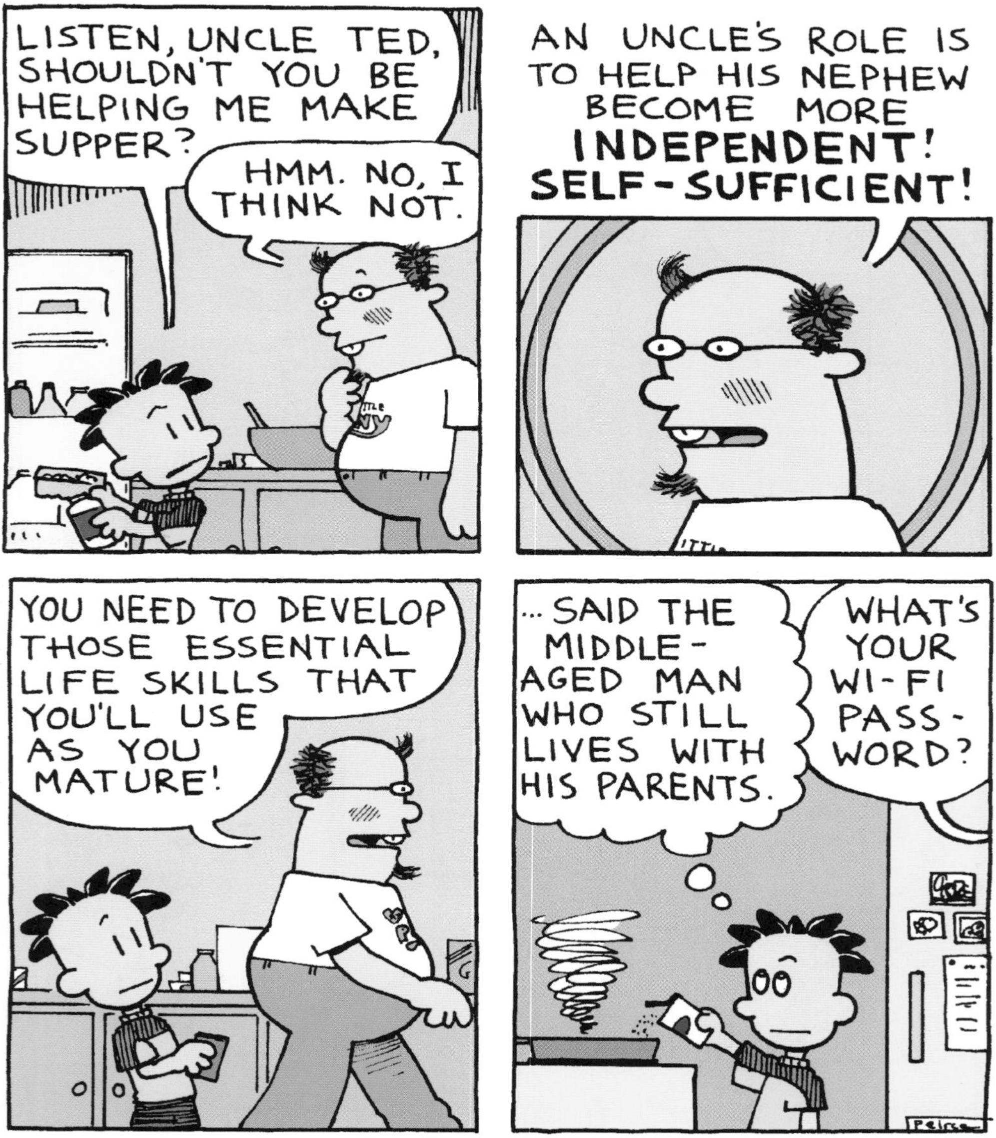

LISTEN, UNCLE TED, SHOULDN'T YOU BE HELPING ME MAKE SUPPER?
HMM. NO, I THINK NOT.
AN UNCLE'S ROLE IS TO HELP HIS NEPHEW BECOME MORE INDEPENDENT! SELF-SUFFICIENT!
YOU NEED TO DEVELOP THOSE ESSENTIAL LIFE SKILLS THAT YOU'LL USE AS YOU MATURE!
...SAID THE MIDDLE-AGED MAN WHO STILL LIVES WITH HIS PARENTS.
WHAT'S YOUR WI-FI PASS-WORD?

HELLO? OH, HEY, FRANCIS. WHAT'S GOIN' ON?
YOU ARE? THAT SOUNDS COOL. THAT SOUNDS **REALLY** COOL. BUT I CAN'T GO.
I JUST CAN'T, THAT'S ALL.
I'M BABYSITTING.
DO YOU **MIND**? I'M TRYING TO WATCH "DEVIOUS MAIDS"!
Peirce

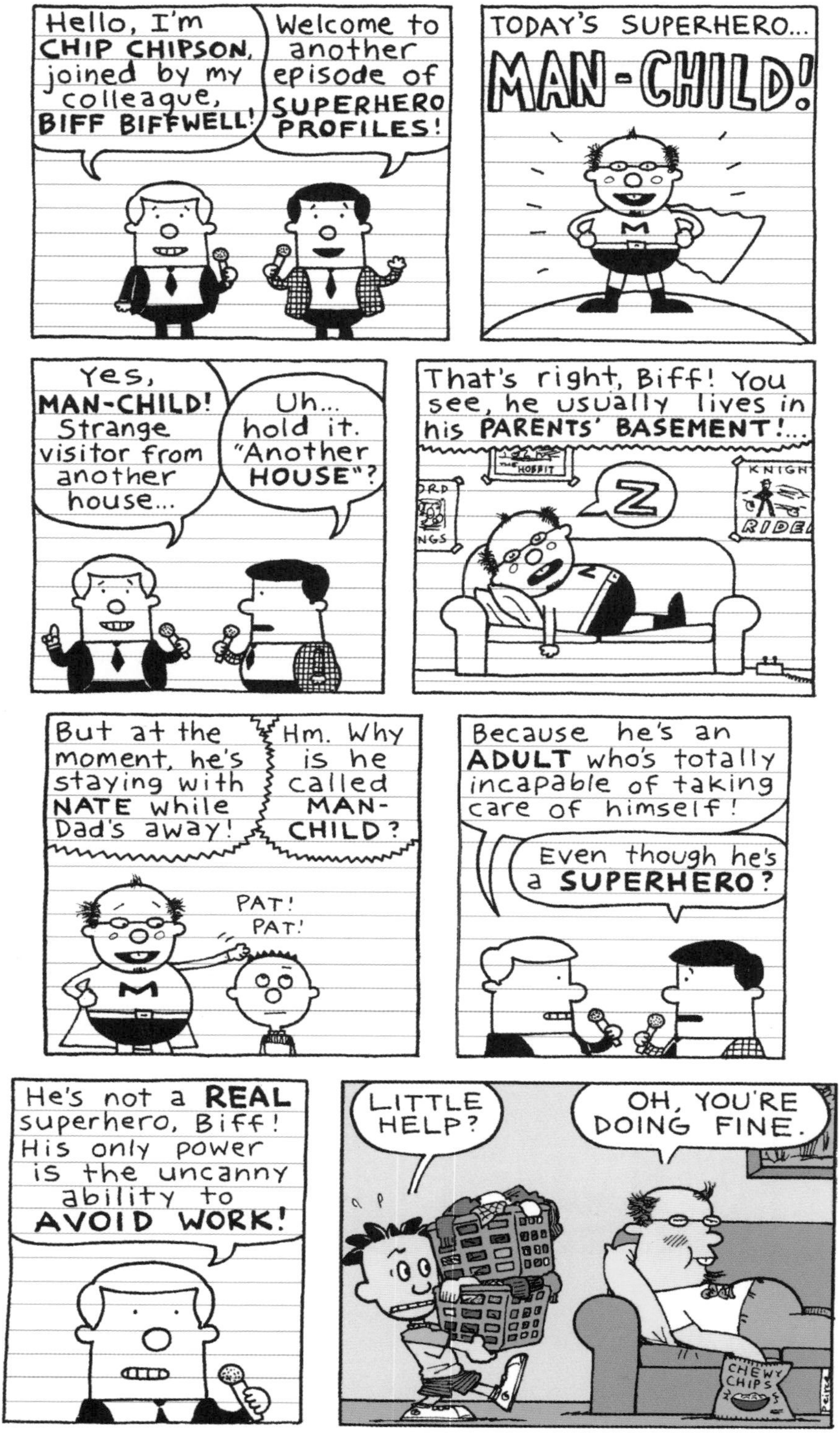
Hello, I'm CHIP CHIPSON, joined by my colleague, BIFF BIFFWELL!
Welcome to another episode of SUPERHERO PROFILES!
TODAY'S SUPERHERO...
MAN-CHILD!
Yes, MAN-CHILD! Strange visitor from another house...
Uh... hold it. "Another HOUSE"?
That's right, Biff! You see, he usually lives in his PARENTS' BASEMENT!...
THE HOBBIT
KNIGHT RIDER
Z
But at the moment, he's staying with NATE while Dad's away!
Hm. Why is he called MAN-CHILD?
PAT! PAT!
Because he's an ADULT who's totally incapable of taking care of himself!
Even though he's a SUPERHERO?
He's not a REAL superhero, Biff! His only power is the uncanny ability to AVOID WORK!
LITTLE HELP?
OH, YOU'RE DOING FINE.
CHEWY CHIPS

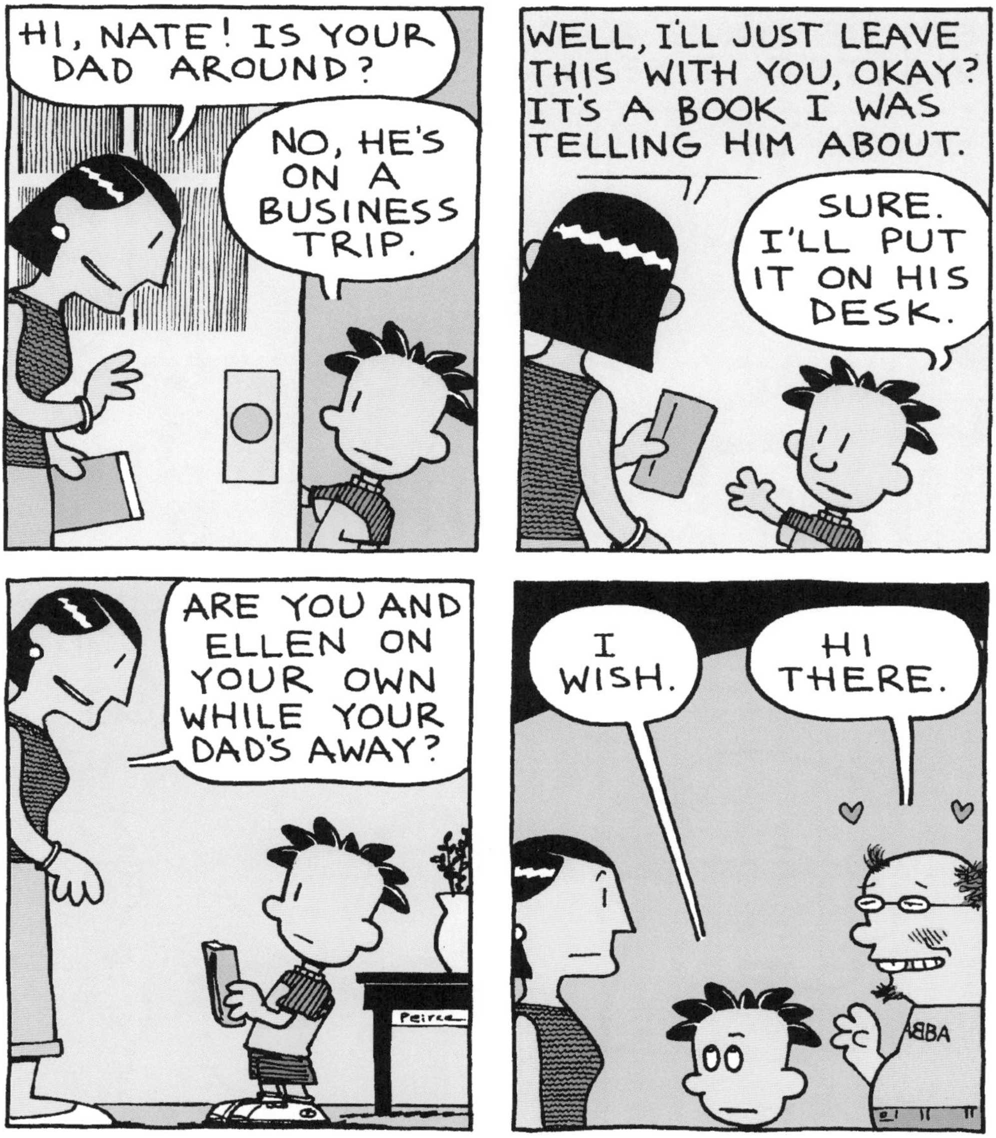
HI, NATE! IS YOUR DAD AROUND?
NO, HE'S ON A BUSINESS TRIP.
WELL, I'LL JUST LEAVE THIS WITH YOU, OKAY? IT'S A BOOK I WAS TELLING HIM ABOUT.
SURE. I'LL PUT IT ON HIS DESK.
ARE YOU AND ELLEN ON YOUR OWN WHILE YOUR DAD'S AWAY?
Peirce
I WISH.
HI THERE.
ABBA

SO! WE HAVE A **VISITOR**, I SEE!
NOT REALLY! JUST A NEIGHBOR!
HI, I'M BETSY.
CHARMED. I'M TED, THE BOY'S UNCLE.
AHEM! I'M A CANCER.
SO, SO TRUE.
SHOCKINGLY ENOUGH, I'M ALSO SINGLE.

TELL ME, BETSY... ARE YOU A FAN OF "SWORD AND SORCERER" MOVIES? BECAUSE I'M—
ER... I REALLY CAN'T CHAT.
BBA
MY HUSBAND IS WAITING IN THE CAR.
BBA
BBA
OUCH.
AND IT WAS GOING SO WELL.
BBA
Peirce

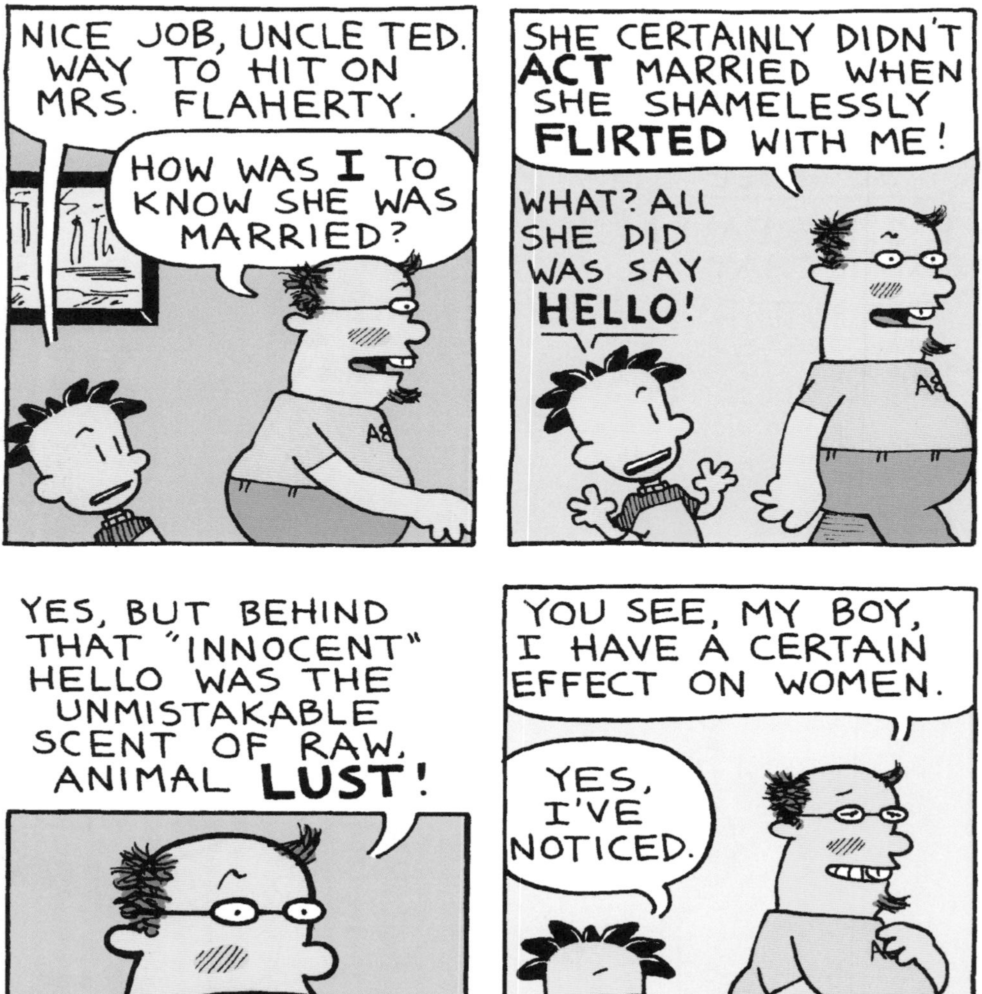
NICE JOB, UNCLE TED. WAY TO HIT ON MRS. FLAHERTY.
HOW WAS **I** TO KNOW SHE WAS MARRIED?
SHE CERTAINLY DIDN'T **ACT** MARRIED WHEN SHE SHAMELESSLY **FLIRTED** WITH ME!
WHAT? ALL SHE DID WAS SAY **HELLO**!
YES, BUT BEHIND THAT "INNOCENT" HELLO WAS THE UNMISTAKABLE SCENT OF RAW, ANIMAL **LUST**!
YOU SEE, MY BOY, I HAVE A CERTAIN EFFECT ON WOMEN.
YES, I'VE NOTICED.

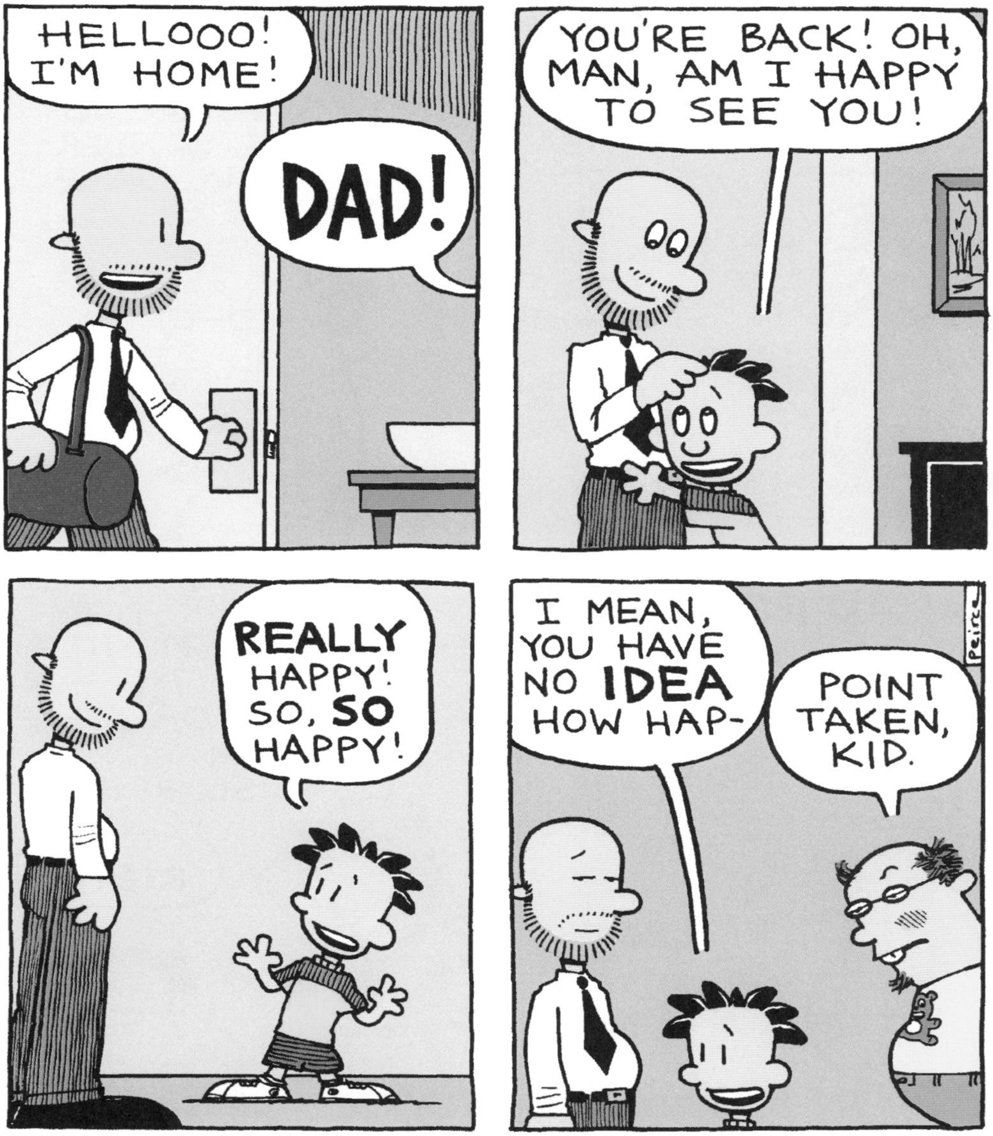
HELLOOO! I'M HOME!
DAD!
YOU'RE BACK! OH, MAN, AM I HAPPY TO SEE YOU!
REALLY HAPPY! SO, SO HAPPY!
I MEAN, YOU HAVE NO IDEA HOW HAP-
POINT TAKEN, KID.
peirce

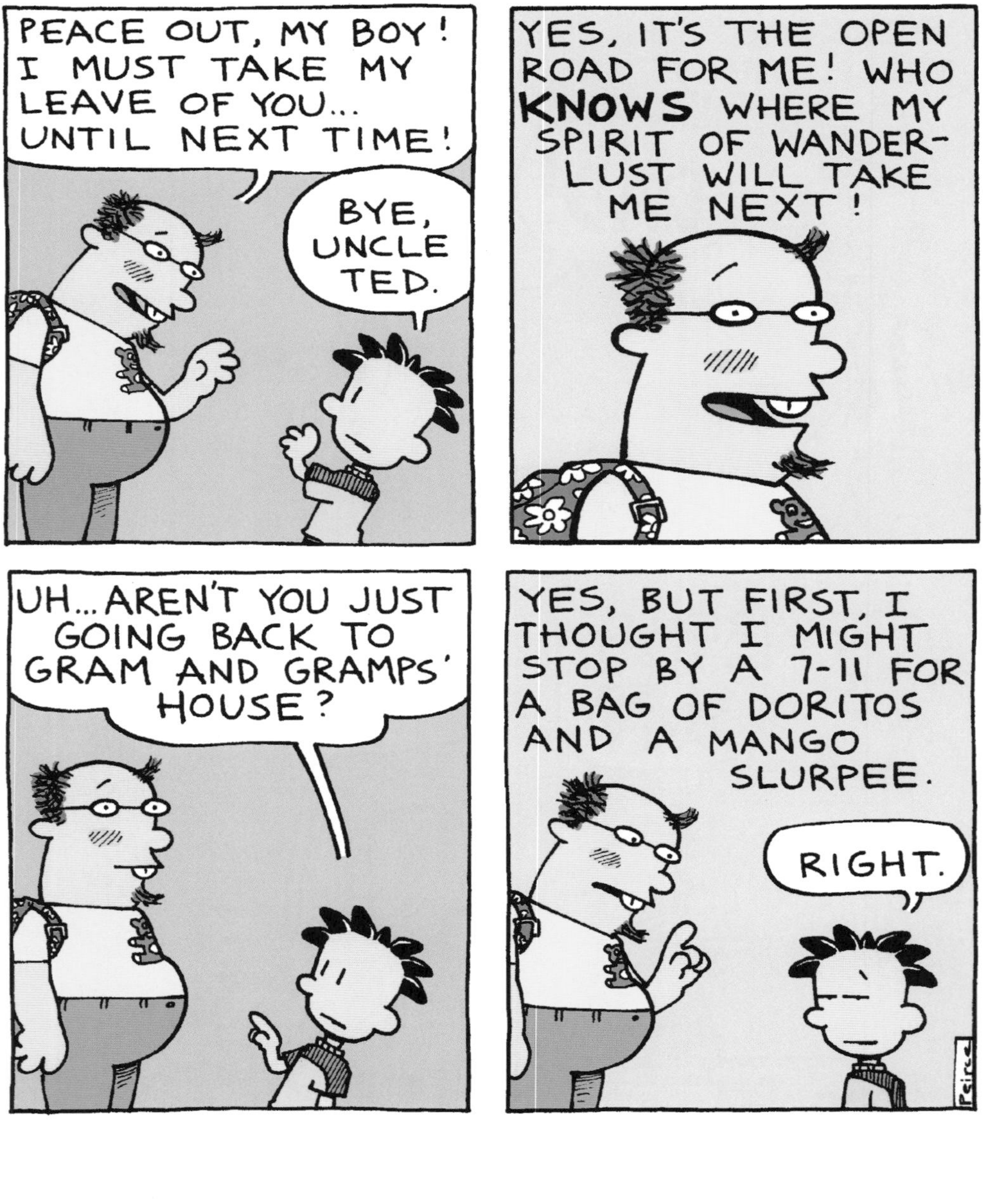
PEACE OUT, MY BOY! I MUST TAKE MY LEAVE OF YOU... UNTIL NEXT TIME!
BYE, UNCLE TED.
YES, IT'S THE OPEN ROAD FOR ME! WHO **KNOWS** WHERE MY SPIRIT OF WANDER-LUST WILL TAKE ME NEXT!
UH... AREN'T YOU JUST GOING BACK TO GRAM AND GRAMPS' HOUSE?
YES, BUT FIRST, I THOUGHT I MIGHT STOP BY A 7-11 FOR A BAG OF DORITOS AND A MANGO SLURPEE.
RIGHT.
Peirce

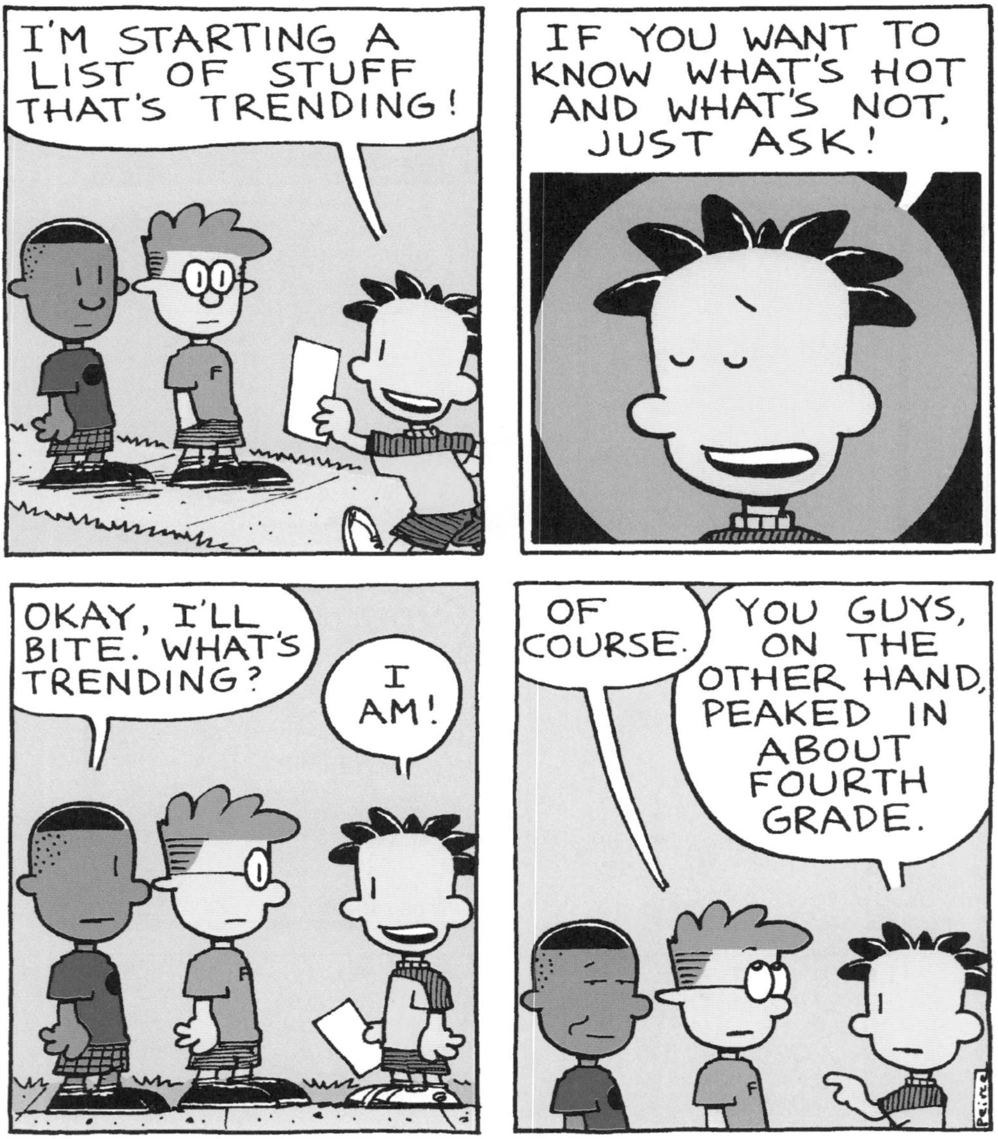
I'M STARTING A LIST OF STUFF THAT'S TRENDING!
IF YOU WANT TO KNOW WHAT'S HOT AND WHAT'S NOT, JUST ASK!
OKAY, I'LL BITE. WHAT'S TRENDING?
I AM!
OF COURSE.
YOU GUYS, ON THE OTHER HAND, PEAKED IN ABOUT FOURTH GRADE.
Peirce

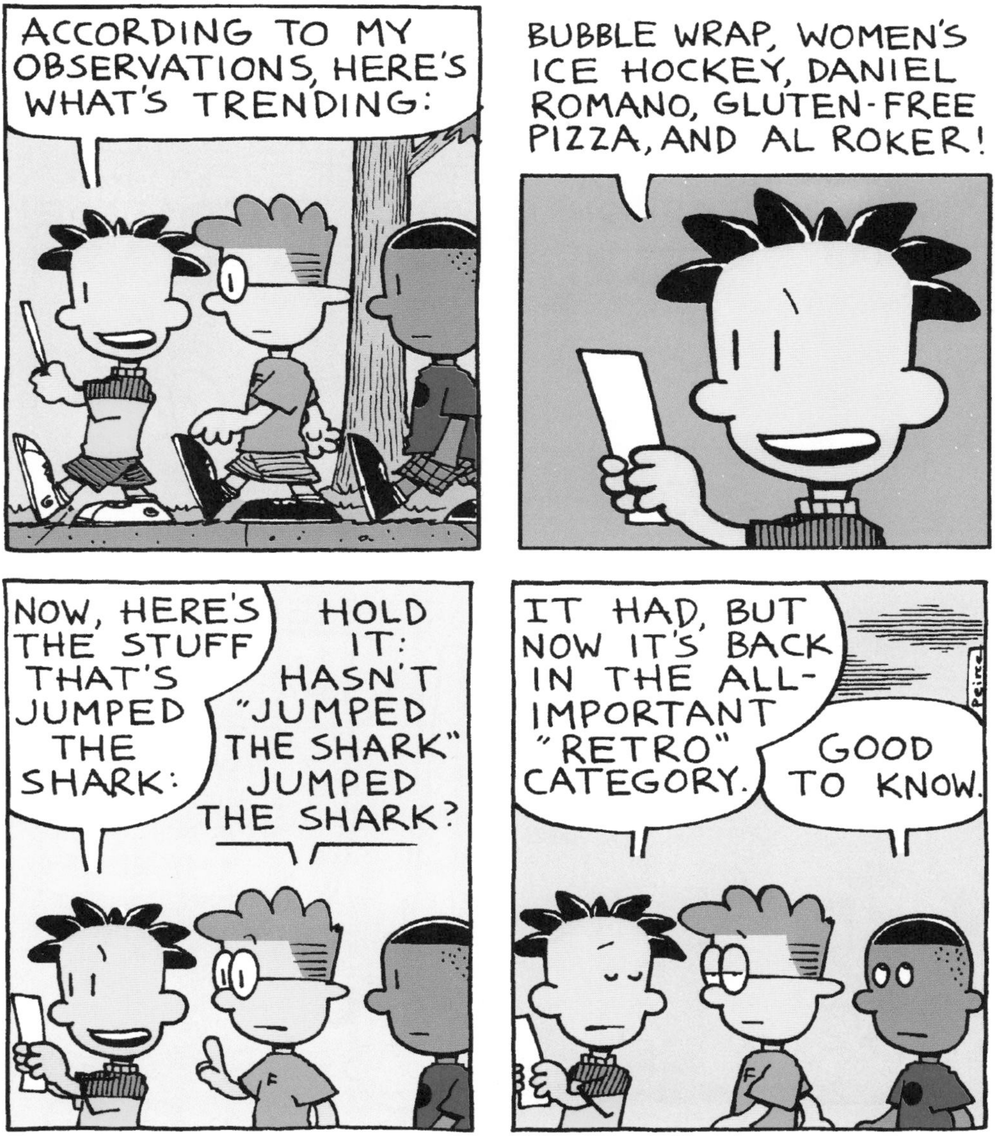
ACCORDING TO MY OBSERVATIONS, HERE'S WHAT'S TRENDING:
BUBBLE WRAP, WOMEN'S ICE HOCKEY, DANIEL ROMANO, GLUTEN-FREE PIZZA, AND AL ROKER!
NOW, HERE'S THE STUFF THAT'S JUMPED THE SHARK:
HOLD IT: HASN'T "JUMPED THE SHARK" JUMPED THE SHARK?
IT HAD, BUT NOW IT'S BACK IN THE ALL-IMPORTANT "RETRO" CATEGORY.
GOOD TO KNOW.
PEIRCE

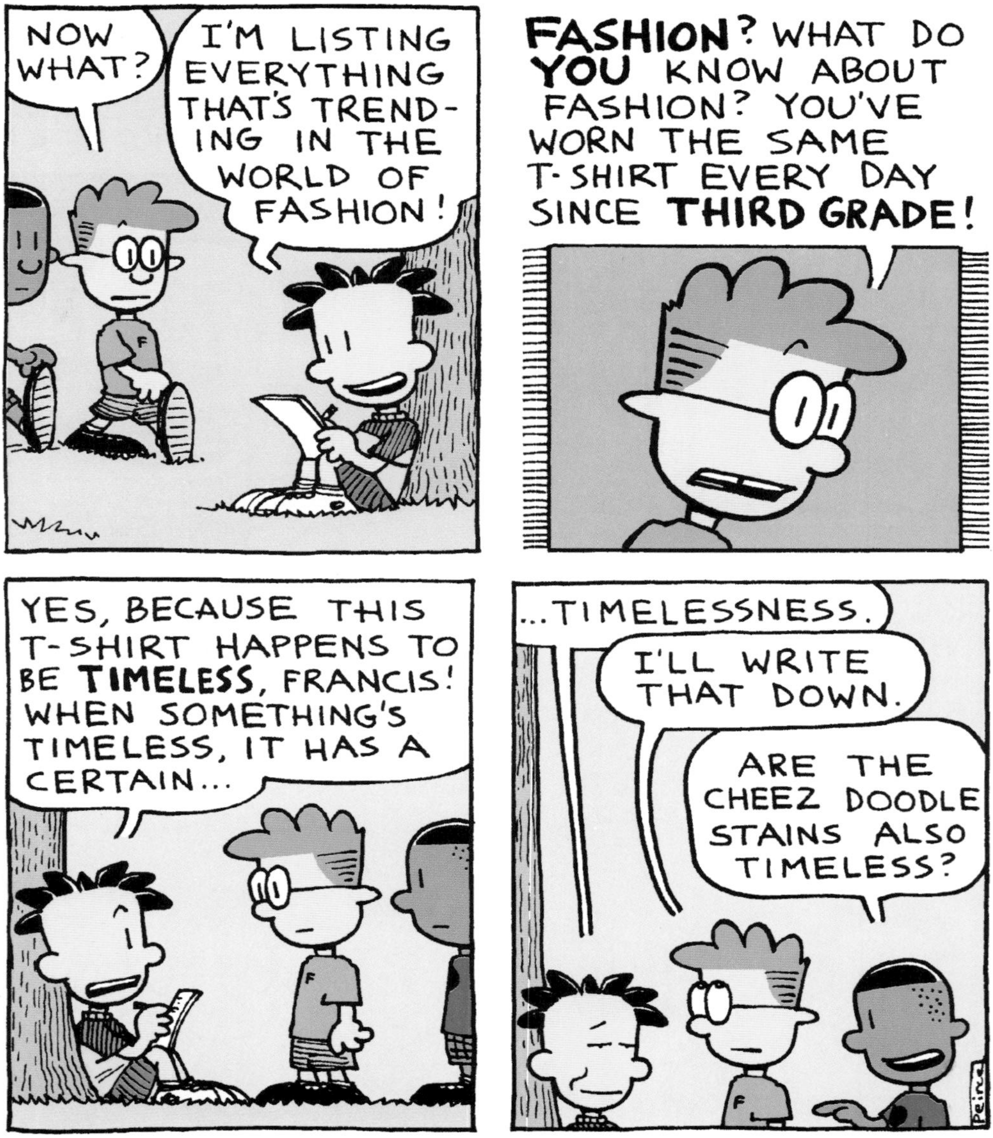
NOW WHAT?
I'M LISTING EVERYTHING THAT'S TREND-ING IN THE WORLD OF FASHION!
FASHION? WHAT DO YOU KNOW ABOUT FASHION? YOU'VE WORN THE SAME T-SHIRT EVERY DAY SINCE THIRD GRADE!
YES, BECAUSE THIS T-SHIRT HAPPENS TO BE TIMELESS, FRANCIS! WHEN SOMETHING'S TIMELESS, IT HAS A CERTAIN...
...TIMELESSNESS.
I'LL WRITE THAT DOWN.
ARE THE CHEEZ DOODLE STAINS ALSO TIMELESS?
peirce

NO OFFENSE, BUT WHY DO **YOU** GET TO BE THE ONE WHO DECIDES WHAT'S TRENDING? WHY CAN'T **I** SAY WHAT'S TRENDING?
FINE. DO IT.
WHATTA YA MEAN?
WE'RE ALL EARS. TELL US SOME-THING THAT'S TRENDING.
OH. OKAY. UMMMMMM MMMMMMMMMMMMMM MMMMMMMMMMMMMMM MMMMMMMMMMMMMM
MMMMMMMMMMMMMMM MMMMMMMMMMMMMMM
INDECISION IS DEFINITELY NOT TRENDING.
SO TRUE.
Peirce

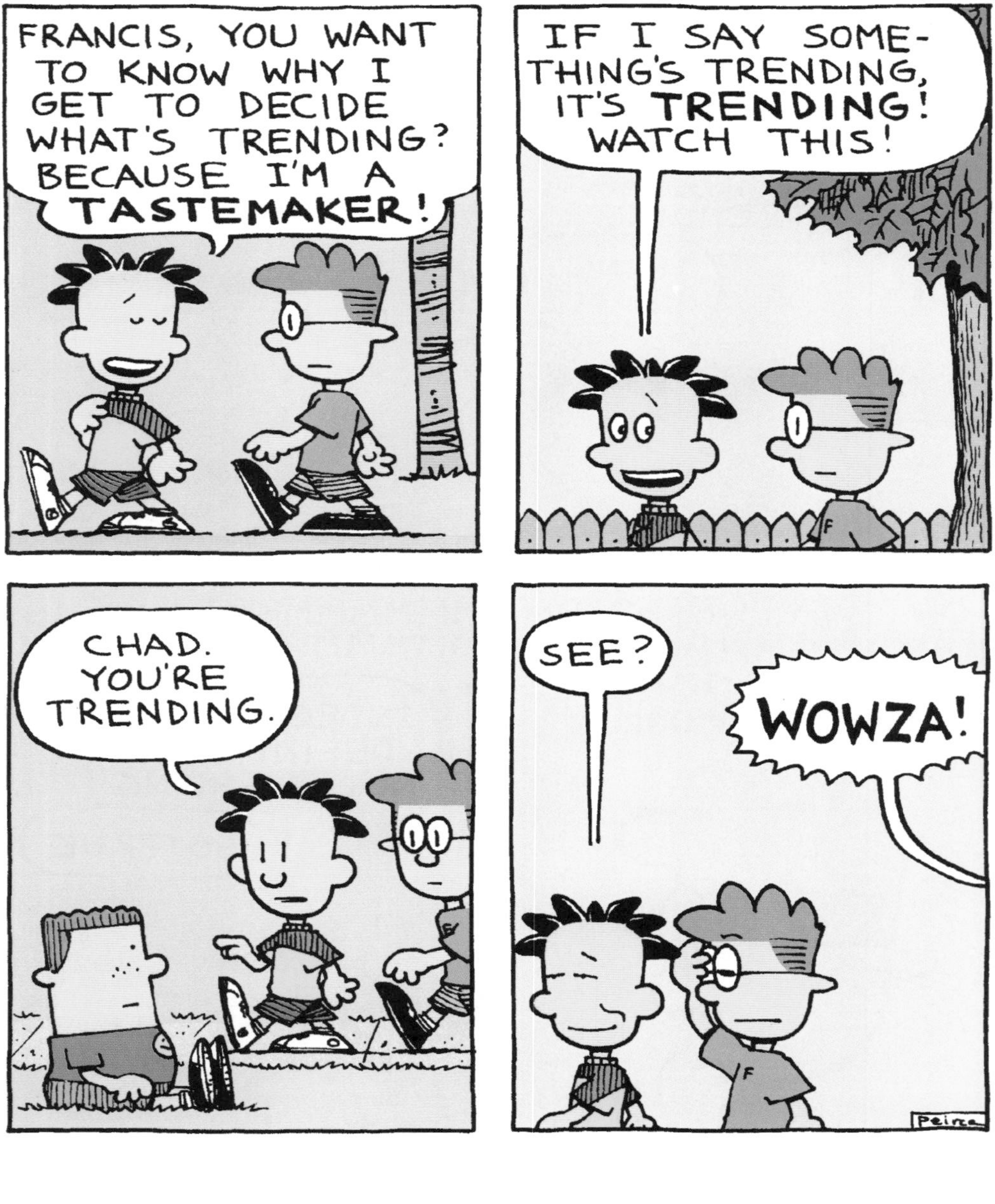
FRANCIS, YOU WANT TO KNOW WHY I GET TO DECIDE WHAT'S TRENDING? BECAUSE I'M A **TASTEMAKER**!
IF I SAY SOMETHING'S TRENDING, IT'S **TRENDING**! WATCH THIS!
CHAD. YOU'RE TRENDING.
SEE?
WOWZA!
Peirce

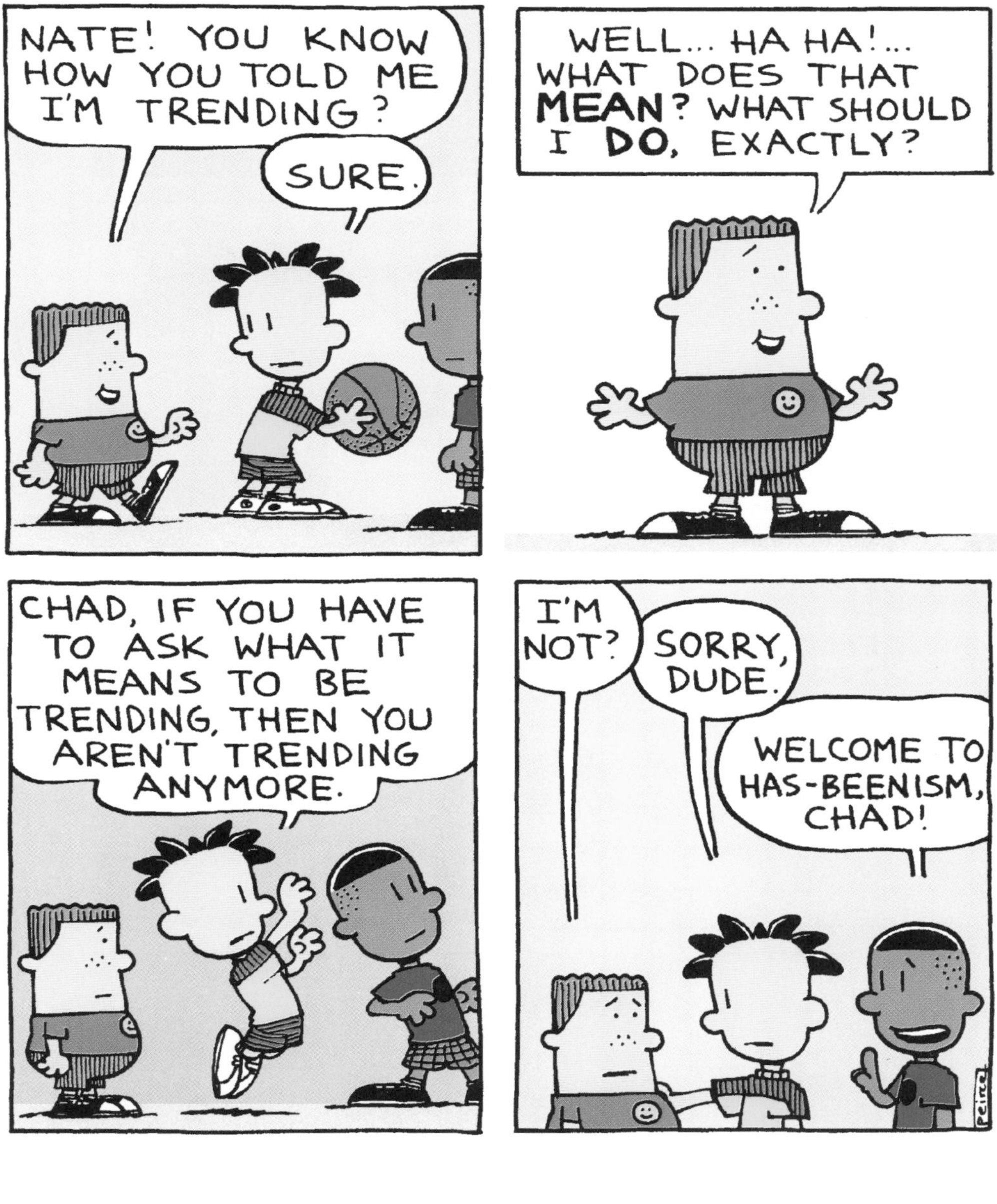
NATE! YOU KNOW HOW YOU TOLD ME I'M TRENDING?
SURE.
WELL... HA HA!... WHAT DOES THAT **MEAN**? WHAT SHOULD I **DO**, EXACTLY?
CHAD, IF YOU HAVE TO ASK WHAT IT MEANS TO BE TRENDING, THEN YOU AREN'T TRENDING ANYMORE.
I'M NOT?
SORRY, DUDE.
WELCOME TO HAS-BEENISM, CHAD!
peirce

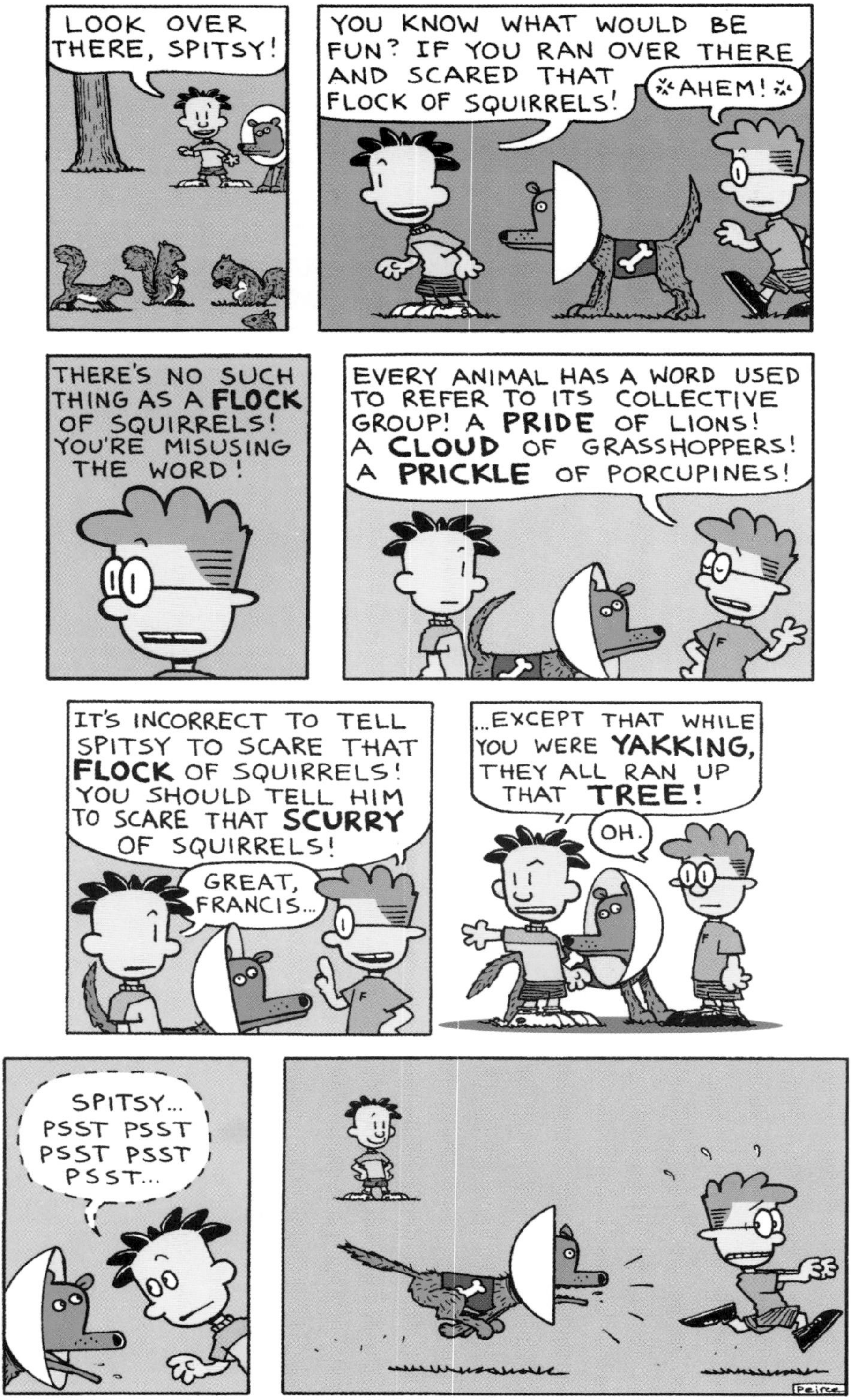
LOOK OVER THERE, SPITSY!
YOU KNOW WHAT WOULD BE FUN? IF YOU RAN OVER THERE AND SCARED THAT FLOCK OF SQUIRRELS!
AHEM!
THERE'S NO SUCH THING AS A FLOCK OF SQUIRRELS! YOU'RE MISUSING THE WORD!
EVERY ANIMAL HAS A WORD USED TO REFER TO ITS COLLECTIVE GROUP! A PRIDE OF LIONS! A CLOUD OF GRASSHOPPERS! A PRICKLE OF PORCUPINES!
IT'S INCORRECT TO TELL SPITSY TO SCARE THAT FLOCK OF SQUIRRELS! YOU SHOULD TELL HIM TO SCARE THAT SCURRY OF SQUIRRELS!
GREAT, FRANCIS...
...EXCEPT THAT WHILE YOU WERE YAKKING, THEY ALL RAN UP THAT TREE!
OH.
SPITSY... PSST PSST PSST PSST PSST...
Peirce

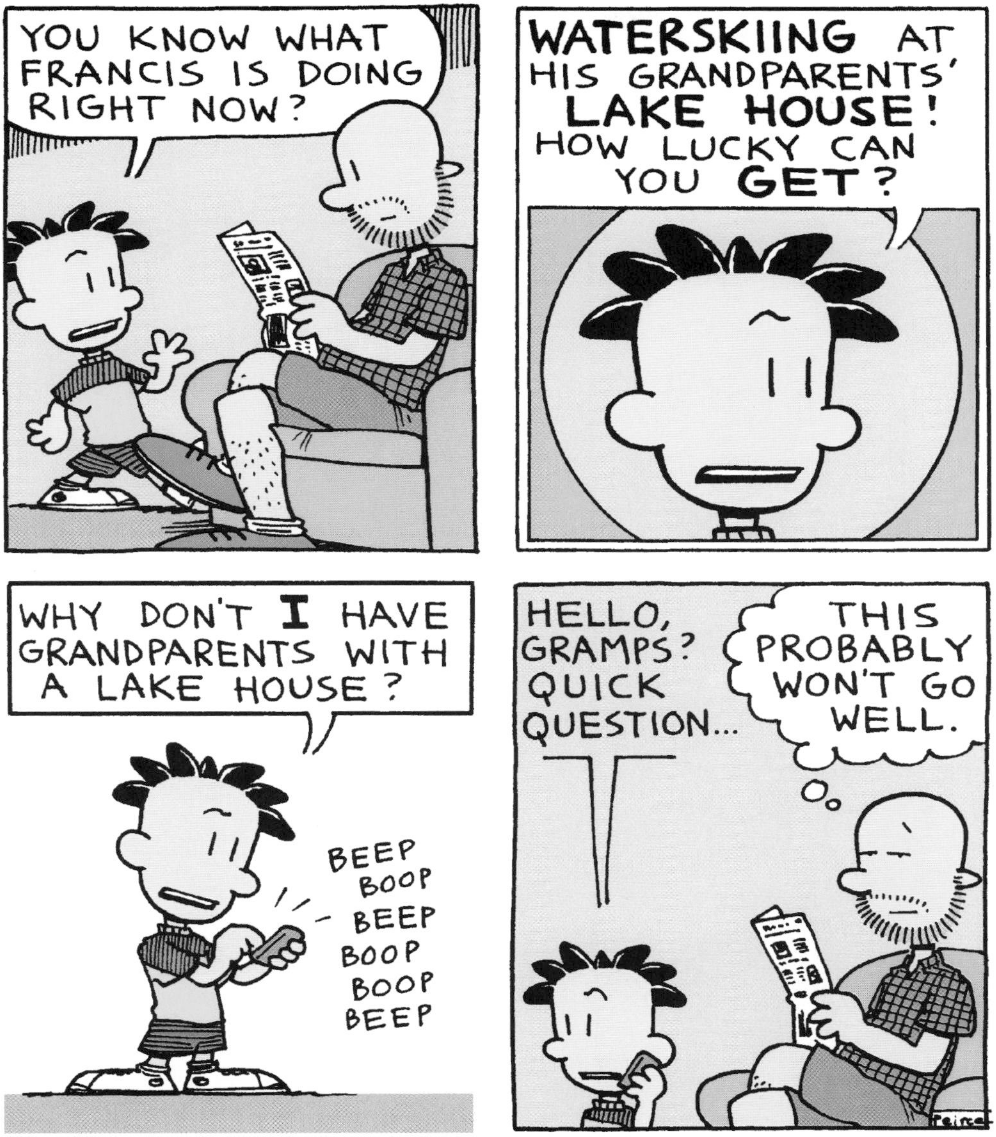
YOU KNOW WHAT FRANCIS IS DOING RIGHT NOW?
WATERSKIING AT HIS GRANDPARENTS' LAKE HOUSE! HOW LUCKY CAN YOU GET?
WHY DON'T I HAVE GRANDPARENTS WITH A LAKE HOUSE?
BEEP BOOP BEEP BOOP BOOP BEEP
HELLO, GRAMPS? QUICK QUESTION...
THIS PROBABLY WON'T GO WELL.
Peirce

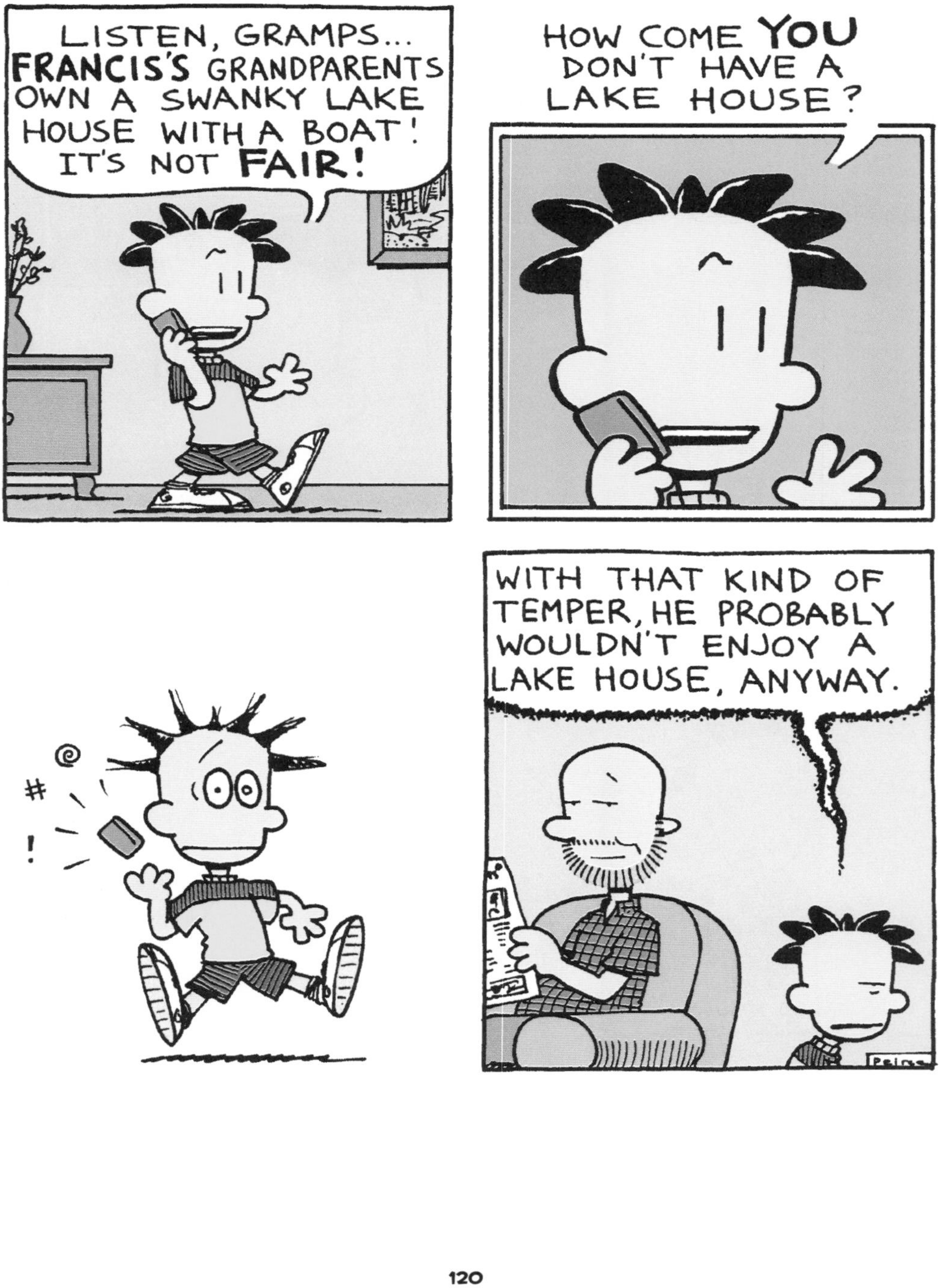
LISTEN, GRAMPS... FRANCIS'S GRANDPARENTS OWN A SWANKY LAKE HOUSE WITH A BOAT! IT'S NOT FAIR!
HOW COME YOU DON'T HAVE A LAKE HOUSE?
#
!
WITH THAT KIND OF TEMPER, HE PROBABLY WOULDN'T ENJOY A LAKE HOUSE, ANYWAY.

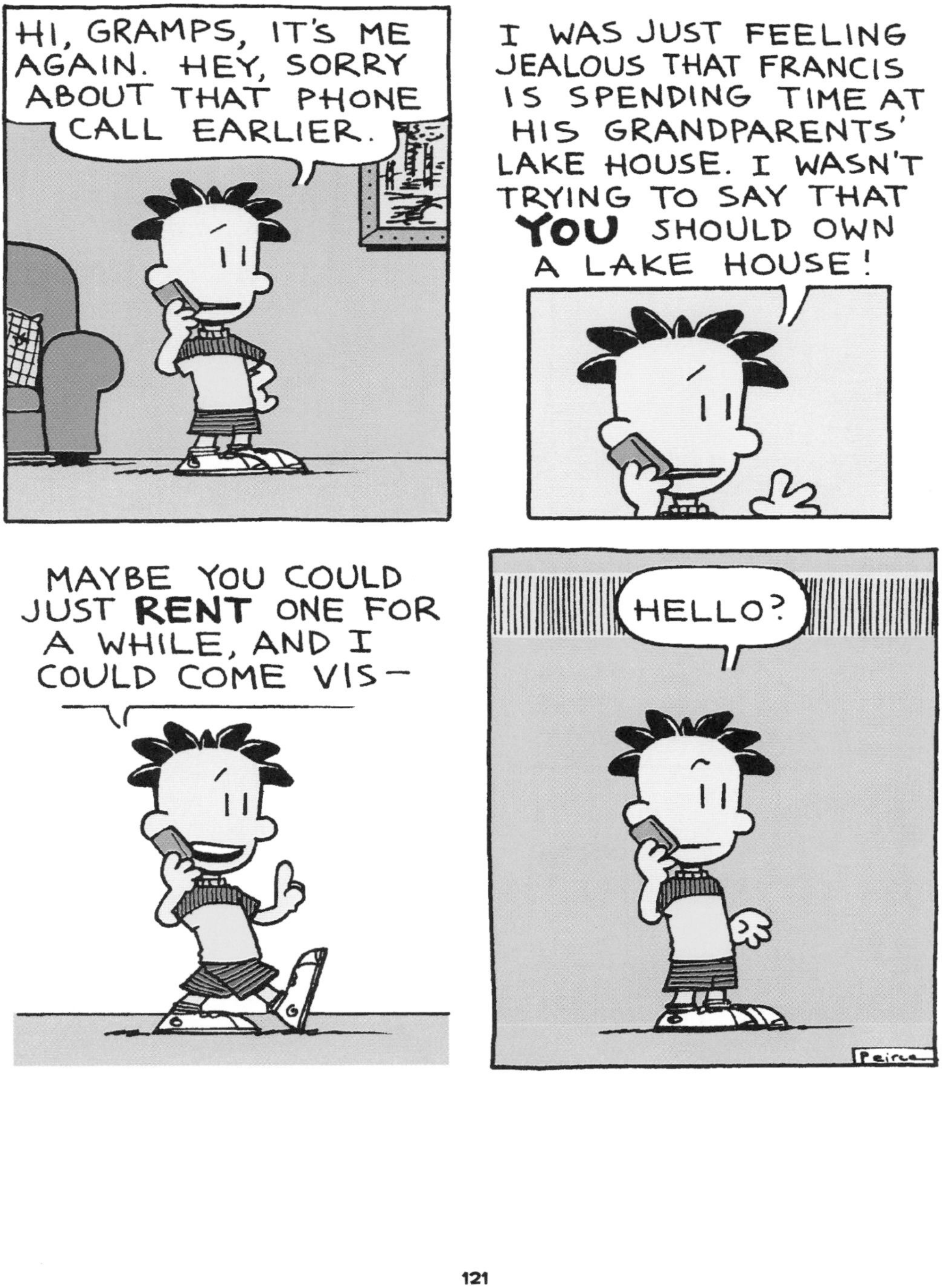
HI, GRAMPS, IT'S ME AGAIN. HEY, SORRY ABOUT THAT PHONE CALL EARLIER.
I WAS JUST FEELING JEALOUS THAT FRANCIS IS SPENDING TIME AT HIS GRANDPARENTS' LAKE HOUSE. I WASN'T TRYING TO SAY THAT **YOU** SHOULD OWN A LAKE HOUSE!
MAYBE YOU COULD JUST **RENT** ONE FOR A WHILE, AND I COULD COME VIS—
HELLO?
Peirce

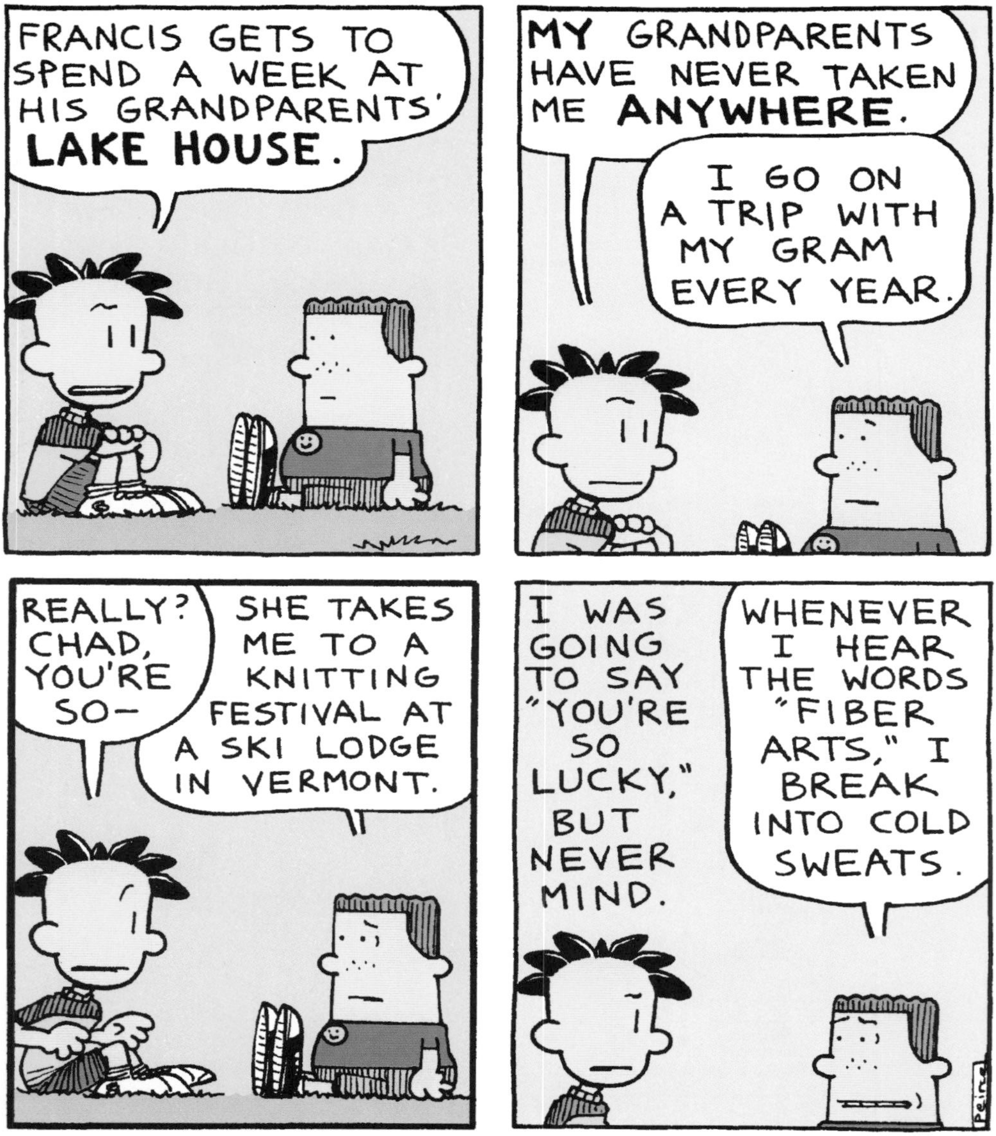
FRANCIS GETS TO SPEND A WEEK AT HIS GRANDPARENTS' **LAKE HOUSE**.
MY GRANDPARENTS HAVE NEVER TAKEN ME **ANYWHERE**.
I GO ON A TRIP WITH MY GRAM EVERY YEAR.
REALLY? CHAD, YOU'RE SO—
SHE TAKES ME TO A KNITTING FESTIVAL AT A SKI LODGE IN VERMONT.
I WAS GOING TO SAY "YOU'RE SO LUCKY," BUT NEVER MIND.
WHENEVER I HEAR THE WORDS "FIBER ARTS," I BREAK INTO COLD SWEATS.
Peirce

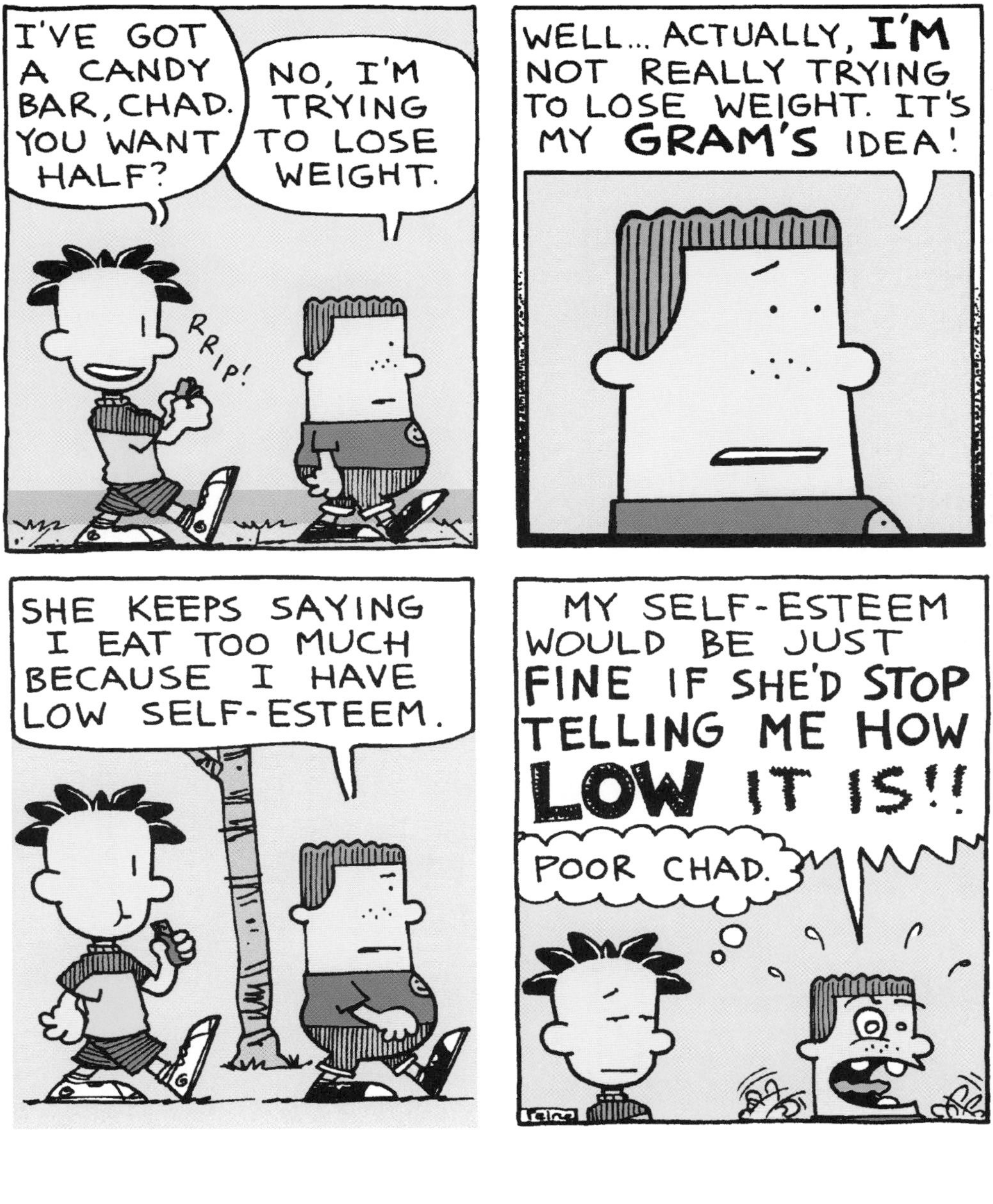
I'VE GOT A CANDY BAR, CHAD. YOU WANT HALF?
NO, I'M TRYING TO LOSE WEIGHT.
RRRIP!
WELL... ACTUALLY, I'M NOT REALLY TRYING TO LOSE WEIGHT. IT'S MY GRAM'S IDEA!
SHE KEEPS SAYING I EAT TOO MUCH BECAUSE I HAVE LOW SELF-ESTEEM.
MY SELF-ESTEEM WOULD BE JUST FINE IF SHE'D STOP TELLING ME HOW LOW IT IS!!
POOR CHAD.

SO YOUR GRANDMA'S ALWAYS BUGGING YOU ABOUT YOUR WEIGHT?

YUP. I JUST WISH SHE'D BE **CONSISTENT** ABOUT IT!

FIRST SHE TELLS ME I NEED TO CONCENTRATE ON GETTING EXERCISE AND EATING HEALTHY...

...BUT WHEN I BRING HOME A GOOD REPORT CARD, WHAT DOES SHE **DO**? TAKES ME OUT FOR **ICE CREAM!**

I THINK A LOT OF GRANDPARENTS ARE SENILE THAT WAY.

HELLO, OPERATOR? GET ME **MIXED MESSAGES!**

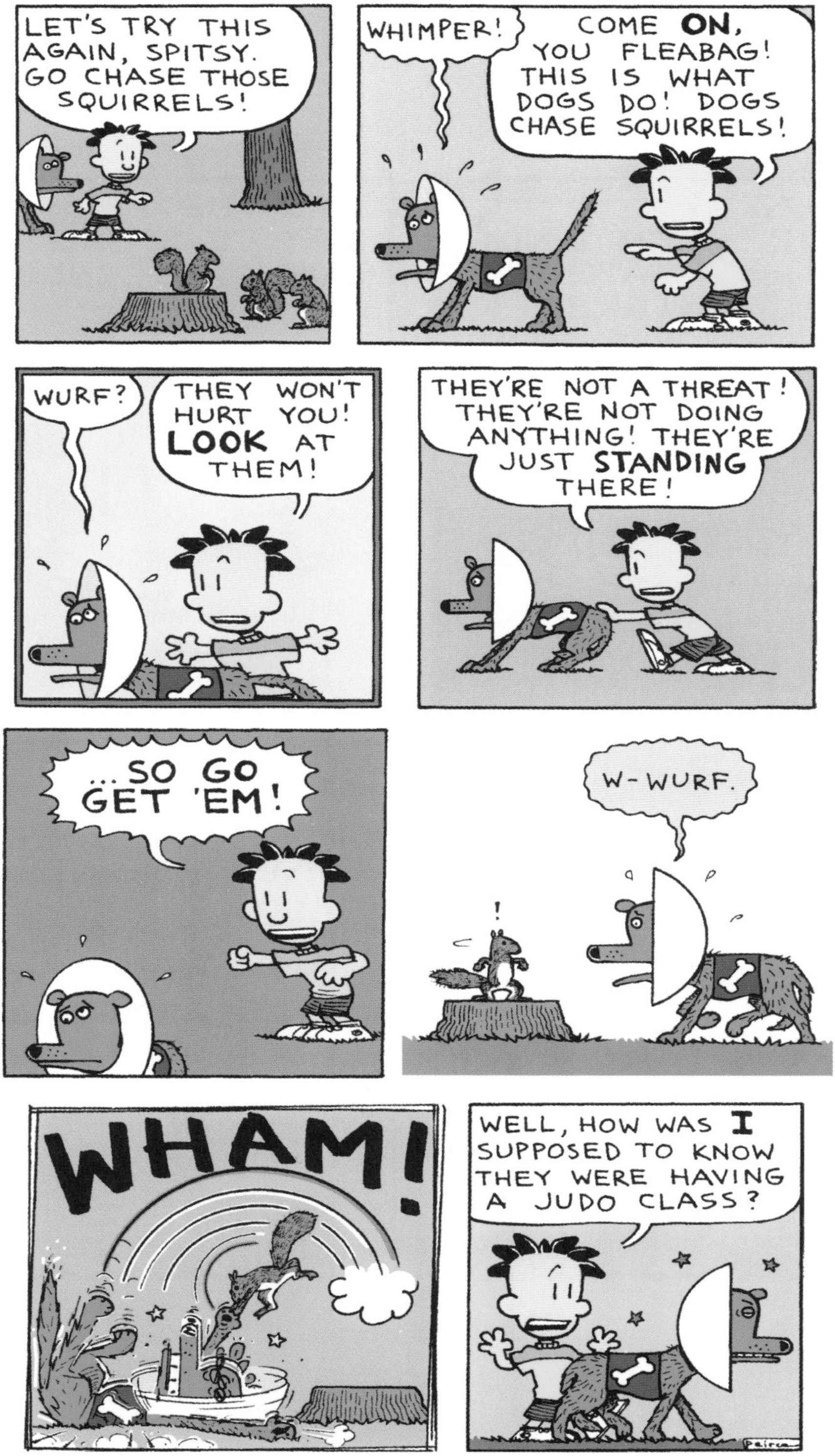

LET'S TRY THIS AGAIN, SPITSY. GO CHASE THOSE SQUIRRELS!
WHIMPER!
COME **ON**, YOU FLEABAG! THIS IS WHAT DOGS DO! DOGS CHASE SQUIRRELS!
WURF?
THEY WON'T HURT YOU! **LOOK** AT THEM!
THEY'RE NOT A THREAT! THEY'RE NOT DOING ANYTHING! THEY'RE JUST **STANDING** THERE!
...SO GO GET 'EM!
W-WURF.
WHAM!
WELL, HOW WAS **I** SUPPOSED TO KNOW THEY WERE HAVING A JUDO CLASS?

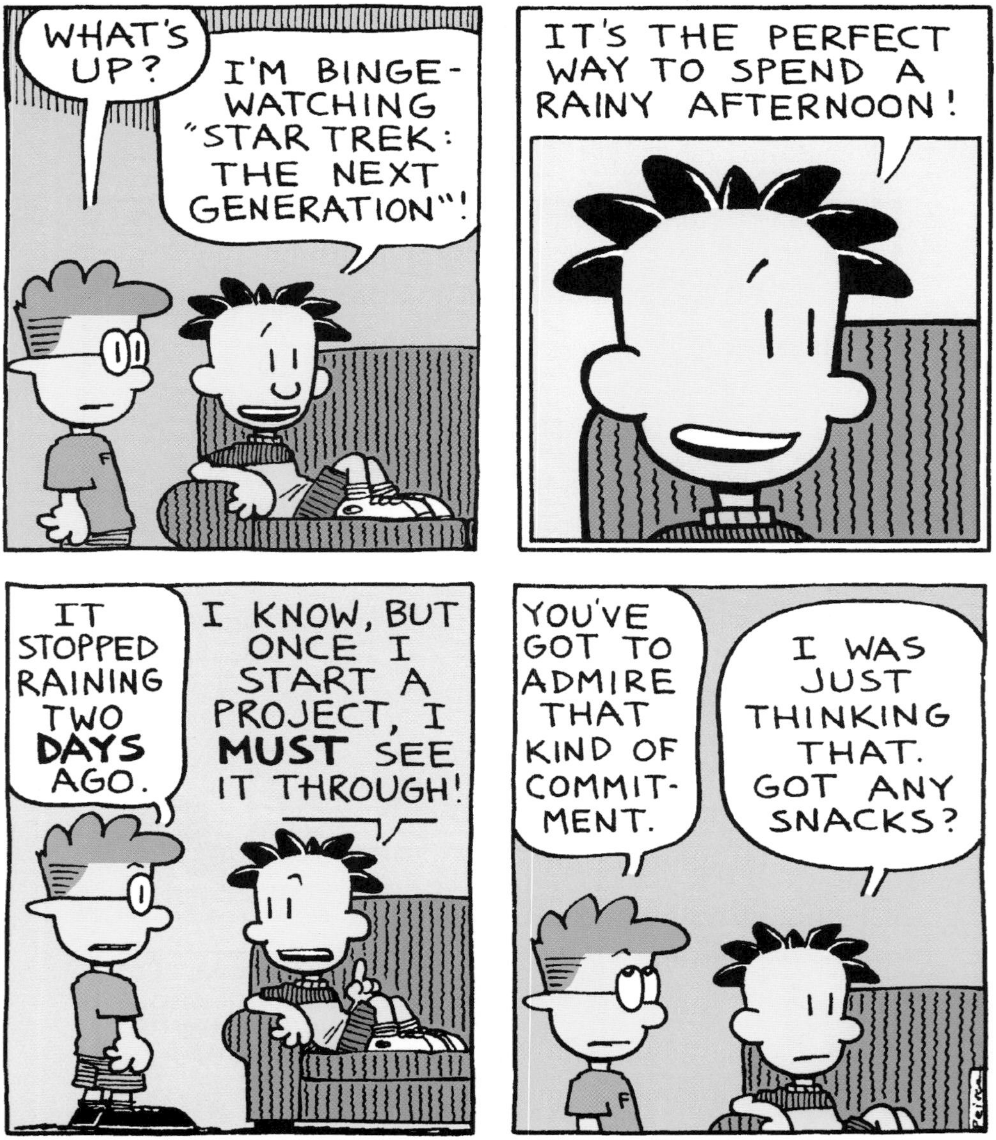
WHAT'S UP?
I'M BINGE-WATCHING "STAR TREK: THE NEXT GENERATION"!
IT'S THE PERFECT WAY TO SPEND A RAINY AFTERNOON!
IT STOPPED RAINING TWO **DAYS** AGO.
I KNOW, BUT ONCE I START A PROJECT, I **MUST** SEE IT THROUGH!
YOU'VE GOT TO ADMIRE THAT KIND OF COMMIT-MENT.
I WAS JUST THINKING THAT. GOT ANY SNACKS?

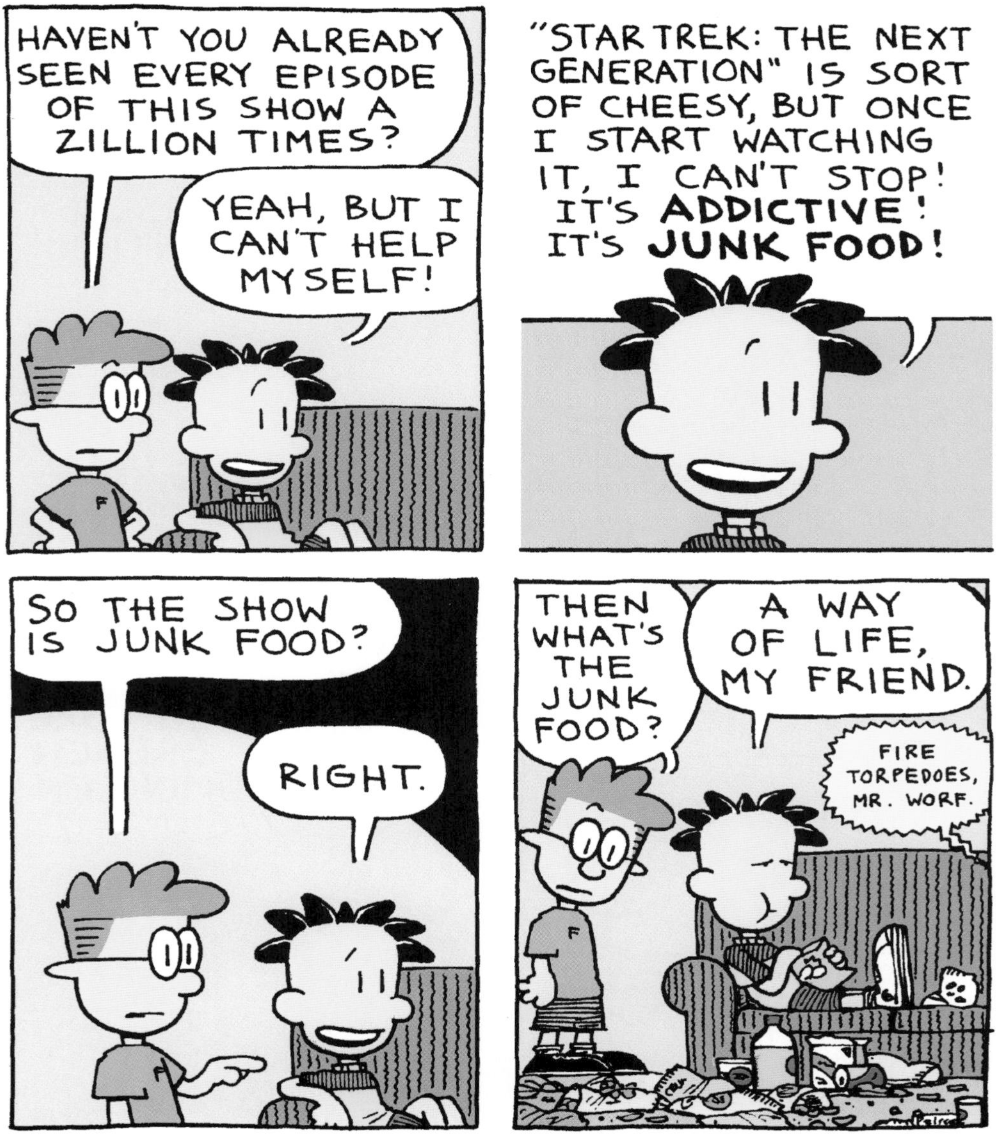
HAVEN'T YOU ALREADY SEEN EVERY EPISODE OF THIS SHOW A ZILLION TIMES?
YEAH, BUT I CAN'T HELP MYSELF!
"STAR TREK: THE NEXT GENERATION" IS SORT OF CHEESY, BUT ONCE I START WATCHING IT, I CAN'T STOP! IT'S ADDICTIVE! IT'S JUNK FOOD!
SO THE SHOW IS JUNK FOOD?
RIGHT.
THEN WHAT'S THE JUNK FOOD?
A WAY OF LIFE, MY FRIEND.
FIRE TORPEDOES, MR. WORF.

WHERE HAVE YOU GUYS BEEN?

I HAD TO DRAG NATE AWAY FROM HIS "STAR TREK: TNG" MARATHON!

DUDE! THAT SHOW'S **OLD!**

SO WHAT?

JUST BECAUSE SOMETHING'S **OLD** DOESN'T MAKE IT ANY LESS **AWESOME!**

COUNSELOR TROI TURNS SIXTY IN MARCH.

OKAY, MAYBE IT MAKES IT A SMIDGE LESS AWESOME.

131

YOU KNOW WHAT'S INSANE? LET'S SAY YOU BUY A BUNCH OF FIVE YELLOWISH-GREEN BANANAS ON MONDAY, AND YOUR PLAN IS TO EAT ONE EACH DAY.

BY THE TIME YOU GET TO **WEDNESDAY,** THE BANANAS ARE ALREADY TURNING YELLOWISH-**BROWN!**

SO YOU'RE LEFT WITH THREE MUSHY, BRUISED BANANAS THAT ARE TOO **NASTY** TO EAT!

HENCE: THE DEMON SPAWN CALLED "BANANA BREAD."

WHEN HE SAID "YOU KNOW WHAT'S INSANE," I THOUGHT HE WAS GOING IN ANOTHER DIRECTION.

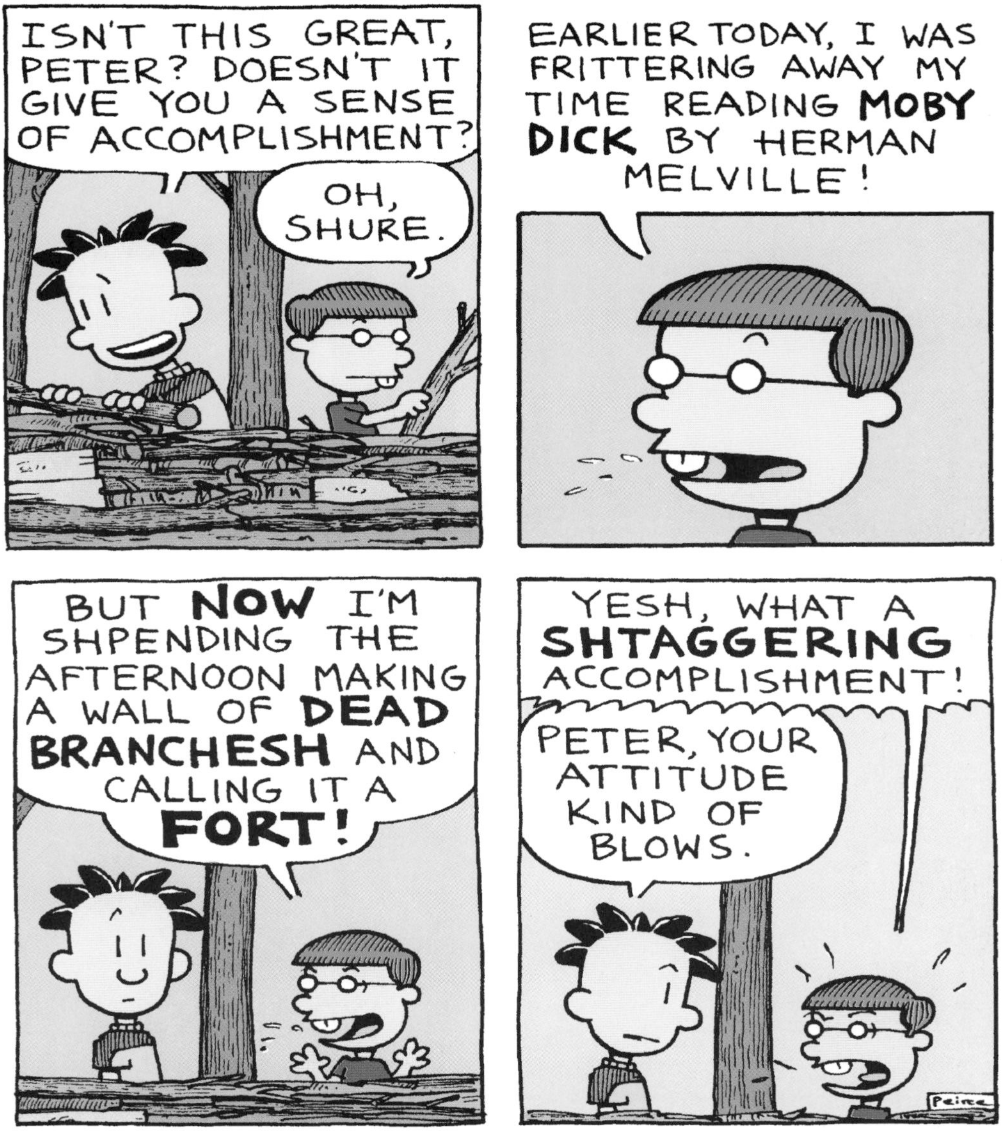
ISN'T THIS GREAT, PETER? DOESN'T IT GIVE YOU A SENSE OF ACCOMPLISHMENT?
OH, SHURE.
EARLIER TODAY, I WAS FRITTERING AWAY MY TIME READING **MOBY DICK** BY HERMAN MELVILLE!
BUT **NOW** I'M SHPENDING THE AFTERNOON MAKING A WALL OF **DEAD BRANCHESH** AND CALLING IT A **FORT!**
YESH, WHAT A **SHTAGGERING** ACCOMPLISHMENT!
PETER, YOUR ATTITUDE KIND OF BLOWS.
Peirce

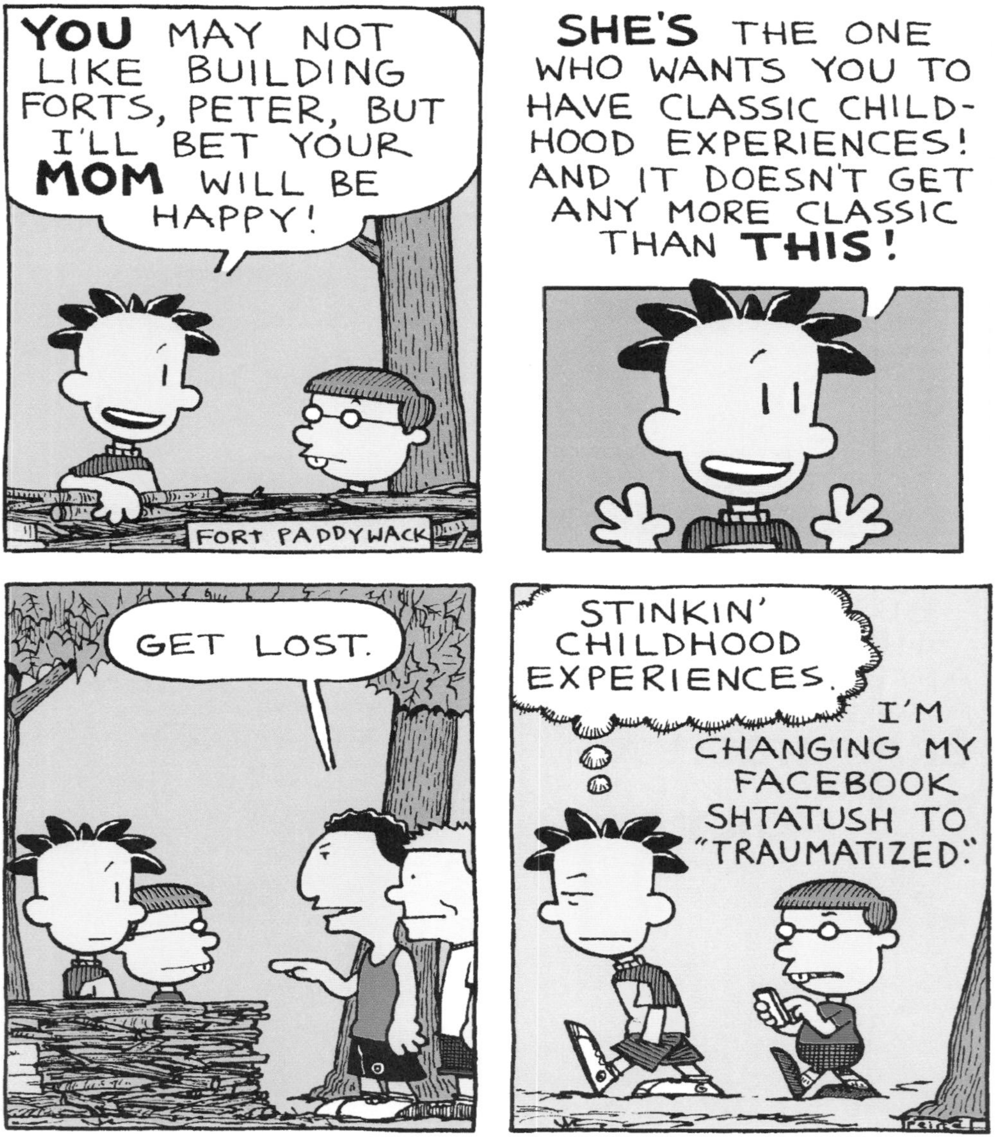
YOU MAY NOT LIKE BUILDING FORTS, PETER, BUT I'LL BET YOUR MOM WILL BE HAPPY!
FORT PADDYWACK
SHE'S THE ONE WHO WANTS YOU TO HAVE CLASSIC CHILD-HOOD EXPERIENCES! AND IT DOESN'T GET ANY MORE CLASSIC THAN THIS!
GET LOST.
STINKIN' CHILDHOOD EXPERIENCES.
I'M CHANGING MY FACEBOOK SHTATUSH TO "TRAUMATIZED."

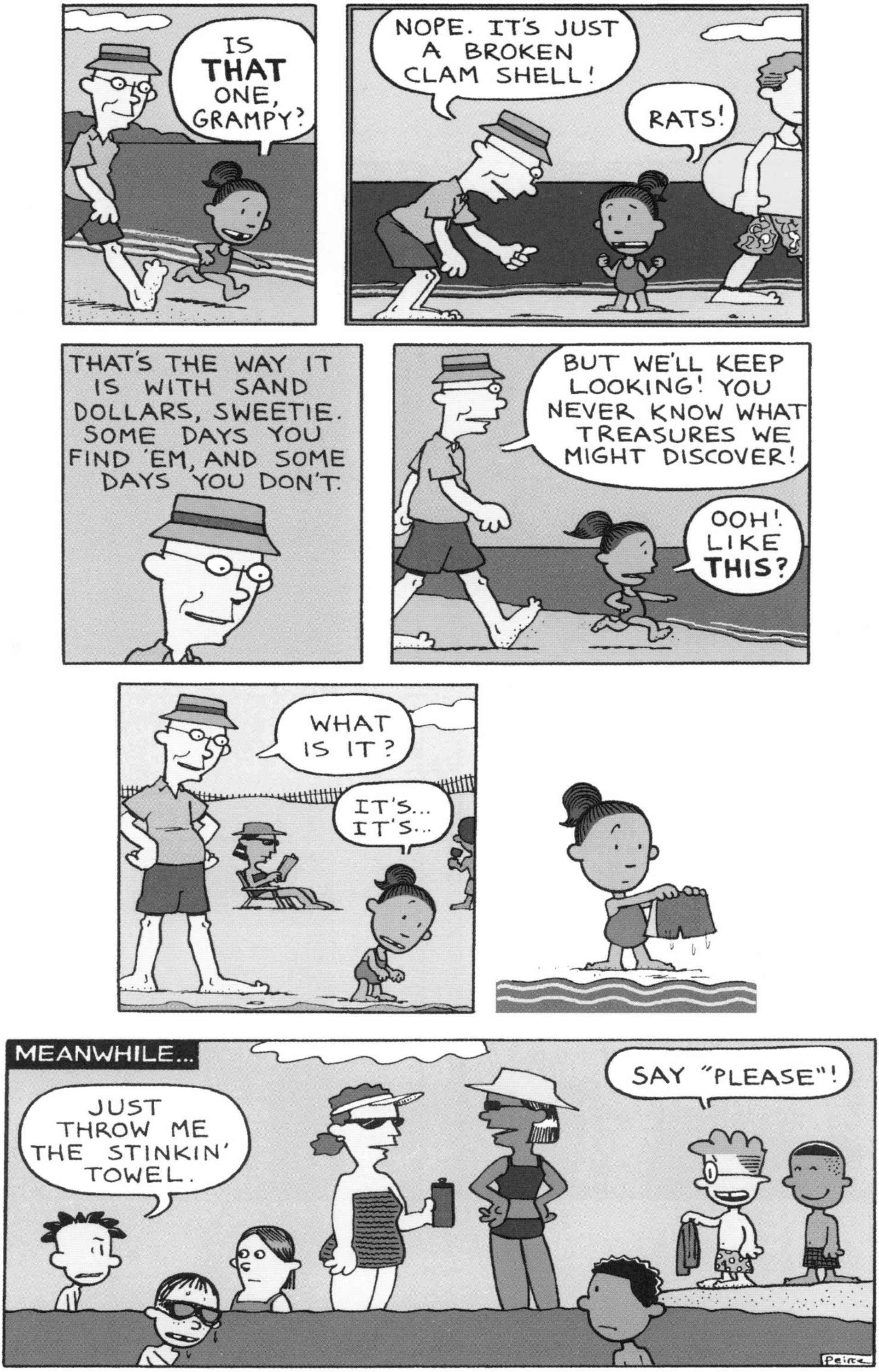
IS THAT ONE, GRAMPY?
NOPE. IT'S JUST A BROKEN CLAM SHELL!
RATS!
THAT'S THE WAY IT IS WITH SAND DOLLARS, SWEETIE. SOME DAYS YOU FIND 'EM, AND SOME DAYS YOU DON'T.
BUT WE'LL KEEP LOOKING! YOU NEVER KNOW WHAT TREASURES WE MIGHT DISCOVER!
OOH! LIKE THIS?
WHAT IS IT?
IT'S... IT'S...
MEANWHILE...
JUST THROW ME THE STINKIN' TOWEL.
SAY "PLEASE"!
Peirce

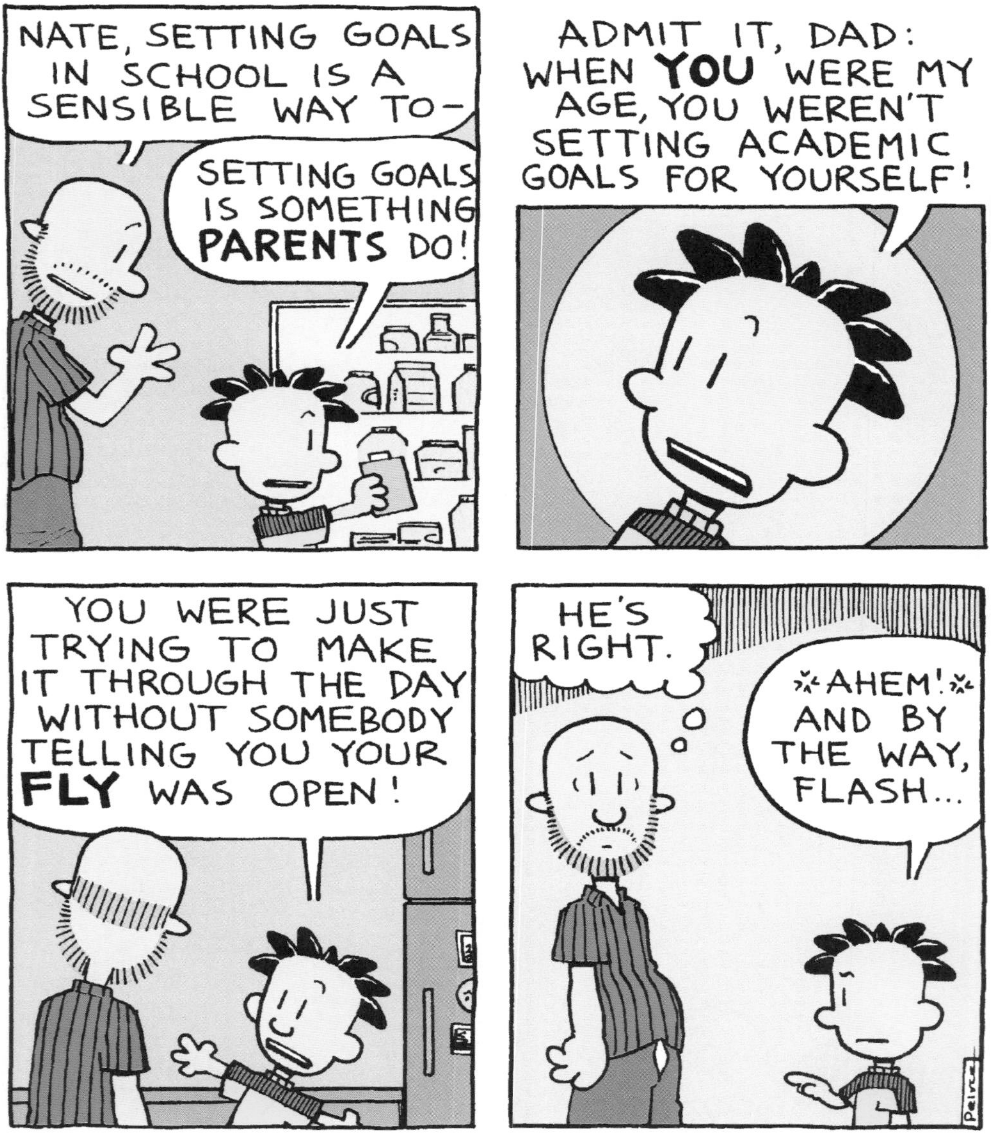
NATE, SETTING GOALS IN SCHOOL IS A SENSIBLE WAY TO–
SETTING GOALS IS SOMETHING **PARENTS** DO!
ADMIT IT, DAD: WHEN **YOU** WERE MY AGE, YOU WEREN'T SETTING ACADEMIC GOALS FOR YOURSELF!
YOU WERE JUST TRYING TO MAKE IT THROUGH THE DAY WITHOUT SOMEBODY TELLING YOU YOUR **FLY** WAS OPEN!
HE'S RIGHT.
AHEM! AND BY THE WAY, FLASH...
Peirce

MY DAD WANTS ME TO SET GOALS FOR MYSELF IN SCHOOL.

MY GRAM'S THE SAME WAY. SHE WANTS ME TO BE A GO-GETTER!

ON THE FIRST DAY OF SCHOOL, SHE ALWAYS SAYS: "CHAD, TRY NOT TO SLIP THROUGH THE CRACKS"!

WHAT DOES "SLIP THROUGH THE CRACKS" MEAN?

IT'S WHEN THE TEACHERS DON'T NOTICE YOU.

SOUNDS LIKE PARADISE.

OH, IT **IS**! DON'T TELL MY GRAM, BUT I **LOOK** FOR THE CRACKS!

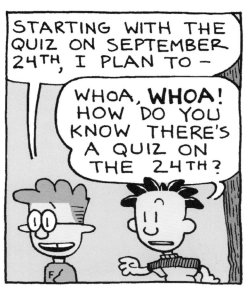

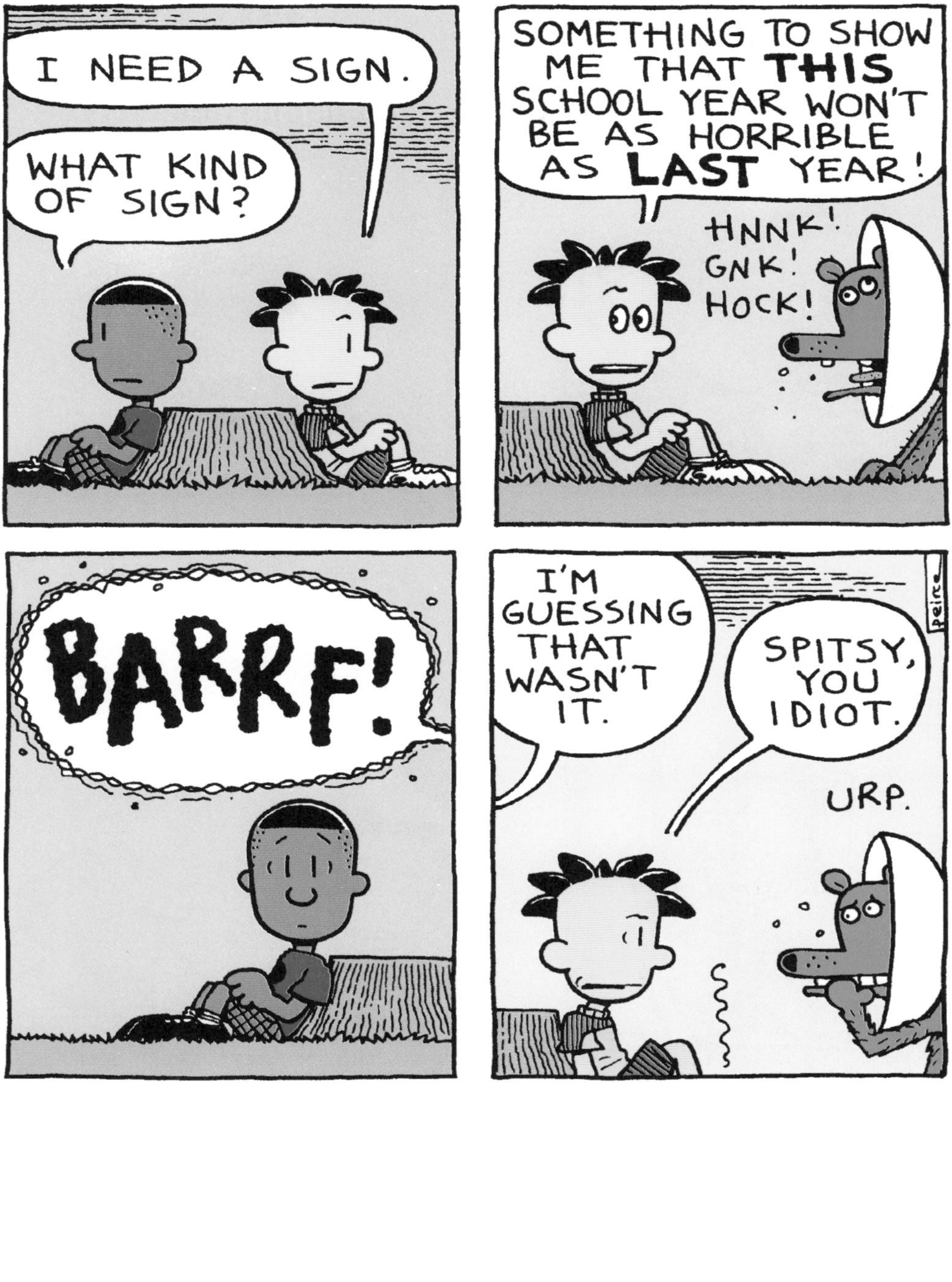
I NEED A SIGN.
WHAT KIND OF SIGN?
SOMETHING TO SHOW ME THAT THIS SCHOOL YEAR WON'T BE AS HORRIBLE AS LAST YEAR!
HNNK! GNK! HOCK!
BARRF!
I'M GUESSING THAT WASN'T IT.
SPITSY, YOU IDIOT.
URP.

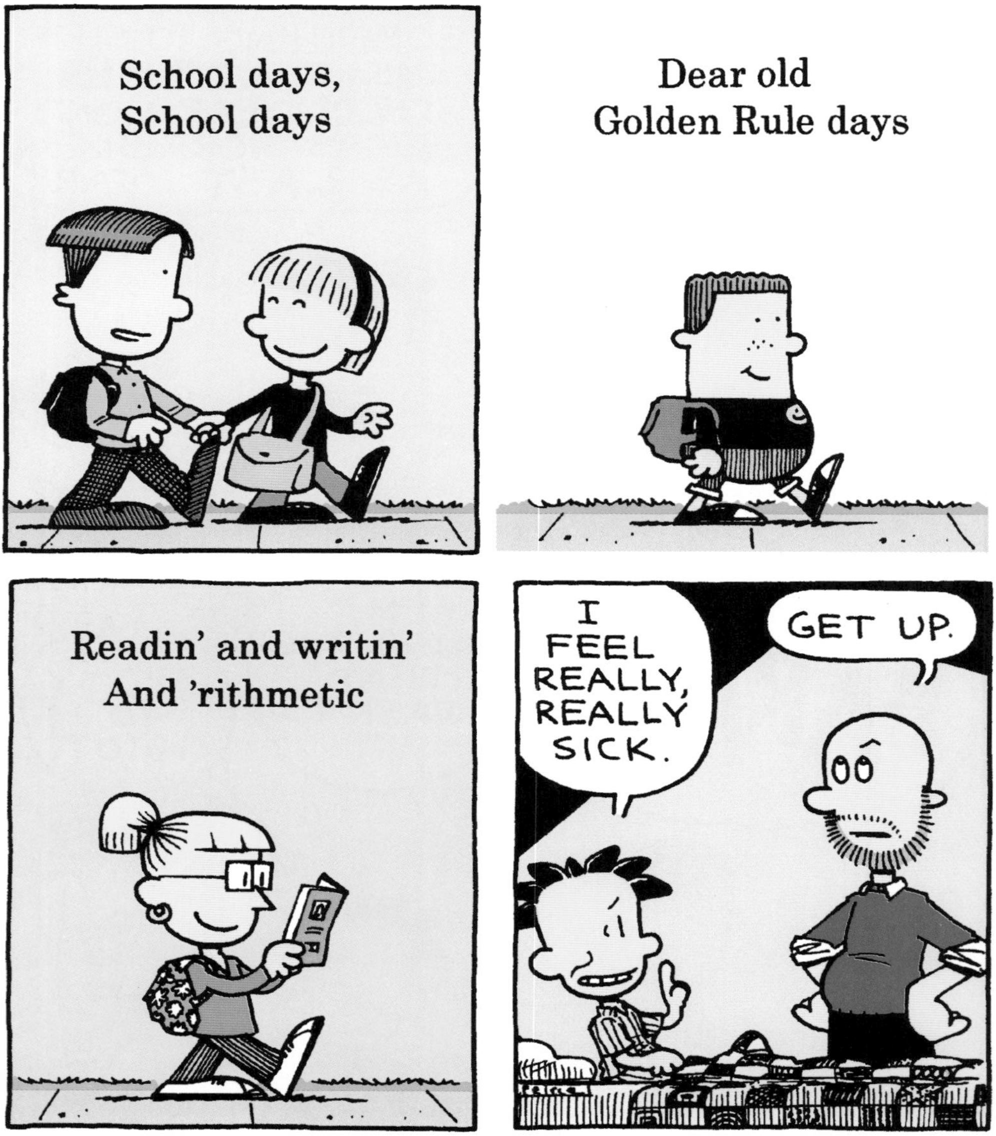
School days,
School days
Dear old
Golden Rule days
Readin' and writin'
And 'rithmetic
I FEEL REALLY, REALLY SICK.
GET UP.

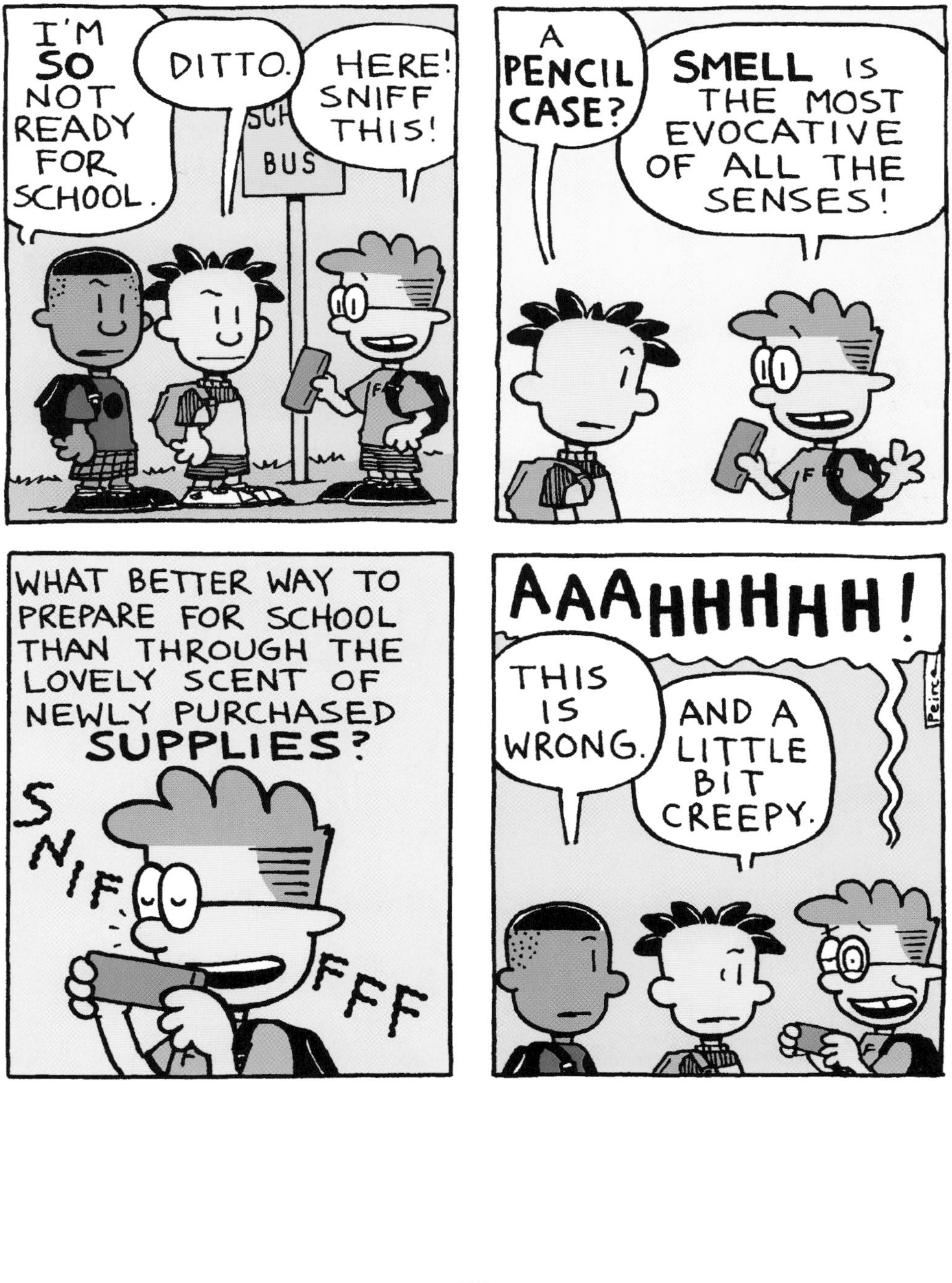
I'M SO NOT READY FOR SCHOOL.
DITTO.
HERE! SNIFF THIS!
SCH
BUS
A PENCIL CASE?
SMELL IS THE MOST EVOCATIVE OF ALL THE SENSES!
WHAT BETTER WAY TO PREPARE FOR SCHOOL THAN THROUGH THE LOVELY SCENT OF NEWLY PURCHASED SUPPLIES?
SNIFFFFF
AAAHHHHHH!
THIS IS WRONG.
AND A LITTLE BIT CREEPY.
Peirce

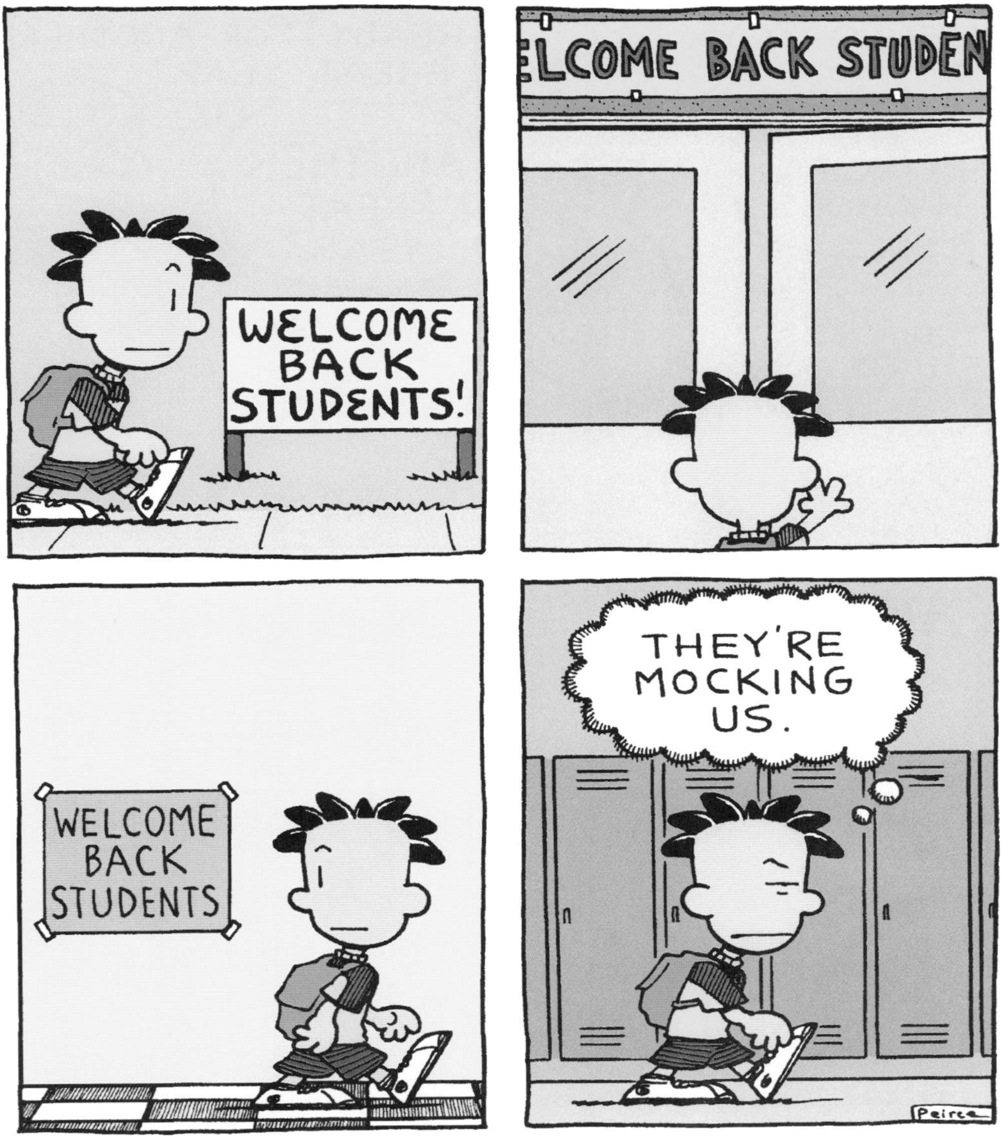
WELCOME BACK STUDENTS!
ELCOME BACK STUDEN
WELCOME BACK STUDENTS
THEY'RE MOCKING US.
Peirce

Check out these and other books from
Andrews McMeel Publishing

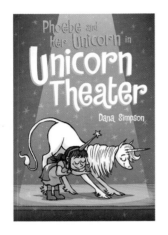

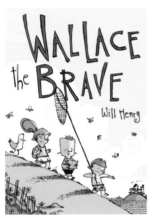

Big Nate is distributed internationally by Andrews McMeel Syndication.

Andrews McMeel Publishing
a division of Andrews McMeel Universal
1130 Walnut Street, Kansas City, Missouri 64106

www.andrewsmcmeel.com

18 19 20 21 22 SDB 10 9 8 7 6 5 4 3 2

ISBN: 978-1-4494-8995-3

Library of Congress Control Number: 2018932793

Made by:
Shenzhen Donnelley Printing Company Ltd.
Address and location of manufacturer:
No. 47, Wuhe Nan Road, Bantian Ind. Zone,
Shenzhen China, 518129
2nd Printing—12/3/18

These strips appeared in newspapers from
March 30, 2014, through September 13, 2014.

Big Nate can be viewed on the Internet at
www.gocomics.com/big_nate.

TAKE AIM...
AT
ADVENTURE!
THRILLS! LAUGHS!

READ

MAX & the Midknights

From LINCOLN PEIRCE,
creator of the
New York Times bestselling
BIG NATE series,
comes a new tale!

HEY! IF YOU LIKE
BIG NATE BOOKS...

...YOU'LL
LOVE
THIS
ONE!

"I LOVED IT!"
−DAV PILKEY,
bestselling author
of the Dog Man
series

"TOO
FUNNY!"
−JEFF KINNEY,
bestselling author
of the Diary of
a Wimpy Kid
series

"This is
the book of
my dreams!"
−WILL, age 9

"Max & the
Midknights are the
heroes we need today!"
−JEFFREY BROWN,
bestselling author of
the Jedi Academy
series

"MAX is
full of
surprises!"
−CHARLIE,
age 10

"I could
not put this
book down!"
−ZOIE, age 11

IT'S
UNANIMOUS!

Creator of BIG NATE
Lincoln Peirce
MAX & the Midknights
"Too funny for one book!" −JEFF KINNEY, author of Diary of a Wimpy Kid   "Fantastic! I loved it!" −DAV PILKEY, author of DOG MAN

rhcbooks.com   RHCB